The Alison Hayes Journey

Book One

INTOXIC

❈ ❈ ⚘ ❄ ❈

Angie Gallion

First edition 2016 (Published by Beech House Press)

Second Edition 2018

Published in the USA by thewordverve inc. (www.thewordverve.com)

eBook ISBN: 978-1-948225-21-2

Paperback ISBN: 978-1-948225-22-9

Library of Congress Control Number: 2018901774

~~~~~
INTOXIC

A Book with Verve

Cover Design, Interior Design, and eBook Formatting
by A.L. Lovell
www.beechhousebooks.com

DEDICATION

For my parents, Nick and Donna.

You were always there
when I came home from
school and all the many
times I came home from life.

You gave me such a good foundation.

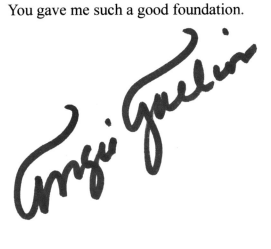

SPECIAL THANKS TO

Alexandra Haynak, from St. Petersburg, Russia, for the use of her beautiful artwork on the cover of this book. Ms. Haynak's work was made available to me through her participation at Pixabay.com, a photo/art sharing site. Pixabay has amazing collections from very talented people all around the world.

JD Jordan for his kind assistance with layout and design of the cover, and for being a great teacher as well as a doer.

Kali Bhargave. Without her encouragement and near insistence, these words would have stayed in my computer, a series of never-ending project pieces.

Janet Fix, my editor, and champion not only of my writing but of all my creative potential.

PART ONE: SPRING

CHAPTER 1

It is raining outside, and I am home alone. Mitch is working evenings at United this week and won't be home until midnight, which is good—I won't have to see him. I don't know where Mom is, just that the trailer was dark and empty when I came home. Milk and soggy Fruit Loops sit souring in a bowl on the table. I wonder which of them left it here. Probably Mitch, since Mom doesn't usually eat food. I tip the contents of the bowl into the sink. The window behind the table is up, and now everything is wet: the floor, the table, the windowsill. I push the window down, leaning over the table, rain splattering against the sill and onto my arm. My skin prickles to gooseflesh, and I use a rag from the counter to mop up all the water so the worn linoleum won't warp, a wasted effort considering the state of everything already. The metallic clang of the rain slapping against the tin roof of our trailer pings out a metallic chant. The lamp is turned over on its side, evidence of the morning

1

battle. I set it right again. I believe Mitch is on his way out, which is good—it's past time.

The fridge is empty, except for some cheese, old cheese, left over from Christmas and wrapped in foil from one of those prepackaged sampler sets. The light in the fridge reflects off the foil and bounces a rectangle of white into the dark kitchen. I flip on the light switch and let the refrigerator door fall shut. I find chicken noodle soup in the cupboard and crackers in the cabinet. There is a pan in the sink, so I wash it and set it on the stove, adding water to noodles, turning the heat up to medium high. The flames lick out beneath the pan, blue fingers grasping at the scarred silver metal. Broth begins to bubble, and I eat a cracker, staving off my hunger while my mind hisses like gas from an unlit stove. I wonder where she is, where she has gone, and when she will return.

In my mind's eye, she is lying dead on the bed with an empty bottle of pills. I go to her room, turn on the light, and there she is, her head turned slightly to the side, her mouth open. Her chest is rising and falling in time with the shallow catching of breath that passes for snoring in the heavily sedated. I run my finger along the disintegrating edge of a bruise along her jawline. She said that she tripped coming up the steps, but I think it looks very fist shaped. I told Mitch that if I ever catch him hitting her, I will kill him. Maybe that's why he is working late this week, waiting until the evidence disappears.

On the bedside table is a glass, and peaking from beneath the bed, I can see the cap of her liquor bottle, her own self-prescribed tranquilizer. I bend down and lift the bottle, tilting it up to see the remains—a shallow pool of clear liquid in the bottom, all that was left to drain from the sides after the last drink was poured. I take her glass, too, and leave her sleeping. I rinse her glass in the sink and tuck the bottle into the trash can alongside another companion. Everything is getting worse and worse and worse. Something should happen to break the cycle, one way or the other, but what? Maybe

Mitch leaving? She was a little better after Ed left, for a little while. I don't know.

I nudge her shoulder. "Mom." She groans and turns to face me, one eye opening to a slit. "Mom. Where's the car?" She groans, turning her face away from me, her hand drawing up to cover her head. "What are you doing here? You should be at work." She draws a deep breath and breathes out enough vodka vapor to stun a horse. "Where is the car?" Did she wreck it? How did she get home?

"S'at work." She groans yet again, her words mushed together like she is talking through mouth full of food.

"What? Your car is at work?" I pause. "Why aren't you at work?"

"Just leave me alone," she mumbles, trying to push me off the edge of her bed.

"Did you get fired?" I ask, my voice ringing in the room. "Mom, did you get fired?"

She tells me again to leave her alone and edges toward the other side of the bed to sit up, weaving when finally upright.

"What happened?" I ask. I demand.

"Leave me alone." There is a sheen of sweat erupting on her lip and forehead. "I'm gonna be sick."

I help her stand up, and she pushes my hand away, weaving toward the bathroom, banging solidly against the doorjamb as she enters. Maybe she did fall on the steps. I listen to her vomit splashing into the bowl and wait. The water in the sink comes on; she sluices the water around her mouth, spits. I am waiting for her when she comes back. Her eyes slide off of me like I am a shadow in the corner.

"Why did you get fired?"

She shrugs, her eyes touching the spot where her glass was, missing it, noticing that the bottle is gone from under the bed. Her eyes flash and flick to me, then the anger is gone as suddenly as it came.

"Were you drunk?" My voice whispers out of me, a sigh, a gasp.

"Lee me 'lone." She flops back into her bed and closes her eyes.

I heave a huge sigh—disgust, anger, and frustration coming out with my breath. Crap. I make my way over her piled clothes and back into the hall, slamming her door behind me. Crap. Crap. Crap. "Goddammit!" I scream, slamming the side of my fist into the front door as I pass. My skin stings. Happy sucky birthday to me.

My soup is hot by the time I return to the kitchen, but my hunger is gone. I wonder what she did at work today. Did she go in drunk or get that way later? I turn back to my soup and dip a cupful out, leaving the rest to grow cold with the fire gone.

The noodles spin in my bowl, and I stare out the window, the water still sluicing in rivulets. Listening to the chant on the roof, I think about the woman lying at the end of the trailer, my mother. The word itself draws up images of something very different. Something that maybe she used to be but isn't now. I don't know. I just know I hate that drunk version.

The rain begins to slacken, and the rivulets running down the window break into drops, clinging to the glass, quivering with the force of gravity pulling them downward. The sun begins to break through the clouds, and I take the remains of my soup, which I haven't touched, and put it and what is left in the pan into a bowl covered with foil in the fridge. Another something to sit and wait for mold.

When I step outside the air is tinged in orange from the sun seeping through the still-roiling clouds. I grab my bike and peddle down our road, avoiding the potholes and puddles, weaving as the spray whistles off of my tires, heading toward Dylan's house, my mood hovering in dark corners until I see his barn break through the tree line.

We've always been friends, since I moved here. Friend by proximity I suppose. I don't know if I want Dylan to be there or if I just want the horses. I used to always want him to be there, but things have changed a bit since I stayed back in sixth grade and he moved into junior high. Even though we never really hung out at school because I am a year younger, that took him to a different school entirely, and we've never really gotten back to where we were. It made a difference, him moving on and me staying behind. Our worlds shifted a step further apart that year, and even though we are still friends, we are not the friends we were. It was stupid for me to have to repeat a grade, but it was the year my mom spent three months in the halfway house and I was left to shunt pretty much on my own. She was clean when she finally came home, and stayed that way for a bit, long enough to get Mitch to come home to her, but it was too late for me. I had already missed too many days of school to pass on, regardless of how my grades turned out. So I stayed behind, and the kids in my class figured I was stupid, even though I'm not, and that changed everything. The kids coming into sixth grade also figured I was stupid because they saw me as going backward. It was a really bad year. By the time I did make it to junior high, I almost didn't care that I was mostly alone in it.

I wheel my bike into the lane and swing off. The ground is soft under my feet, and the muck sucks up around my shoes and makes a low, thooping sound as I pull away. The clouds tumble just above the barn, and the soft, orange glow fades as the sun is forced back behind the shifting clouds. It could rain again at any second. Thunder growls around me, and the newly budded leaves on the trees turn their light sides up against the wind. In the distance, a flash of lightening slashes through the grey. The grass is bright, vivid with color after the long winter, shimmering when the errant sun sparkles across it. Not that there has been much sun over the last week, with one storm system rolling in after another. But the buds on the trees and bushes lining the lane are beginning to pop, just ready to open.

The barn stands to the left of the house. The gingerbread house, with its white siding, deep green shutters, and orange roof. It's a beautiful house. In the spring and fall, it blends with the colors of the trees around it, and in the winter, it's a splash of color against an otherwise desolate landscape. As I come through the paddock, I see the horses, nuzzling at the trough, waiting for their feed. There are three of them: Pride, the white Arabian; Adelaide, the chestnut; and Chessa, the red with a thick blaze on her face. Chessa and Adelaide are Morgans, with finely shaped heads but not as delicately boned as the Arabian. With the three of them nuzzling at each other and watching the front of the barn so intensely, I know Dylan must be there, portioning out oats and grains for the feeding. I hesitate and almost turn back, but then I slip inside. There he is, just as I thought, filling the pail with oats and cracked corn. The naked bulb overhead swings, throwing shadows across the walls. I lean against the jamb, just watching. He won't see me until he turns to come out.

He is dressed in blue jeans and a white T-shirt. His rubber boots come up to his knees. He leans into the feed bin and back out, pouring oats and corn into three separate buckets. He is liquid motion. He has very loose limbs that don't seem hindered by joints or bones. He is hanging the buckets for the horses when his dad, Jake, arrives in the doorway beside me. I jump, bringing my hand to my neck.

"Didn't mean to scare you." He says in his very calm, well-mannered voice. I like Dylan's dad okay, but he makes me nervous.

"You didn't." I smile and look away, feeling my face flood with color. I step closer to the wall, giving him more berth to pass through.

"Dyl, dinner's on," he calls from where he stands beside me. Dylan turns and grins when he sees me. I raise my hand and wave. "Have you eaten, Alison?"

"Yes sir, I ate at home."

"That's too bad, there's enough for thrashers." Jake smiles, displaying large, somewhat crooked teeth.

"She'll eat." Dylan closes the feed bin. "Won't ya, sneaky?" It's not so much a question and neither of them wait for a response. He really hasn't changed. It's just me. I'm the awkward creature in the corner of the room, the one drooling and farting and gnawing on the carpet.

"Great, I'll tell Vaude to set a plate." Then Jake turns on his heel and is gone, loping toward the back door as Dylan reaches up and pulls the beaded chain to make the light go out.

"Ya sneakin' up on me, Al?" He makes his way toward me.

"Not really." He drops his arm over my shoulder, and I duck under before he can catch me in a headlock. He never hurts me, he just doesn't let me get away. It's something he's done for years, a holdover from younger days when we'd wrestle across the living room floor, trying to pin each other. That was before he hit his growing spurt and gained about sixty pounds on me, and before we both hit puberty. I like it though, his arm resting across my shoulder, the fingers dangling, following the curve of his wrist. I like his closeness. But today I feel so prickly that I have to shrug my spines away so I don't poke him.

"How ya been?" We walk toward the back door, swaying slightly, squishing into the wet grass. I haven't been around much this spring.

"All right, I guess." I pause. "Mitch is working late this week." I don't mention that my stupid mother got herself fired today. I'm not ready to divulge that personal tragedy yet. "You know you don't have to feed me."

"Thought so. His truck wasn't there when I went by. I looked for you after school." He ignored my last comment, and my stomach turns over.

"I caught the bus." We've reached the back door, and he swings it open. "I thought you had your student council thing tonight."

"Got cancelled. John's got the flu, and Mindy had cheerleading." We step inside, and he bends to pull off his boots, removing his arm from my shoulder. I kick my shoes off, too, and leave them, covered in muck, outside the door beside the welcome mat. I can hear Jake and Vaude talking as Dylan pulls up his socks, and we pad our way to the dining room. I love Dylan's house. It's very clean, with cream-colored carpets and vaulted ceilings. The dining room opens out from the kitchen, where Vaude and Jake are putting the finishing touches into a salad.

Even though I love the house, I don't like being inside it. There should be signs that say "DO NOT TOUCH" across everything. I feel like I'm going to run into something or spill cranberry juice on the carpets. It used to be homier, but now it's pristine, like newly fallen snow. The carpets still smell new. It's overwhelming, all that white, and when I get overwhelmed or nervous, I get very quiet, like a hummingbird, hovering, but never quite touching down.

Jake and Vaude are smart and funny, and they seem to love each other too much to have been married forever like they have. What makes that work for some people and not for others? I can't imagine Mom ever making a salad with someone. Actually I can't honestly imagine Mom cutting up a salad—maybe an olive for her martini. She's not a fan of "rabbit food," and when it comes right down to it, mealtimes are certainly not events in my house. Maybe that's the problem, not enough roughage. But Dylan's family is nothing like mine, and I sometimes find myself wondering what my life would have been if Jake and Vaude had been my parents instead. Would they be talking about colleges for me and planning our summer trip to Alaska or something? What if I had won the family jackpot and Dylan had been dealt the snake eyes.

"How is your mother?" Vaude asks, as she always does, polite and mannerly.

"She is fine." I answer as I always do. "Thank you for asking." Vaude was my seventh-grade history and English teacher, which was odd but nice, since she already knew me so well.

We eat lasagna, garlic bread, and salad. I watch them and listen as they talk about their days. This is how it's supposed to be: a FAMILY, in great big capital letters. I wonder if they are different when they're alone. Do they fight and yell and throw whatever is handy? I glance at their flawless walls and know there is no throwing of anything in this house. Still, I wonder if they keep the peace until the house is empty and then let it rip, when nobody can hear. They seem almost too much like "family," the way families are supposed to be, like it just comes easy and natural. Unlike my family, where the basic form of talking is yelling and the general topic is complaint. I wonder if that is the difference, what makes them the "Haves" and us the "Have Nots."

CHAPTER 2

I t is Friday night, the night of the Spring Dance at school. I know Dylan is there with Kelci Bancroft, the latest in his little girlfriend train. Her family owns the local market, and her mother teaches with Vaude at the junior high. Kelci has been a part of my life almost as long as Dylan. When I first moved here, we were friends, all through the first year. We were the two redheads that year, with hers fire-orange and mine auburn. She has three freckles on her face, right at the bridge of her nose. She is pale and magnificent. If the truth be told, she was probably my first crush. I was in love with her easy confidence and laugh, all calm grace and glow. She was Dylan's friend first, and he introduced us. The three of us used to ride bikes and play together, and I thought this was the best place in the world to live. That lasted about a year, until I invited Kelci to spend the night, and she realized in a very clear way that she was part of the "Haves" and I was not, and unlike Dylan, it mattered to her, or maybe it mattered to her mother.

So, Dylan is off dining and dancing with the future homecoming queen of Charleston, and I am waiting for dusk and for the moment when our trailer will be overrun, as it sometimes is in the spring and summer. The guys Mitch works with at the shop and their girlfriends, and some of the people my mom knows at the plant, they arrive, and drinks get poured and spilled, and we all settle on the logs circling a fire pit. We sit out under the stars listening to the Calversons belting out bluegrass on a guitar, a mandolin, and a fiddle. I love our Friday nights. I love the music, the crackling of the fire, and the pungent smell of weed being passed around me. It's one of the only times I feel like a part of something bigger than me. More than once I know I crawled into bed with a buzz, just from sitting in the haze. Some nights the party is at somebody else's house, and I am left home alone while they go. Sometimes they don't make it back until the morning. Tonight there is a lot of beer in the fridge, and my mother is putting chips and salsa out on the table. I am happy the party is here tonight. I would hate to be alone while Dylan is off with Kelci.

She is drinking rum and coke, her socializing drink. Her hair is newly colored, blazing auburn, and her lips are painted to match her hair. When I came home from school today, I found her sitting on the back step with her hair piled on top of her head, smoking while her hair processed. She was dressed in blue jeans and a bra, not wanting to get the chemical on her shirt. She did not look happy, and when I asked her how it was going, she just gave me a roll of her eyes and looked back out toward the woods.

I'm surprised we are having the fires tonight, since she just got let go at work and a lot of the people who will be here are people she used to work with, but Mitch has already filled the pit with broken limbs and brush from the woods, and apparently that was a battle she did not win. Perhaps that explains her rolled eyes. I go back outside as dusk settles over the fields to sit on our front steps and watch as the budding limbs of the maple tree splits the face of the moon. I wait for the droves to arrive.

My mother is animated, and her surly attitude seems to have washed away with the chemical rinse from her hair. She is flushed with the rum in her blood. She is really at her best when there are groups around, as if she were made to be a hostess and had somehow been misplaced into this life of ours. I watch Mitch's small movements as he talks to his friends, watch as they connect, then separate. There is peace tonight. Mom and Mitch are a unit, a connected front. The veneer that covers the cracks in their relationship is opaque, and the chasms cannot be seen. They are trying maybe too hard, maybe, because they know they are at the end. The past two nights have been filled with fighting, and I know Mitch is pretty pissed about her losing her job, even though she says it was because Venetta has always hated her. It's always somebody else's fault, never hers. The world is out to get her. She is putting on a good show tonight though, and if you didn't know us, you would think we were just your normal everyday average family. Nothing about her tonight screams that we are broken, that she is broken, that we are defective.

They come in the house, drinking beer and smoking cigarettes, snacking on chips and salsa and little hot dogs in croissants, taking beer from the fridge and mixing the liquor with soda on the counter. I make my way out to the logs around the fire pit and sit, waiting for the fire to catch and begin to crackle. I am mostly invisible in this crowd, and I sit like a ghost, watching them all with their talking and flirting. I sit with them on the logs until my face feels crisp with the heat of the flames and my eyes feel dry and scratchy. I catch sight of Theresa Calverson's backside slipping into the woods and take a quick look around to see who else is missing.

I retreat to the trailer, and I realize that Mitch is the only other person missing. Son of a bitch. I head inside, not wanting to see the wrath of Demon Mother when they return. She will go off the rails when she figures it out, and if she catches sight of them coming out of the woods, one after the other, I can only imagine the hell and its frozen state. I'm sick to my stomach with my new little bit of knowledge and stop in the kitchen, where my mom is deep in conversation with Jenny about the unfair treatment she received in being fired. I can't tell if Jenny is buying it, but she is listening with a sympathetic look. She smiles at me as I wave and nod my way past. I'm grateful that nobody has taken over my bedroom, as sometimes happens. I lock my door behind me and slide down the wall, blocking the door. I pick up my book and start to read. Smoke has covered my hair and filled my eyes. I feel alone, with all of these people here. I was fine until I saw slutty Theresa slinking into the woods. She doesn't care if she screws everything up for us. It makes me sad and angry. Finally I give up on reading and take my sketchpad and start to draw. I sketch eyes. Left eyes, right eyes. Eyes with brows and without. I then move to noses, big ones and small ones. Roman and ski slope. It's a strange composition. I can always draw, even when my mind is humming and whirring with a million different thoughts.

When I stand up and stretch, all the bones down my spine crack and snap into place and I look out the window, through the straggly branches of the pine, to see if Mitch has returned, but it has gotten full dark, and I can only see the shapes of the dancers around the flame without any definition to their features. My mind rolls off of Mitch and to Dylan off with Kelci at the Spring Dance. I wonder if they will have sex. I wonder if they are having sex right now. What a freaking horrible day. He dated Shelby Dycus for four months last year, and if the bathroom walls are to be believed, he is quite a "stud."

I wish everybody would leave, so I can be alone, really alone, not just lonely. I settle on my bed and stare up at the ceiling while the Calversons cut into another song. They get more rhythmic and rambunctious as the night goes on and the beer in the fridge becomes depleted. The limbs from the old evergreen tree at the corner of the trailer is scraping against the side of the house, like a spoon on a metal washboard, adding a whole new element to the music bouncing through my screen. The sketchpad slips from the edge of my bed, fluttering to the floor, as I fall asleep, bluegrass in my head.

CHAPTER 3

The sun is shining through my window and there are low rumblings from the rest of the house. I've been awake for some time, listening. The smoke from the fire last night still hangs in the air, heavy and stale, waiting for a stout wind to drive it off. Three weeks have passed since our first Friday Fire, and I suspect there will be no more to follow. The rumblings between Mom and Mitch have been on a progressive upswing over the last few weeks. She knows about Mitch and Theresa, and I wonder if she knew before I saw them sneaking off together. She flat-out called Theresa a whore last night. We were all there, just hanging out by the fire. Jud was tuning his guitar and Mitch had just gone inside to get another beer. Mom was talking to Tabby Johnson and didn't seem to notice him going.

Then Theresa slid herself upright, a snake gaining legs, and made a stealthy step to pass by my mother toward the trailer. If I hadn't seen it myself, I wouldn't have believed it, but my mother's arm snapped out and grabbed a hunk of Theresa's hair, yanking her clean off her feet. She fell on her butt with a loud "oomph," the wind completely knocked out of her. My mom said, "Look, you stupid whore, if you think you're going into my home to make time with my man, you better think again."

Theresa sat for a second, rubbing her head and then her ass before standing up. "You are a fucking crazy bitch."

"Maybe so, but at least I don't have to fuck my friends' men."

I have to admit, I was pretty impressed. Don't play with my mother. She'll mess you up.

None of that went over well with the Calverson boys, and it wasn't long after Theresa left that the boys packed up their instruments and went as well, passing dirty looks back at my mother and then at Mitch as he saw them leaving down the drive.

I spend several hours listening to them screaming after that, waiting to hear something physical, worthy of my involvement. Mitch calls my mother crazy, proclaiming his innocence with the intensity that only a true liar can muster. Finally, the front door slams—Mitch has left the arena, which is generally what he does when she is being "insane," or when he realizes she isn't buying his bullshit. The door opens again, and my mother yells something through it, but I can't make out her words. Mitch's truck sputters to life, and he backs down the driveway, throwing white rock as he goes. There is an absence of sound, until the floor creaks again as she moves from living room to kitchen, words growling loose on her tongue, clipped.

The next step is more booze, probably switching to vodka, her preferred "pitiful me" drink, maybe some vomit at some point, maybe not. I hear the clink of metal on glass, and then she is moving through living room and into her bedroom. Her door closes, and the TV in her room begins to hum.

At some point she goes dark, and the world is silent. I crawl into my own bed, grateful she didn't come to me to hash out her emotions, her anger, which she sometimes does, complaining about her sorry lot in life and how nobody loves her. Why isn't she ever enough? Thank God we didn't have to have that conversation again. I don't think I could have handled it.

This morning she is grumbling through the house again. I hear her stomping, opening the medicine cabinet, and I'm sure she feels like shit. Every few minutes I hear her say something—inaudible, half-mumbled words, talking to herself, saying what she should have said last night. What she should have said to Mitch, what she would say to Mitch when he grew balls enough to come home. I've heard similar rumblings often enough to know the gist. I listen long enough to know the general topic. I wonder if he has finally had enough and will be gone for good.

A couple of years ago he'd been seeing some woman and actually left us to live with his "whore." When he was gone for about a month, my mom ended up in the psych ward after a drunk dial to her friend Faye, who called the police saying that my mom threatened to kill herself. Three days in the psych ward turned into a stint in the halfway house and three months of me getting by as best I could on my own. Hence my double time in sixth grade.

By the time she got out of the halfway house, Mitch had been visiting her there for a month, and when she came home, he came with her. Things were better for a while after that. We even ate dinners together, mealtime events. Mitch said there would be no other women, and my mother stopped drinking. For a while.

I leave my bed and go into the bathroom. Something thumps against the wall, and my mother lets out another yell. She is out of vodka. Thoughts of my life drip through my mind while the water dribbles from the lime-encrusted showerhead, falling weakly into the tub. It's a frustrating shower, not enough water pressure to fully rinse off the soap, and by the time I get out, the water has run cold. I dry, dress, and wrap my long, uncombed hair in the towel to squeeze the water out. I lean over the basin and study myself in the mirror, looking for breakouts and imperfections. I look like my mother, sad to say. My green eyes are her green eyes. My cheekbones are hers; my chin is hers. Only my lips are my own, though maybe they came from my father, whomever he may be. My hair comes from her, too, and no matter how much I hate it, I look like mom did when she was young. I hope I don't look like her when I am old, but I suspect I probably will. Life sucks.

I take the towel from my hair and toss it over the shower rod, shaking my hair to untangle it. I grab my backpack from beside the bed and load it with my sketchpad, charcoals, and pencils before stepping softly back into the hall and out the back door, closing it with a quiet click. When I pass under her window, I can hear her TV. I wonder if he's going to come back this time. I push my mother and her problems out of my mind as I escape into the early morning sunshine.

Our trailer sits on about an acre of land, and behind it, the woods go all the way to the back side of the Winthrop pastures. Ed bought our land and put the trailer here as a consolation for walking out of our lives, or maybe for something else, I've always wondered if it was for the something else. My mom and I were going to build a house, a real stick-and-stone house, because we were going to make a better life than the one that had left us behind. Our plans got delayed until they ended up in the scrap pile. We talked about "the House" a lot those first couple of months, and one Saturday, we even staked out the perimeter. Those months—before there was a new man—when we tried to be "just us girls" felt strange, almost pretend. Mom has never been very good without a man, or with one either, for that matter. Through the months, through the men, and as the months slipped to years, the stakes grew weathered and eventually got turned under by the lawnmower. Eventually "The House" disappeared from our imaginations, and the trailer rattled more and grew more sorely used as the seasons of east central Illinois marched past.

I shoulder the backpack, stepping over one of the few remaining stakes, and head into the woods, dew from the grass seeping into my shoes, soaking my socks. Summer has come with open skies, and the shadows from the canopy above dance through the woods. The green gloom of the underbrush is peaceful, solitary, melancholy. It is my favorite place. Monday and Tuesday are finals, and then it will officially be summer. The heat has already settled, and the farmers have put their crops out. Little green shoots are already sprouting from the black soil.

Not far into the underbrush there is a wire fence that separates our yard from what we call "the woods." We didn't put the fence up—it was here when we came—and it was rusty and loose even then. I climb through the barbs and manage my way through the dense growth until I find the path, one of many that run all through the woods, radiating from one main trail. Dylan told me the main trail was once a railroad bed that they stopped using after a series of train wrecks down in the gully around the turn of the century. There are no rails now, no remnants from those rails; in fact, it seems unlikely a rail ever ran here. I can't imagine where it was coming from and going to. Regardless of its origin, the trail makes for an excellent horseback ride and a pretty good hike.

The series of smaller trails have been worn out from the main. Today I take one of these and climb the hill leading up to Donovan's Ridge. From the ridge, you can look down into the gully and, through the trees, watch deer as they come to the creek to water. I settle myself on a ledge just below the top of Donovan's Ridge and dangle my feet. It's a steep drop, almost a cliff, and the ledge juts out slightly from the side of the hill. I watch for the longest time as birds flit through the trees, and the longer I sit, the more birds appear, growing comfortable with my presence, my silence. I feel my blood slowing in my veins. My breath slows, too, and the echoing of their words and of my thoughts slip away. When the trailer is small in my mind and my mother is very far away, I pull out my drawings and open to one that I've been working on for my final art project. It's of three horses running in a storm. This is what I do, to get away from everything: I draw. Someday I'm going to have a studio with my prints mounted for display. That's my dream anyway.

Voices echo along the gully and come to me through the trees. I lift my eyes and search the sun-dappled paths for the intruders. The voices continue for a few minutes before I spot them. Two people, a boy and a girl on horseback. I know the boy is Dylan, because I recognize Pride. The other horse is Chessa, I can tell by the pudge around her middle and the blaze on her face. I can't quite make out the person riding. She's wearing a baseball cap, and at this distance, I wouldn't be able to see her face anyway. For a second I think it might be Vaude, but then the laughter rolls up, and I recognize the pretty voice of Kelci Bancroft.

My throat tightens, and I close my sketchpad, watching through the trees. They're at the base of the gully now, just coming up to the creek. For a few minutes I can't hear anything from them, but I have a perfect view. Dylan leads, and although I'm sure Kelci hasn't spent much time on a horse in her life, she looks pretty comfortable. Of course, Chessa's about the calmest thing ever; anybody could look comfortable on her. I am jealous she is riding Chessa, my horse. There was a time when a Saturday morning meant we were riding—Dylan and me. They cross over the creek, and Dylan turns Pride toward the slope that leads up to the back side of Donovan's Ridge, the very path I took not even an hour before. The path itself wraps around the base of the ridge and then begins to zigzag up the slope. It's the only way up and the only way down. I'm trapped here on my ledge, and unless I hide, I'm going to have to speak to them. I glance around anyway, just in case some portal to another dimension has opened to allow my escape, knowing that hiding behind a tree would be no use and would make me look incredibly stupid if they happened upon me. I take a deep breath and keep my seat. I force my eyes back to my sketch, not working on it, just studying it, waiting for the inevitable.

Since the Spring Dance, it seems I always see Kelci and Dylan together. In big bold letters, TOGETHER. I walk into the lunchroom at school, and there they sit. I walk down the hall and see him at his locker, with her a step away. I bet they did have sex after the dance. I bet they are having sex now. I've managed to avoid them, mostly, turning the other way or walking a different route to classes when I know my path will cross one of theirs. I feel the same anger that I remember when Kelci came to spend the night and promptly toppled off the fence into the land of the upper echelon. I've avoided them. There won't be any of the questions this time. I remember, with a sick sense of shame, the day I caught Kelci outside our math class shortly before we finished the sixth grade, and I asked her why she was mad at me, wanting to make peace, amends, and go back to the easy comfort of being friends. "I'm not mad at you, Alison. It's just things are different now. I'm going to junior high next year." As if that explained everything, and I guess it did in a way, because I wasn't. The writing was well on the wall by then. I had missed too much school; my performance was not satisfactory. That was the end of it, while her new group of friends pressed past me, taking her with them into class. I remember sitting there, as class poked by, trying to follow my math equations through puddled tears that I couldn't repress. I remember hearing whispers behind me, clearly the word "dirty," and knowing they were talking about me. Every giggle for days seemed to be at my expense.

Finally, after what seems to be hours, the underbrush begins to crackle as they move closer to the top of the ridge. The birds stop twittering and hunker down on their branches. The two of them will be on me in a few minutes. I can't very well pretend I didn't know they were there, with all the noise and bits of their conversation coming at me. I don't want them to think I was eavesdropping, even as I've been spying. I should have known that they would be heading to the ridge, and I should have left as soon as I'd heard their voices coming from the trail. After all, that's how I came to know about Donovan's Ridge, riding with Dylan. He comes up here a lot, to think or just to sit and watch the world. If I'm honest, when I came here this morning I was probably hoping to run into him, especially after avoiding him for so long. I wanted to hear his voice and touch base again, to know that everything was going to be okay. So, I wanted to see him, but not like this, not with her.

I put my sketchpad into my pack and shoulder it. I should have already done this, been ready to go. I should have circled around and down and found a way to pass by them without being seen. Instead I just sat here dumbly until they are almost here. Idiot. I scramble off my ledge and up onto the actual ridge just as they come around the last bend. I am straightening up as Dylan tells Kelci to watch out for a low-hanging limb. How nice it would have been to see her knocked off. That would have been worth the humiliation of being caught. She tilts in her saddle and maneuvers past the obstacle. Damn.

She spies me and is the first to speak. "Hi." Her face breaks into her cheerleader smile, and you would think we were still the best of friends. Her eyes rake from my face to my men's t-shirt to my cut off blue jeans, stained yellow from being washed too often in the well water at the trailer. Dirty. The word washes through my mind. I wish for a split second that I had actually taken the time to brush my hair, to have done something to make myself less of a ragamuffin. But here I stand, ragamuffin to a tee. I smile and nod, unable to make words, which frustrates me. I should have been ready to seem okay, but I wasn't. Idiot. In the same split second she assessed me, I assessed her, in her blingy Jordache jeans and teal polo shirt with the collar flipped up, so cool, so hip. These are the girls Dylan dates— Shelby Dycus with her huge, perky boobs, and Kelci Bancroft with her gorgeous hair and clothes. Dylan doesn't date people like me.

Dylan turns and sees me then, too. His smile is easy and comfortable, so familiar, and for that split second, I hate him for his good looks and easy fucking life. He looks like he's been enjoying his ride. He has color in his cheeks, just below the surface of his tan, from the heat of the morning.

"Hey, Ali. Surprised to see you up here this morning." Which of course really means that he has not thought of me until now, so of course he couldn't have expected me. It's almost a sucker punch to my stomach, understanding so suddenly that I am less to him than he is to me. I'm just the poor kid from down the street. The poor kid he tries to be nice to. He thinks I am young. Much younger than he, even though I am not. He thinks of me like he would a poor cousin. I am that person, and Kelci is the girlfriend.

I finally find a voice, although it sounds like someone else's. "Yeah, well, you know. It's a pretty morning." I move from one foot to the other, tugging at the fringe on my shorts, which suddenly seems too high up my leg for decent, as he slips down from the saddle. He loops Pride's reins over a limb and steps back to help Kelci down, and then we are all standing eye to eye to eye.

"Sure is. I thought Kelci'd like to see the view."

"It's amazing," Kelci breaks in, showing the appropriate enthusiasm. "I've lived here my whole life, and this is the first time I've ever been out here."

"Really?" I don't know what else to say, but it's slowly dawning on me that they were planning on sticking around up here for a while, and they were planning on it without me here. They are probably going to have sex up here. God. "Well, hey, enjoy. I've got to get on back home. So, I guess I'll see you all at school." But, again, my functions fail, and I am unable to move.

"You want to hang out a bit, then I'll give you a ride back down?" Dylan asks, but he feels it, too—the something awkward in the three of us standing here looking at each other. I give him credit, though, for trying to be the nice guy.

"No, that's okay. But thanks. I have to go."

"That's too bad," Kelci says, smiling again, not really meaning it, her cheerleader smile. For a split second I imagine shoving her over the ledge, but as soon as the satisfaction of seeing her start to fall enters my head, the image is gone. I meet her eyes, set just above those three cute little freckles that dot across the bridge of her nose. I wonder if I hate her more for not liking me as much as I liked her or for the fact that she and Dylan seem a matched set. There is something dark and wrong inside of me, I know it. Something hateful. Something evil. Something dirty.

"Well, see ya." I shoulder past them and hope they don't turn to watch my somewhat clumsy descent down the zigzagging trail. I glance up once and can see them silhouetted into the sky, his arm draped across her shoulder, hip to hip, her tinkling little girl laugh bouncing down the hill to chase me on my way. Bitch. Bitch. Bitch. By the time I reach the bottom of the slope, tears are stinging my eyes, making the path difficult to see. I wipe my eyes and make my way across the gully, breaking from the trails and setting off through the underbrush, so as not to have them overtake me on their return ride.

CHAPTER 4

I come out of the woods into our backyard. Mitch's truck is still not here, but a blue Ford is sitting in the driveway instead. I recognize the car; it belongs to my mom's friend, Faye, whom I have known for years and don't like. She is the reason Mom ended up in the psych ward the last time. She is the reason I had to redo sixth grade, and I hate her for it. I open the door and slip into the living room, wondering why she has come this morning. The trailer is bustling with activity. My mother is stacking bags beside the door, while Faye and a man loiter in the living room.

It takes me just a minutes for my eyes to adjust to the dimness after being outside. My mother is talking, but what she is saying doesn't register. The man is hefty with a shock of reddish-brown hair and a neatly trimmed mustache. A real lumberjack man. Mom's voice finally comes through to me. "Did you hear me? Alison?"

"Huh, I'm sorry, what?" I ask, feeling stupid and slightly dizzy from my descent from the ridge into our shadowed hell.

"Pack some things. We're getting out of here."

"Where are we going?"

"Don't ask me questions. Just get some clothes." The utter exasperation and annoyance of her tone is like a slap in the face, as if I am the cause of all her turmoil. Her breath hits me, and I know she has been drinking. Her breath is fresh with vodka, not the stale rum and coke that she drinks at the Friday Fires—because vodka doesn't have a scent, which must be some universal belief held by all drunks and disproved by every other person with a sense of smell. She has a wild look around her eyes, and I know better than to push it, so I hustle down the hall and fill my backpack with underwear and clothes, not mentioning that the trailer is ours and Mitch should leave, not us. I wish he would get here. Maybe he could make this right, either by putting them back together or by moving out himself, but who knows where he has gone. He's probably gone to Theresa. Faye comes back into my room and sits down on the bed. Suddenly I realize that I am crying again.

"Honey, you okay?"

"Sure. Why not?" As if it were every day that your world comes unhinged, even if it hadn't been great before. But I'm more upset about seeing Dylan with Kelci than about my mom leaving Mitch—I don't really care about that one way or the other. It is not like it's a first. What has me crying is the stumbling, tumbling walk back through the woods, arguing to myself about why I don't care whom he dates and how I don't even care about him anyway. Trying to tell myself how I don't need him and don't even really want him. It's just that it's her. Damnit. But standing here in my room, packing clothes for another run, all I want is have him here, regardless of the awkwardness of our meeting up on Donovan's Ridge. I need him to be here for me, and he isn't. I need somebody to be here for me. Why am I not ever enough? The thought echoes in my head, bounding from the grey walls of my brain, transforming from a thought into a memory of my mother's voice saying the exact same thing.

"You're going to stay with us for a while, okay?"

"I can't leave. This is our home. Anyway, I have finals this week." All the way back from the stupid ridge, I hoped he would overtake me, having left Kelci on the ledge. I wanted him to come for me.

What is wrong with me? I'm still packing, even as my mind tells me I am a fool. Such a stupid little fool. Why would he come for me when he had her already? I can't compete with that.

When I first met Faye, she told me to call her Aunt Faye, which I never have done. She and my mother used to make a big deal about being self-proclaimed sisters. I've heard the story of my mother's life in bits and pieces, stuttered starts and halted stops. I wonder what version of herself she has given Faye.

"Rob works here in town. He'll bring you."

I had almost forgotten that we were in a conversation, of sorts, so it draws me up, and I look at her perplexed.

"Who the hell is Rob?" This is insane. I haven't seen Faye in over a year, and now she's here telling me that I'm going to stay with her and some guy named Rob is going to bring me to school.

"Honey, he's my fiancé. He lives with me." As if this should all be common knowledge. Last I'd heard, she was married to some guy name Johnny. I narrow my eyes and almost ask about Johnny, but I think better of it. Faye is not the most tolerant person I know.

"I don't want to go." I'm grabbing things off of my dresser and shelves, whining, and putting them back down in different places. "Why can't I just stay here?"

"Honey, that just isn't a good idea." She says it with strained patience.

"Why not?"

"You can't just stay here with Mitch. Not alone." She drops her voice. "You've turned into a very pretty girl. Who knows what he might try with your mother not here to protect you?"

"I can take care of myself," I say, annoyed. Her lowered, conspiratorial tone is infuriating to me. She thinks Mitch would come on to me, and that somehow my self-absorbed, alcohol-addled mother protects me from such. She never protected me from Ed; I can't imagine she would now. She'd probably kick me out for taking her man. I actually laugh. "Protect me? That's rich." I don't believe "protect Alison" has ever been high on my mother's rather short list of priorities. Regardless, Faye's implication, her insult to Mitch, perhaps her close touch on a festered wound that lives in the dark, creepy corners of my soul, resounds deep inside me. All of the frustration and anger I've been feeling about everything else comes pounding out of my mouth against this accusation. I throw as much scorn and disgust as I can muster into my voice. "Mitch would never do anything to me. He's a good person." I'm not really sure why I am defending him. He is maybe not such a good person, and didn't I spend half the night last night waiting to hear him hit her? But defend him I do. "You don't live here. You don't know him. You don't know her. You don't know any of us, Aunt Faye." I spit my words out with contempt, my tone speaking of the times that I had pulled her down the hall and into her bed because she was passed out on the floor, even though I would never dare utter such things. These are our secrets. Our dirty little secrets. Or the time she got so drunk she threw up in the bathtub and passed out. That was a fun one to clean up. I think of the accusations she has thrown out time and again, and I know that Mitch finds other women. Half of what I say is mumbled, under my breath, a practice I've learned from my mother. Contempt and disgust is a language I didn't even know I had in me, but it tumbles from my lips to poison the already dank air between Faye and me.

I could go on. Making my own accusations, my own judgments, my own injured existence giving me that right, but Faye's hand slams across my face. I spin into the wall and nearly tumble off my feet. I catch the edge of the dresser and right myself. Nobody has ever hit me before. Nobody. Even with all of the other craziness in my life, I've never felt the sting of a slap or a fist, and I stand in dumb silence, my hand holding my cheek, my lips parted with the shock.

"Shut up. Do you hear me?" she hisses at me as she whirls around the bed, her eyes wide and excited. She grabs my elbow and shakes me. "Your mother may let you talk to her like that, but I will not. She has had a tough time of it, and I will not have you making it any harder for her. Do you hear me?" She releases my arms, but her grey eyes, the color of a storm, bore into me, holding me as if chained. The muscles in her jaws twitch. "Now, you get your shit together and shut up."

I nod my head dumbly. Who would have thunk she would hold such a powerful whop? I pick up my backpack, and she again takes my arm, steering me to the living room, which is now vacant, as Rob and my mother have gone outside to load her things into the car. Faye rushes me down the front steps, with urgency, as if the trailer were set to ignite. I'm bundled in the backseat with my mother. Rob drives, and Faye keeps turning in her seat and reaching back to pat my mother's knee. I stare out the window as we drive through town on 16. Faye lives just on the west side of Mattoon, in the spoils from her last divorce. She's had three. No wonder she and my mother understand each other so well.

CHAPTER 5

The small, yellow house sits at the end of a cul-de-sac in a subdivision called Green Meadows. It's a nice little ranch-style house with a white wooden fence going across the front. Faye and her third husband, Johnny, bought it together shortly after they married. There is a piano in the living room that she also got in the settlement, and I wonder if she plays or if it is just for show. Rob, I finally discover, is husband number three's brother, and I suspect one of the reasons for that split up. I bet Thanksgiving in this family is a whole bundle of happiness.

My mother is tucked into the bed in the guestroom, her lips parted, drool spilling onto the pillow. She sleeps, wrapped up like a kitten, purring lightly.

"She'll feel better when she wakes up," Faye says to me as she brushes past me, leaving my mother to sleep it off.

"Doubt it," I say, but not until Faye has moved on down the hall and cannot hear me. I'm not sure I really want to cross her path right now. My cheek is still hot where her palm landed. But I know that when my mother wakes up, she will feel like shit and will wonder how the hell we got here. She will not remember the drunken, certainly pathetic phone call she placed, which resulted in our rescue. I stare down at her for quite some time, wondering how she will extract us from this situation. Will she confess that she doesn't remember calling? Will she admit that she had any fault in the relationship falling apart? Will she present herself as a great victim and Mitch as a horrid, abusive man who took advantage of her generosity of spirit until she could stand it no more? It is impossible to say. I hope I'm here when she wakes up and wants to know where the fuck we are.

I finally leave the room and find Faye and Rob deep in conversation at the kitchen table. I stand at the sliding glass doors and stare out into the backyard. I refuse to make myself invisible. She forced me to be here, so she's just going to have to look at me. She clearly mistakes my hostile silence for fear or worry, which it is not. I'm just numb, waiting for the day to move forward so my mother will call Mitch to come get us and we will go back to normal, whatever that is.

"Honey, I know you're worried. She'll be better when she doesn't get treated like that anymore." The concern in her voice must be for Rob's benefit. She's made it pretty clear how she feels about me, and concern isn't high.

"Treated like what?" My voice ricochets off the glass, and I stare at my faint reflection. I purposefully keep my voice low and modulated, intentionally calm. Does she not understand that my mother likes to be treated like that? She likes drama and drunken brawls. She likes a man who will fight for her, with her. She likes it a little rough.

"You know how that man treats her." I can hear her click her tongue on the roof of her mouth, something some of the girls at school do when they are stating the obvious.

"He doesn't treat her badly," I say, turning to face Mitch's accusers. I mean, Mitch isn't perfect, but he's always been decent to me, and from what I've seen, he's been decent to her. I wouldn't put up with her if I didn't have to. She picks most of the fights, or worse, alcohol picks them.

"Sometimes men don't know how to express themselves, and they get a little too physical. You're lucky you haven't had to see any of it." She is smug, sitting there, feeling that she has done her good deed for poor Alice.

"Seen what? You think he beats her? Is that what she tells you?" My voice rises, and I'm afraid for a second that it will shatter. It's become crystalline and brittle. I remember the fist-sized bruise on her jawline and try to think back to other moments when I have seen bruises. I let out a strangled laugh and turn back to look out the window.

"You aren't there all the time. Things happen. She tries so hard to shelter you from it." Again, the vision of the mother, the protector, the shelterer. What a load of crap. She sips from her coffee. "She wants to make sure you are safe. Better to get you out of the environment while he moves on, rather than risk it." She pauses, staring past me, out into the yard, "It's not just the physical either. There's emotional and psychological, too." I can tell from her tone that she is thinking of herself now, of the abuse she has suffered. Why do people ever get together? It never ends well, and it's not even good until it ends. "When you grow up a little more, maybe you'll understand." As if I were an idiot who she must help "to see." I think Faye has read way too many self-help books for people with too many divorces. There is abuse in our house, that is true, but it is in the bottle, of the bottle, because of the bottle. It is the bottle.

I set my jaw and return her stare through the reflection of the door. I've seen a lot of their fights, and I've seen a lot of different occasions when I thought he'd haul off and smack her, but he never has, at least not in front of me. I've seen her strike out at him, and once I even saw her throw a knife at him. It wasn't her fault, of course; she was drunk. That's what he said to me later. But never once have I seen him raise a hand to her. Maybe he does, behind closed doors. But mostly I think he just leaves when he starts to feel like he wants to hit her, which is probably more effective. I think she wants him to hit her. I can hear it in the ways she picks and picks and picks. That's probably a really horrible thing to think about somebody, that they want to get hit, but I think it all the same. She's loved all of her men best after a good throw-down. When they made her feel their power over her. I don't dare voice any of this to Faye.

"I know this is hard for you to understand, but sometimes people do bad things."

"I'm not stupid, I know what you're talking about, but Mitch didn't do what you're saying he did. I mean, I've seen her hit him, but never him hitting her." I remember him saying "Elvis has left the building" with his best radio-announcer voice as he climbed into his truck. Then he would wink at me, and I always knew that everything would be okay. He would give her some time to calm down. He would come back. They would all apologize, and the cycle would begin all over again.

"Alison, you were not always there."

Beat that dead horse. I am so tired of hearing her voice, wheedling, whiny. Pathetic.

"And you were never there, so what makes you think you know more about it than I do?" I step to the phone, dialing our number. The phone rings, but he doesn't pick up. He isn't there. If he does leave, I wonder if I could convince him to take me with him. Even as the thought crosses my mind, I know he never would, and I know I could never ask him. How could I? How could he? It would look too wrong. Anyway, what would I do, move in with him and Theresa? Now that would be something. I feel tears welling in my eyes, and I force them back down. I will not allow myself to cry in front of these people. I put the phone back in the cradle, and I wish I were over at Dylan's, up in the loft. I leave Rob and Faye sitting at the table and retreat to the back deck, where I sit, watching a fly buzz over the grill.

The door creaks open, and I'm joined on the deck by Rob. His heft tilts the deck. "Alison?" He pauses. "Can I sit down?"

"You live here. I don't." My voice is rude, and I have a moment where I'm ashamed, but I close myself to the feeling and set my face with as much ice as I can muster.

He eases his rather large body into the other deck chair but doesn't say anything for a few minutes. Then, "I know this is really tough on you."

Why do adults say stuff like that? He's never met me before, and here he is thinking he knows something about me. Jerk. I want to say that he doesn't know anything about it so he just should stay out of it, but I keep my mouth shut.

He goes on. "We're just trying to help. Your mom, she calls here all the time, crying about how miserable and scared she is. She wants to leave, but has no place to go. She's tried to make him go, but he won't. She's very unhappy."

I hadn't known that mom called Faye all the time. I'm ashamed that she does, talking to people about things that aren't any of their business. Does she really call them and say she is scared? Really?

"Then she should go. Mitch and I would be okay. I don't want to leave. We get along fine."

"Alison, you know you couldn't stay there with just that man. What would people think?"

Suddenly I have the urge to laugh, loudly and hysterically, and I know that if I start, I will not stop. What do you think people think anyway? I want to ask. Apparently they think my mother is beaten regularly, and I am diddled by the nicest of the men my mother has ever brought home.

"That's great, that everybody wants to help," I say. "But I want to go home. It doesn't have anything to do with me."

"When you talk to Mitch, you can work that out. But who knows when he'll make it back? Come on, how about we go get something to eat?"

I can hear Faye working in the kitchen, and I realize that my stomach is empty, even though I'm not sure that I can think of eating.

When my mother wakes up, she joins us in the kitchen. Damn, I missed the waking. Dark circles rim her eyes, only some of it the flaky mascara left over from last night, and she looks like she has been crying. She and Faye talk in hushed tones, and I try to listen.

I try to catch her words so I can contradict her or at least know for myself what she is saying. I can feel my mother looking at me, but I refuse to meet her eyes.

Tonight I sleep on the floor in the guest bedroom, my mother sleeps on the bed. I hear her get up twice in the night and unzip her bag. In the darkness I hear the clink of her rings against a glass bottle as she drinks. The faint odor of the vodka radiates through the room. When I wake the next morning the bottle is tucked under her pillow, the cap barely visible. The room is vaporous with the smell of it. Funny, scentless vodka. Maybe you can only really smell it after you've cleaned up somebody else's vodka vomit. Maybe.

Around noon on Sunday, my mother calls Mitch. I hear her talking in her "I want to make peace" voice. She is meek and mild, seeking forgiveness. An hour later Mitch pulls into the drive to take us home. Faye does not come to the door to see us go. She does not help carry the many bags that my mother shunted from our trailer. Rob, who may actually be an okay guy, does help carry our stuff to the truck. He even shakes Mitch's hand, comrades, fighting the good fight against all these crazy bitches. Faye thinks my mother is making a big mistake going back, and as we climb into the truck, she calls out through her screen door, "Alice, don't call me if you aren't willing to fix it. You hear me? Don't call me."

CHAPTER 6

"Where were you this weekend?" Dylan asks when I run into him at school on Monday. I am on my way to my history final, and he is heading to civics.

"We went to visit my aunt." I shift my eyes away from him on the word "aunt."

"I stopped by Saturday afternoon, and Mitch said he didn't know where you were."

"I was with my mom." I really don't want to talk to him about this. He won't understand. Him with his perfect family and his perfect house and now his perfect girlfriend. The last sight of him, holding Kelci up on the ridge, blurs across my vision, and I try to blink it away.

"Want a ride tonight?" He drops his arm over my shoulder, and I feel my back tense.

"No, I'll just catch the bus." Don't touch me. I want to scream at him. How dare he?

"You sure? We can swing by and get an ice cream." He knows my fondness for Dairy Queen, but he must also feel the tension in my frame because he lets his arm fall from my shoulders, and I step aside, less within his reach.

"No." A look crosses over his face, and for a second I'm sorry for my ugly tone, but I can't go back now. My voice is softer when I speak again, but just as cold. "Listen, we're just from different worlds, you know? It's better if I don't get to see the water if I can't swim. Okay?" I had no idea, until I hear my voice outside of me that I even thought that, but now that the words are in the air, I know it is true. I do feel that way. I don't know if it's about dating him or just about his perfect life with his perfect mom and dad, his perfect house and barns and horses. I had stopped beside him, delivering my words, but now I walk on, leaving him to stare after me. To hell with him. I'm angry at everybody and everything, and I want to hold on to my anger because at least I know what to expect of it.

His hand folds around my forearm when I am only a few steps away and draws me back. "Look, I am trying to help you. You're not the only one with a fucked-up family." He hisses the last three words. His voice rises on the word "help," and a snake roils in my stomach. I hear my mother's voice ringing in my head: "I don't want no charity." She's said it more than once when I've mentioned some nice thing he has offered to do.

"Oh," I say, offended, "You want to help me? What do you know about anything, Mr. Perfect?"

"I know more than you think." He straightens his back, elevating his height a couple of inches, towering. "You aren't the only one who has had a drunk. I knew a guy who was a bad drunk. Really bad." He is close in my face, his cheeks flushed and angry.

"Good for you, Dylan. Good for you. I'm so proud of you. You've had a drunk . . . what does that even mean? My mother isn't a drunk. You don't know anything about us. Just stay away from me." I shake my arm down hard and break his hold on me. I turn, in my dingy t-shirt and jeans, and jog down the hall.

Later, after history, English, lunch and PE, I am heading toward my last class of the day, art. I'm still sour and surly, and I imagine a black cloud gathering around me, like an angry little Pigpen with his swirling scribbled dark cloud of dirt. That's me—Pigpen. Mean and dirty.

There are twelve people in my art class, and I make my way to the table I share with Pete and Tonya. Tonya once lived just down the road from us in a little, grey, asphalt-sided house, and we used to do stuff together. Then her dad left, and Tonya and her mom moved to town. The three of us sitting here are all mismatched and broken. Pete's being raised by his grandparents because his parents dumped him when he was three. Two years ago, Tonya's dad tried to come back, and when her mom wouldn't take him back, he called and left a long, rambling message on their answering machine that ended with a bullet blowing his brain out the back of his head. We are broken. I don't even know my real father's name, but still, my life isn't as bad as what they may have dealt with. Pete's Grandma is great, though, so he's okay.

They've been dating for two years, Tonya and Pete. They'll be together forever because they know each other's trauma. She's pretty in a quiet, "don't look at me" way, with freckles and a chin that recedes to meet her neck. Her final project is a watercolor sunset over a clear ocean. She's the best with watercolors in our class and has even done a couple of paintings to sell. She's more talented than I am. Pete is putting the last few touches on his final project, a sculpture made from plaster of Paris. It looks slightly obscene, the bulbous white forms melding together. Like a pair of fat women nestling into each other. He used condoms to pour the plaster in, then held them until they set. It is a very lazy art project but suits Peter Walston just fine. He only took this class because he loves Tonya. Pete is less talented than I am.

"How you been?" His eyes are shaded by heavy brows, and his smile is crooked, like lopsided, but seriously crooked. When he was thirteen, he ran into a fire hydrant on his bike. The scar across his forehead is mostly covered by his hair, but the damage to his mouth is clear. He lost several teeth and now has a denture for almost a whole side of his mouth. He flips his false teeth in and out at will, and more than once he's been sent to the office for freaking out a sub.

"All right." I'm still grumpy and not much in the mood for general conversation.

We settle down to put the finishing touches on our projects. After we finish, we are free to do whatever we want, as long as the rest of the class isn't disrupted. Tonya is putting her finishing touches on her painting, but I'm done with my project and so is Pete, and I can tell he's in the mood to chatter.

"I saw you talking to the Prince this morning."

I look up at him and realize that his question about how I am doing wasn't just a standard howdy. I hadn't realized there was anybody even around when I was talking to Dylan.

"Yes." I nod and go back to sketching eyes and noses, hoping the conversation is at an end.

"He looked a little worried after you walked off."

"Hm," I say, trying not to encourage him, but not sure I want him to stop, either. "Yeah. Oh well."

"He seems to really like you." Pete is still looking at me, I can tell. I hear his teeth flip out and back in, a small, sucking thwoop.

"Well, he shouldn't. I'm not nice."

"I can tell." His sarcasm is dripping.

"Holy hell." I look up at him. "Can we move on to a different subject?"

He shrugs, and we sit in silence, me looking out the window, waiting for the time to pass.

"I think he is nice," Tonya says, not looking up.

"What?" I ask.

"Dylan," she says. "He's always been a good guy."

"It's easy to be a good guy when the whole world is handed to you on a plate."

When I finally look up Tonya is looking at me with a sad look around her eyes and her lips open a bit.

"What?" I ask, annoyed.

"I thought you guys were tight."

"We're friends. I mean, I guess we're friends." I'm not really sure what tight is, but I certainly wouldn't dare to claim it today.

"Well, I remember when his brother died. I don't think he's had much handed to him on a plate." She turns back to her art, moving her body slightly away from me, to the side, distancing herself.

I look at Pete, and he shrugs.

"What are you talking about?" I ask. I am irritated because I was ready for a Dylan-bashing, and here she goes talking him up.

A look passes between Pete and Tonya, and Pete sticks his third finger in his mouth, chewing at his already shredded nails. She shrugs and goes back to her painting.

"It's not my place to tell you. It's not. But when his brother died, it was really bad for a long time. I guess that was before you moved here." Her voice trails off. "I shouldn't have said anything. Sorry."

"Dylan doesn't have a brother." My voice rises, petulant. He's been my best friend since I moved here. Wouldn't I have known if he had a brother?

Tonya shrugs. "It's not my story to tell. I'm sorry I brought it up. Just don't think his life has always been easy."

We work on in silence, my mind hissing and steaming. I feel like I've been abandoned or tossed aside, and I have to remind myself that Dylan and I are just friends, if even that. That's all we've ever been, and maybe not even so much of that. The whole world seems to be collapsing. My mother got fired for being drunk on the job, she and Mitch are breaking up, I'm jealous because Dylan can date and I don't think I will ever be able to, my clothes are all tinged yellow because of the well water at out trailer, I haven't eaten anything other than peanut butter and jelly for dinner in a lifetime, and my life just sucks, in a general, dirty, have-not kind of way. Now I find out that my best friend has a freaking brother that he never even mentioned to me.

It is not a comfortable silence, but after a few minutes, the conversations around the room filter back over our table and drown our silence out.

My mind rings with thoughts of Dylan, the image of him, dropping line by line, unbidden onto a blank sheet. His pale-blue eyes, the way his cheeks flush just under his skin when he works or when we ride in the morning chill. When I think of him my stomach flips. Is that love? I hear his laughter in my head. Not a condemning laughter like my mother's, or mocking laughter like Pete's, just his calm, amused, and always-easy laughter. Then I flash to the sight of him and her up on the ridge, leaning into each other, and my jealous little soul goes another shade darker, heading toward hunter, just past evergreen.

But there are other things going on inside of me, things older and different than Dylan in my life. The accusation Faye leveled against Mitch has ripped a festering wound open that I had left untended and dirty for years. Why did she have to bring that up? Why did her bringing it up cause such vivid memories of bath time with Daddy Eddy. I close my eyes and shake my head, trying to rattle the memories back to darkness.

I wonder if the reason I don't know Dylan at all, apparently, is because if I let myself know him, then maybe at some point he would want to take me out, and then at some point he may want to touch me, and then I would kill him.

CHAPTER 7

When I get home, Mom is working in the kitchen. Mitch is out in the shed, rebuilding the carburetor for the lawnmower. "Hi," Mom says as I walk into the smells that are radiating from the heated oven. "Dinner will be ready in just a few minutes. Go wash up." I tell her that it smells good and head toward the bathroom, feeling more than a little like Dorothy dropping into Oz.

We share a family dinner of pot roast with carrots and baby potatoes. This is my mom's best meal. She brings it out when she is trying to fit the part.

I manage to put Dylan out of my mind, watching the show unfolding around me. They share a bottle of wine, my mother's "good girl" drink, and I have milk. By the end of the meal, the mists of illusion are still thick, and I wonder when reality will start to settle back in and the fairy folk will return to their island. After dinner, I help with the dishes while Mitch goes to take a shower. They're going to a movie this evening, a proper date. Mom hums softly while we put things away and I wipe the table.

It was nice, in a surreal sort of way. It was an event. After they leave, I settle down in my room to study for my algebra exam. I've just begun when the phone rings. "Hello."

"Hello, is Alison in?" a man's voice says to me over the wire.

"This is she."

"Alison, hi, this is Rob Cartwright." It takes me a second to figure out who he is, but then it hits me: it's Faye's Rob.

"Well, hi." Then I tell him my mom's not in, forgetting that he had just asked specifically for me.

"No, no, I'm calling for you. I don't know if this would be something you're interested in, but my boss is looking for some help this summer, and I thought you'd be perfect. You're mom told us you were wanting to get a summer job."

Which I am, since next year, I'll get to do driver's ed and would love to get a car. I wonder when she would have said that, though, and why. I've never said anything of the kind to her. Maybe she meant she was looking for a summer job, now that she is unemployed again.

"I am. What's the job?"

"Well, I work over there at Billups Hardware, and it'd mostly be for filing, but sometimes helping with customers and that sort of thing. It wouldn't be many hours, but it'd be some spending money. Well, anyway. I just thought of you and thought you might like to stop by and talk to old man Billups and see what it's all about."

I am excited. A job is money, and money is freedom.

"Thank you," I say. "I really appreciate you thinking of me." It seems like a genuine kindness, and those are so rare that I hope there isn't something hiding beneath the surface.

When Mom and Mitch come home from the movie, there is laughter. I am already in bed, I made sure to be in bed, just in case it hadn't gone well, but I can hear them, bursting through the door and spilling into the living room, bumping into each other. I wonder if they made the movie or just stopped off at the bar instead. I slip out from under the covers and crack the door, just enough to see down the hall. I can see them, my mother's smiling face, that pretty face, leaning close to his, his arm around her waist. She is still young.

Too young for me to be so old, as she often reminds me. When the front door falls shut, they are enveloped in darkness, and I close my door, still listening. I hear their voices traveling down the hall to their room at the other end of the trailer. Once their bedroom door closes, I can no longer understand their words and climb back into bed, listening to the low murmur of their voices, broken occasionally by laughter, until silence falls. I think the bar won—a good drinking night—but I am not sure.

My mind hums with thoughts of a job. A job means less time in the house and more money. More money means more freedom, and if I can manage to save enough for a car next year, I will be so much closer to not being stuck here. Tomorrow I will go by Billups Hardware and talk to Mr. Billups. I try to think of what I should say to convince him that I can do that job. I'm sixteen, so Mom won't have to sign anything for me to work, but she may still tell me no. Surely she won't refuse. My mind hiccups on that. She might, depending on her mood and blood-alcohol content. She won't like it, although she might like it if she thinks she can get the money off me. I rub my hands over my eyes and know that she will try to get the money off me. It will be better if she doesn't know. I'll just not mention the job at all.

CHAPTER 8

Billups Hardware is of the Ace variety, in a low-slung, glass-fronted building with wood stacked beneath four pole barns out back. I walk in to the main building, and the scents of motor oil, metal, paint thinner, and cardboard hit my nose even before the bell on the door is finished dinging. It's a very Mitch smell, and I feel a little awkward walking into the building. It feels like a very man place, and I stand frozen for a second, thinking that maybe this isn't such a good idea. Then I see Rob, a friendly smile on his face as he holds up a small bag and keys an item number into the register. A woman stands opposite him, and my panic wanes. Not just a man place, then. He glances up, making polite small talk with the dark-haired woman he is helping, her hair teased up like a little halo around her head. He sees me, nods, and beckons me over. The woman pays. Rob puts her two paintbrushes, package of X-acto knives, and two pints of paint into a paper bag.

I scan the aisles until I hear him thank his customer and the ding above the door as she goes out. He greets me with a warm, open smile, and I feel my own mouth spreading. "Thanks for the phone call last night," I say. He nods, as if to say it was nothing.

"When Billups said he wanted to hire a high schooler, I knew you'd be great." He steps out from behind the counter, and I follow him. "Let's go meet the man."

Mr. Billups looks like Santa Claus. White-haired and bearded with overalls and a t-shirt covering his paunch. I have a split second fear that he will sit me across his lap and ask me "What do you want, Little Girl?" He does not. Thank God. He greets me with a handshake, large calloused hands that completely fold over my own, and invites me into his office. I sit across from him, and he asks, "How old are you?"

"Fifteen." He nods. Damn. "I mean sixteen, I just turned."

"You're folks okay with you getting a job."

My "folk" could give a shit less and isn't going to know, but I don't say anything of the kind. Instead I say, "Yes, Sir," maybe too quickly. "They are very supportive." Did I really just say that?

"Do you have transportation?"

"I have a bike." He smiles, and I half expect a jolly Ho Ho Ho. My answers are okay; I've passed, so far. He rustles over his desk and peels an application from a pad, sliding it across to me. I smile and look through the application.

"You can fill that out and bring it back. You can have the job if you want it."

"That was easy." I smile and give just a little laugh.

"Rob told me good things."

Bless Rob, who certainly shouldn't have had anything good to say about me. I was nothing if not rude at his house.

Mr. Billups offers me a tour of the store, and I follow him with my application in my hand. He motions to plumbing fixtures and piping, then tools, paints, woodworking. Finally we are at the back of the store, and he goes toward a dark stairwell, and my throat begins to close with that old familiar lump. I hesitate at the bottom until he reaches the top and flips on the light. I swallow around my lump. He has already moved past the steps and is waiting for me in the file room, a loft that overhangs that back quarter of the store. He doesn't seem to have noticed my hesitation, and I am grateful. I would have said I was just a little scared of the dark. Even as embarrassing as that is, it is better than saying I was afraid for a minute that he was leading me into a dark place so he could grope me, which would probably make him change his mind about hiring me.

He talks me through the filing system, which is simple but also overwhelming. I feel my pulse pumping up, and I wonder if I am ready for this, for a job. What if I screw it all up?

"So, what do you think?" Mr. Billups asks, his arms spreading wide to display his files and, beyond the windows, his store. He is proud. He has built this.

"I think I'd love to work for you, Mr. Billups." Seriously, who wouldn't want to be an elf? I promise to fill out the application and get it back the next day.

And I did. I am grateful that I don't have to worry about a waiver, since there is no sober parental unit able to sign anything. The next afternoon when I show up with the application, Mr. Billups neatly places it in a "to be filed" box without so much as looking at it and turns me over to Rob to start teaching me the register. I finish my shift at eight and ride my bike home, grateful that it is staying light a little later, but even so, the sun has dropped low to the horizon as I ride. I hope not to get run over by my own mother on her way home from wherever she goes these days. Mr. Billups said we'd start with four hours a night for three nights a week until school is out, and then we'd plan for the summer.

I'm a little worried about what my mother will say when I get home late. Will she be angry that she didn't know where I was, worried, thinking something bad had happened? I pedal a little faster, hoping to make it "less bad," but when the trailer comes into view at full dusk, I am relieved because it is dark and neither Mitch nor my mother's car is parked in the yard.

Throughout the rest of the school year, all of two and a half weeks and into the summer, I work at my little job without anybody being the wiser. My mother never once asks where I have been or what I was doing, and it may even be accurate to say that she hasn't noticed anything different in my routine. I have thought for a long time that she doesn't really notice me in her life except the inconvenience of me being there, needing stuff. I ride my bike most days to get to the store and home again, and it feels like the best thing in the world to have a little stash of money growing and to have someplace to be where people act like people are supposed to.

I'm so busy that I don't even have to try to force Dylan out of my mind. I'm so busy that I almost don't think of him at all. It feels good to be busy, to be the one who doesn't have time, the one who has something better to do. I stop going past his house on any pretext with the hope of catching sight of him. He hasn't given a second thought to my sudden absence—he doesn't really care, except when it strokes his ego to be doing something good for the poor kid, his charity kid. I close the door as the beggar in our friendship and focus, very intently, on doing a good job for Mr. Billups so someday I can get out of the trailer, away from my mother, and out of this damn town. Someday I am going to have something, and if I want that, then I'm going to have to do it myself. There are no knights coming to the rescue. I don't want charity.

PART TWO: SUMMER

CHAPTER 9

Dylan shows up at my house this morning. I hear his voice outside my window, talking to Mitch. "Hey, Mitch. Is Alison up yet?"

"I think I heard her around." I scurry through the house and exit onto the front steps before he has mounted them. I do not want him to come inside. "Dirty" echoes in my head, making my skin crawl. The element of the fairyland that had permeated the house for a few short weeks has lifted and left in its stead the tension and scent of vodka and normalcy. My mother still hasn't found a job, and I can tell Mitch is not going to be that "take care of you" kind of guy. She did get a call back from one of the nursing homes and has an interview set up for Monday morning at ten. I'm keeping my fingers crossed, although I think maybe housekeeping is not her best bet.

"Hey." He startles at my sudden appearance and takes a step back. I'm surprised to see him. I've been maintaining my distance since school has been out. Actually, I've been avoiding him since I blasted him in the hall.

"Can we talk?" he asks. I nod and steer him around the back of the trailer, away from all ears. Neither one of us say anything for a few minutes as we walk toward the line of the woods.

"Did I do something?" His voice is quiet, "Like to piss you off?"

My shoulder bumps against his arm. It feels strong and familiar, and I let myself bump against him again because it felt so good the first time. "No. Not really. Not you, so much. I'm just pissed off."

"I'm sorry."

"Not your fault." I look down, watching our feet trudge through the grass. I'm suddenly unsure of why I've been so angry at him at all.

"I'm sure some of it is." He bumps against me, and I smile. Suddenly all the distance and space between us begins to slip away, and he is my oldest friend. My only true friend.

"Maybe some." I smile slightly, "Sort of."

"So I sort of did something?" His voice is still quiet, trying to make peace without understanding the war.

"No, really, you didn't. I mean I think it's really just me." I know I'm going to have to explain that, so I trudge on with, "I think I've just been in a bad mood and didn't really want to talk about it."

"And now?"

"I'm still in a bad mood." I glance up at him, but drop my eyes from his as quickly as they meet. "I may always have been in a bad mood." I think about telling him that I was just jealous and let it be that, but I hesitate to bring Kelci into it.

"Do you want to talk about it?"

"I may never want to talk about it. Not really." And I laugh, because I'm nervous, not because I think it's funny. There is an intensity in him that I'm not used to. He's not my buddy Dylan right now. I'm not quite sure who he is.

"Can we?" He has stopped walking. I remember telling him that we were from different worlds and that I didn't want to see the water if I couldn't swim. I called him Mr. Perfect, like a petty bitch. I'm sure he remembers it, too, but that's a much bigger conversation than I am up for. I take a few more steps, but then stop, too, watching a barn swallow zooming toward the woods.

"How's Kelci?" I ask, bringing the bitch up anyway, steering safely to something I'm able to cope with.

"I don't know. I haven't seen her."

"You two are quite the couple." There, I've said it. It's out there, and we can talk about it and stay away from the real stuff.

"No. Not really." His tone is tolerant, controlled, slightly annoyed. "Is that why you've been so distant with me lately? Because I took her out a few times?"

"No. I'm just busy. Anyway, I mean, it's none of my business. Who you go out with."

His laughter breaks the tension, and his arm falls over my shoulder, drawing me toward him. "We're not going out anymore. She's just a friend. That's it. You know she's going out with David now." David Delaney is the football quarterback. They're a perfect match. He pauses. "I thought you knew that."

"No." I let myself lean into him, "I just started seeing you and her together all the time. At the ridge, at school. I was jealous, I guess." Like she was taking you away from me. I do not say the last but know from the look on his face that he clearly sees it written on my face.

"You were jealous." He says it like it's a joke, like he's got some power over me. My jaw tightens, and I know he sees it because he drops the mocking tone. He has no idea the jealousy I feel, the least of which is about him and his dating rituals. But his face grows serious and his hand slides onto my shoulder. "Come on, Al, nobody can take me from you. We are linked, you know?" He gives me a squeeze, and we've reached the edge of the woods. I nod but don't know what he means, we are no more linked than me and the kid who lives across the street.

"Don't say that," I say, feeling pissed again. We are nothing. We are just friends . . . what is there to take away? Friends by proximity more than by likeness.

"I'm sorry?" he says, clearly confused, but he lets out a long breath. "Come on. Don't be mad." He bumps me, "I didn't come here to make you mad. I've missed you."

"Right." I draw the word out, long and sarcastic.

"Seriously," he says, and I start to feel like a small-minded idiot. "Are you still mad?"

"No. I'm not mad. I've missed you, too," I admit grudgingly. We sit on the fire logs and catch up. He asks about the Friday Fires, and I explain that we don't have them anymore. "You should have seen it," I say. "Mom went after Theresa across the fire. Pulled her through it by her hair. It was very caveman." I laugh a little at the memory. "You should have seen the looks. It was awesome." He chuckles a bit, but clearly it was something you had to be there for, and he isn't as amused as I was. "I mean it wasn't funny at the time, I guess, but it's kinda funny from a distance. Maybe."

"Sounds like quite a scene," he finally concedes. We sit for about twenty minutes, me drawing with a stick in what remains of the ashes from the last fire, with a shard of glass left behind, somebody's broken bottle, and him resting his elbows on his knees, plucking blades of grass from the weeds. I slide my thumb along the sharp edge of the shard and a neat little pool of blood wells from the cut. It doesn't hurt. It just sends a peaceful pop through my head.

"I got a job," I say, putting the well of blood into my mouth.

"Really?" he asks, noticing my thumb in my mouth, I draw it out and smash the small slice onto my knee. A frown creases his forehead when he sees the small drop of blood in the ashes, and I brush it under the ashes with my foot. I start talking quickly, telling him about Billups and how much I love being there. His frown disappears.

"That's awesome," he says, his face splitting wide, and I get such a surge of pride that I actually blush.

We are sitting there, me feeling giddy with his praise, or with the little slice on my thumb, when the back door of the trailer opens and my mother comes spilling down the stairs. We turn and watch her approach, weaving slightly as she comes. "I thought you'd like some lemonade." She hands us each a glass. The one she gives Dylan is half empty because it has sloshed out during her weeble-wobble stroll. She notices and goes to correct the problem by taking my glass and handing it to Dylan, giving me the other one. All the while she is talking, babbling almost, in circles, "Damn yard," she giggles, "it's like a fleet of moles have been at it. I swear Mitch needs to flatten it before somebody gets hurt. It's like a flock of moles . . ." and she giggles again. "Somebody could have a nasty fall walking in these mole holes." Giggle. Her words are precise, not sloppy, the way the movies show people when they drink. With Mom, it's her thoughts that get dizzy not her diction. The logic fumbles in circles as the words tumble out of her mouth. To follow the meandering subjects require a certain amount of mental gymnastics. If I didn't know her, I wouldn't necessarily think she was drunk, I would maybe think she was flighty, dingy, even dumb.

"You should let Mitch know," I say, hoping to send her weaving back to the house.

"My, it's hot out here." She sits down on the log beside Dylan, who is politely drinking his lemonade. He's been around my mom more than once when she's drunk, so I know he sees it, heck, he probably smells it with her sitting so close.

He acts like he doesn't notice anything. "Thank you for the lemonade," he says, always polite, such good manners from down the road. "It sure is hot," he adds, as if Mom being completely sodden, is no big deal. At least she isn't upset about anything; at least she isn't fighting about anything. She sits, leaning back, fanning herself with her hand, fingers spread, not making much of a breeze, but drawing attention to the long lines of her neck.

"Oh dear," she says with a glance down her body, "I've missed a button." Her shirt is buttoned scant, and she laughs, saying, "Oh well, not like anybody is going to be looking at me." With that, her hand taps down on Dylan's leg, and she starts to stand up, nearly tumbles back, but Dylan reaches up and steadies her tilt. She fumbles with the buttons. I stand up and reach to take her elbow. "Come on, let me take you in. You should rest."

"Let go of me." She slaps my arm away, and her eyes flash, and she turns to Dylan. "Do you see how she treats me, like I'm an invalid?" She says it like two words, In Valid. Then she laughs, a girlish, tinkling laugh. She smiles and pats my arms, repositioning herself in the frame. "You kids enjoy your lemonade." She begins the slow meandering steps back to the trailer, her hips swinging wide, her best Marilyn Monroe, still fumbling with her buttons. I hate her with every ounce of my soul. By the time she is reaching for the door to the trailer, her buttons have been undone and her shirttail flaps in the breeze.

Dylan has known for years that my home life is all screwed up. His knowing that life isn't great isn't the same as him seeing it firsthand. I'm disgusted and embarrassed when she turns and waves, her black bra cutting a stark contrast across the paleness of her doughy skin. I'm mortified as she totters on the top step, fumbling with the door, and for more than a split second, I wish she would fall.

CHAPTER 10

"Let's get out of here." We leave the plastic glasses on the ground beside the log, nestled in amongst the ashes.

We are about a third of a mile into the underbrush, almost to the main trail when he breaks the silence. "Do you want to talk about it?"

"No. I don't know why she does that crap." The disgust and fury rolls off of me in waves.

"Because she's sick." His voice is calm.

"She's not sick, Dylan. She's a drunk." I spit the words out, as if I am the drinker, trying to remove the taste from my mouth. I am so tired of excuses for the stupid shit she does.

"How often does she drink?" Although he knows my family is a mess, he hasn't really begun to see exactly what a mess it all is.

"When she's awake." It's a cold statement. I know the first thing she does when she wakes up is pour a drink. I know because I hear it, the clink of her rings on the bottle. Some mornings I hear her climbing on a chair to reach one of her many hiding places.

"Can we talk about it?" His voice is tentative, hesitant.

"What is there to talk about? I wish I knew who my father was so I could go and live with him." It pops out of my mouth as if it were really something I had thought about, something I wanted. I haven't thought of my father in years. The last time I asked her who he was, she trashed the house telling me what an ungrateful little brat I was and that he didn't want a damn thing to do with either of us.

We walk in silence for several paces, my mind playing back the reel of her tottering on the top step, her black bra cutting her visage and her loose shirt flapping against her wobble. I am so embarrassed. Dirty. "I just don't understand why she keeps doing it."

"Because she's an alcoholic, and that's what they do, she can't just stop. It doesn't usually work that way."

"See that on a public service pamphlet?" I'm irritated that he, with his perfect family, presumes to know something about the mess in which I live. The way he says it makes it not her fault, like she is a victim of it, with a great bottle of rum running after her, holding her down, and pouring itself down her gullet.

Dylan expels air from his nose in a humph sound. "Something like that. I know more than you might think."

"What? Did you do a report on it once, give a speech maybe? Good job. Well, I'm living it, my friend." We walk on in silence, my embarrassment and anger bubbling against each other until they mix into a soupy, brown sludge. I feel tears building along my lashes, and I blink quickly to dispel them. Maybe he and I really are from worlds too far apart to be bridged. We've just reached for each other after such a long, lonely absence, and here comes Mother, busting it back to pieces. Is there anything she doesn't destroy? "Sorry, that was uncalled for." A single, angry tear drops over the rim of my eyelids, and suddenly he has stopped our forward progress, drawn me around to face him. He wraps me into the solid space created by his arms. I take a deep breath, drawing back but without force. We touch . . . I mean, we've always touched, but with my cheek pressing so firmly on his chest and the scent of him so strong in my nose . . . this is something else all over again. I draw in a shuddering breath and close my eyes. I'll take this—this one hug, this one moment in time where

I am not lost and alone and outside of him. The tension melts through my shoulders, and I let my own arms draw up to him, hooking my thumbs in the hoops of his waistband. I could stay here, right here, and never move again. I could disappear right here. I feel his breath across my hair, ruffling it like a breeze.

"Can we talk about it?" he asks, and the calmness in his voice grates against my jagged nerves, drawing me back from the edge of calm, as he repeats this question, his mantra for the day.

I shake my head into his chest. "There's nothing to say." And I laugh angrily, pulling myself free from him and beginning our journey yet again. His hand reaches out and takes my elbow, turning me back. His eyes lock on mine, and I don't pull away.

"Look, Al, I know. I understand. I want to help you." I step away from him and glance back toward the way we've come. Him wanting to help me makes me feel pathetic, his charity case. It's the worst thing he could have said to me.

"Can you make her stop drinking?"

"No. I can't." His voice is low, calm.

"Then I guess there's just not a lot you can do, huh?" A fleeting look passes his face, and I'm not sure if it's pain or anger or some mixture of the two, maybe frustration.

"Come on. Let's go." He doesn't sound angry or upset. He sounds resolved and determined. I follow him through a narrow stretch before we come out to the pasture. We pass the grazing horses and climb the ladder in the barn that leads to the hayloft. Dylan opens the hay door and light floods in, catching dust streaming in the air, and I sit cross-legged on the hay-strewn floor while he paces. This is one of his "get away" places. I have found him here many times over the years when he has been upset or angry or just needed to be alone. I assume we have come here so nobody will notice us, so we can talk in private. My stomach churns, and I do not want to have a conversation about this with him. I do not want to share with him the life I live. I pluck a piece of hay from the floor and slowly set about shredding it, my mind working out just how I can make it all sound not so bad.

"So what do you understand?" I ask him without looking away from my busy fingers. Maybe if I can get him to tell me what he thinks he knows, I can leave it at that and he'll be none the wiser. He comes and stands in front of me, his back against a bale of hay.

"I understand that it has gotten a lot worse, these last few years. A lot worse this year. I know that Mitch has women and your mom drinks, a lot. I know that they fight, and I know that because I can hear them sometimes." I glance sharply up at him at this last and feel my cheeks flush. Dirty. Cheap. Trashy. I look back down quickly. His laying out my life, like a supper, surprises me. I had not realized that it was so transparent, that I was so transparent. I had not realized that the sounds from our acre of land would filter to his house. Is that why he wasn't amused by my story about Mom and Theresa, because he heard the whole thing? I'm surprised to feel the sting of tears in my eyes and don't know if I can speak.

"I know that you are the most stubborn person I know. Jake says that I have to let you come to me, not to push it." He stands above me, looking down at me, looking older than we are. "But Al, you never come to me. You just build your walls all by yourself, and in the process you shut everybody out. I used to think I knew everything about you, even more than I knew myself. Now I don't. I don't know anything anymore." With these last words, he touches his hand to mine, and I let him. He has settled on the floor beside me, not close but near.

His words hit a chord inside of me, touching on a lot of feelings at once. Anger that he has talked about me to Jake; embarrassment for that, too; curiosity at exactly what has been said; sadness that he feels locked out; comfort that he cares enough to feel locked out. "You're my best friend," I say, glancing up at him, thinking of how I really want to talk to him and tell him how much he means to me, how much I love him. My eyes rest on his lips, before I drop them.

He squeezes my hand. "That's why I wish you would talk to me."

"There's nothing to talk about." I start to pull my hand away, but he closes both of his around it.

"Don't."

"It's embarrassing. It makes me feel pathetic." Trashy. Dirty.

"It shouldn't. It isn't anything you've done, or even about you." I draw my hand out and slide across the floor to sit beside him, my back against a bale of hay. "Come on, Al. Talk to me."

I shake my head. I wouldn't even know where to start. It is his voice that finally breaks the silence. "Fine, then I'll talk," he says, his voice sounding resigned. "I knew a man once; he was bad," he starts quietly, but when I say nothing he goes on. He is telling a story, like we are sitting around a campfire. I remember him saying this to me in the hall that last day, and I glance up at him. "His name was Jake, and he drank Jim Beam, and he was the life of the party. He was fun when he'd had just the right amount. He'd try anything. 'You want to ski off the roof into the front yard? Great, let me get the video camera.'" His voice shifts when he speaks for this other person. "He didn't care. And he'd try anything, too. He was invincible. It didn't matter that he'd broken his leg more than once and had nearly broken his back from doing stupid human tricks. He once told me that he jumped off the bridge in St Louis, going over the Mississippi, just for the hell of it." I've turned toward him, watching him talk, his eyes are focused somewhere in the distance above his arms, which are propped on his raised knees. Did he just say the guy's name was Jake? His Jake? "He was a ton of fun, a real FUN drunk. To a point. But then just past that point, watch out. It'd happen so damn quickly, too. No warning, like a switch going off, then he went mean. Really mean. He put his wife in the hospital with a broken jaw once. He threw a half-empty bottle at one of his sons once, and I had to get stitches. If it had hit half an inch lower, I would have lost my eye." My mouth is hanging open. I have stopped breathing entirely. "He hurt a lot of people while he was drinking, and he never remembered anything the next day."

I draw a shuddering breath. "Jake?" He closes his eyes on mine and nods. "No way."

He nods. "He lost my brother in a boating accident and didn't even know he'd rented a boat." He is still holding my eyes, and I want to touch him. I want to trace that scar above his eye. His words seep slowly through my shock-thickened head. He paints this picture of a broken family, another broken family, and I am unable to make it correlate to the family I know.

"It's not like nobody knew what was going on, they just didn't know what to do to help." He looks wrecked, strangely destroyed, deflated.

I bring his hand up to my lips and let my breath pass over his skin. I have no words, I try to reconcile all that he has said, and the one thing that finally comes from my mouth is, "Tonya said you had a brother."

"I did. I should have told you."

"I had no idea. How old was he?"

"He was nine. I was eight." His voice has flattened.

Dylan was ten when I moved here. How did I not know? I find my voice. "I'm so sorry. How did I not know?"

"I didn't talk about it. Ever." He smiles a little. "By the time I could talk about it, I realized what your family was like and I didn't want to bring it all up."

"God, it's not like that. For me, I mean, sure she drinks and there are problems, but it's nothing like that." I feel relieved, like everything will be okay because his life is better now.

"But it's still not good. I know it's not."

"Not good, but not always bad." I try to tell him the success stories, but they sound pathetic even to me. When I say that we've had milk for two weeks in a row, I go silent, realizing that I am doing my family, my mother no favors. I almost tell him that she made pot roast not too long ago but know that he would see the fact that I was impressed by that, a hot dinner once in a blue moon, is a testament to our dysfunction. All of it makes us sound so trashy. Dirty. Dylan traces the lines on my palm as he listens to my long pauses and short sentences. Finally I stop all together and draw my hands over my face, hiding myself from him. I can feel his eyes on me, pale and intense. I haven't cried, which makes me proud. There is some relief at having some little bit of my broken story outside of me, sitting there on the floor of the loft in a jumbled heap of ick. He tilts his head and rests it lightly on top of mine.

"Is it just alcohol?" I nod. His voice is muffled against my hair. "Do you think she's an alcoholic?"

"I know she's a drunk," I say, conceding.

"Isn't it the same thing?" he asks as I take up a new shred of hay.

"I don't know." The term "alcoholic" brings up images of bums in the doorways of city streets sleeping under newspapers. "I mean, she's not a bum, she has a job, she's not like an alcoholic." Of course, she doesn't have a job. An interview for Monday, but that is not a job.

"Jake had a job. A good job. Most alcoholics aren't bums. They don't usually live out of dumpsters."

I shrug my shoulders. "But, things have been better, lately." I pause, thinking over the last few weeks, and I know that it isn't really better, just more closely covered, less visible to me since I started working at Billups. That's all. I don't want to talk anymore, and he must see it. "Come on, let's go for a ride." He nods and rises to hand me down the ladder.

We saddle the horses, Pride and Adelaide, and we leave the farm through the back gate that leads directly into the woods. It's a bright, lazy morning. The summer heat is sizzling, draining the energy from all things except for mosquitoes and black flies. Adelaide's tail swishes constantly, warning flies from her flanks as we step through the underbrush and onto the trail. Dylan pushes Pride into a gallop, and Adelaide follows suit, unbidden. He has a strange, intense expression on his face, and I wonder what is running in his mind. We gallop only through the open trail and return to a walk when we reach deeper into the woods. The saddle leather creaks with the motion. The flies and mosquitos hum in my ears. We cross over the creek, neither of us talking, the tension in his shoulders making him jerky in his seat, just riding, but not his normal riding. We ride, silent, intense, listening to the birds in the trees, smacking at the bold midge that dares to land and feeling the sun as it comes through the canopy to touch our skin.

Dylan leads me through a smaller trail that branches off from the main and down a path that is nearly overgrown. The trees are thick, and we pick our way carefully. He points through the trees, and I follow his hand, spying a buck drinking from a pond. His horns are still fuzzy with youth, and the three little points on each are rounded. I've never been through this section of the woods before. I never thought the woods would have spaces I had not yet explored after all these years. I try to draw this pond into my mind, but it is nowhere in my memory. To the left I can hear water rumbling and gurgling over rocks in a streambed. Dylan reins Pride to a stop and slides from his back just as we enter a small clearing. I feel like I have crossed into another world.

CHAPTER 11

The air in the clearing hangs like a cloud—the mist has not yet burned off. On the far side of the clearing, there is a small, lopsided building, tilting precariously, leaning close to a tree for support. It is bathed in a spray of light from the canopy above. We tether the horses, and Dylan drops his arm across my shoulder, allowing me to lean into him. When he speaks, his voice is low, almost hushed.

"Daecus and I used to play out here when we were kids. Vaude always used to say that Dake was just like Dad had been when he was a kid and I was more like her." He pauses. "He was mad at me the day it happened. Mad because I didn't want to go on a boat. I wanted to stay behind and read. He called me his "little woman" as he and Dake left. I stayed at the tent. When they weren't back by night I found the guy who cleaned the toilets. He called the ranger who came and put me in his golf cart, and we rode around the perimeter of the lake. We found the boat but no sign of Daecus or Jake. He called the police and called a search party. We found Jake about three miles from the lake, almost to the road going through the forest. He was asleep next to a tree, but Daecus was not there. Jake never could say what happened, but two days later, they found his body caught at the spillway."

"I can't believe you never told me," I say, feeling strange and empty.

"When you moved here, I was still making stuff up, and I never talked about him. Nobody did."

"What was he like?"

"Not me." He laughs. "He was always that kid climbing trees and jumping off of things. He had no fear. He was trouble. You know the kind, just reckless, fearless, and I was always telling him that he was going to break his leg. He did, actually. Once. Right over there." He points toward the slanting building. "He climbed that tree, about thirty feet up, maybe not quite, but pretty high, and he jumped out of the tree and landed on the roof. See how it leans? That's how that happened." He shakes his head. "I haven't thought of that in a long time."

"Jake never remembered what happened on the boat?" I ask, and Dylan shakes his head.

"That's horrible." I reach my hand up and hold his fingertips where they dangle over my shoulder. We've come to the building and he leads me to the little overhang, and we sit on the rough-hewn bench that is there.

"This was my place. Had been our place, but after he was gone, I kept coming, trying to sort things out. It was pretty rough for a while."

I feel like I should say something but I can't think of a thing that doesn't sound lame. I've never heard him talk like this, so serious and intense. "Why'd you stop coming here?" A stupid question. What difference does it make?

"I didn't have to hide anymore." His voice is distant, soft, almost reverent.

I match the softness of his voice. "What were you hiding from?"

"Mostly my Dad." Now he laughs a sharp-edged hoot. I'm confused, but I don't say anything. "I've wanted to tell you for so long."

He leans against the building, and for a second, I think the building will give way and crash down, but it holds fast. I watch Dylan, his eyes distant and faraway. The light streaming through the canopy casts him in gold, and he shifts around, settling down on the rough-hewn bench beside the wonky building, putting himself in the cool shadows of its walls. His finger lifts to trace the small half-moon above his right eye, cutting into his brow, disturbing the growth pattern there. His eyes are intense on me, and suddenly I see the scar differently. It's no longer just one of his features. I can see the stitch marks, now, clear as day, white against the surrounding tan. The pit of my stomach falls away, and for a second, I begin to feel trapped, frightened, but I'm not sure why I should be. Dylan's voice goes on, still soft, distant. "He was a bad drunk."

I lift my finger to his brow, tracing his scar. "Not anymore?"

He shakes his head, taking my hand, drawing me around to sit in front of him, in the hollow of him. I am stunned, silent, unable to reconcile, not just his revelation, but his arms around me. My pulse is fluttering, and my mouth is dry. His breath rushes past my ear, and I melt a little into him, my flesh rising to bumps all down my arms. "I remember waking up in the middle of the night, hearing him stumble into the kitchen, yelling because the table was in his way." His voice is nearly a whisper, as if he is frightened to put this into the world, frightened of the consequences. I try to imagine Jake as this person, and I can't. The picture Dylan paints is so dark, such a stark contrast to the reality I see at their home. "It just got worse. Over time, the older we got." I notice the "we" and feel a pang for the lost brother.

"Why didn't you ever tell me?"

"I don't know. I don't talk about it. It wasn't really his fault. There was an investigation at the time. It was just an accident, a very bad accident." An accident, I think, an accident, a very bad accident. But how do you go on after that? How does a family survive? How can a woman love a man who lost, let drown, her son? How can a man still live with himself afterward? "I don't remember a lot about that year. She blamed him, and he was drinking more. Trying to get away from whatever guilt he felt, I guess. It wasn't his fault. But he felt like hell."

"Wasn't his fault?" I ask, incredulous, angry. Maybe it wouldn't have happened if he hadn't been drinking, drunk, unaware, heedless. I want to say these things. I want to say that none of this is okay, but I am afraid that if I say anything, he will stop talking. He draws a breath, and I lean deeper into him. His fingertips rub along my cheek.

"Well, maybe, it was his fault. It was certainly his job to keep my brother safe, but we couldn't fix it and we had to get past it. We had to get past the blaming. Blame. I'm surprised we made it through. I pretended that I didn't have a brother, or that he was off at summer camp. I started lying to people about everything. I made up stories about how my uncle from Australia, who doesn't exist, was going to come and take me home with him to his kangaroo farm. I had a whole reality based out of these lies, and I guess I pretty much lived there for a while." I remember the story about his uncle and his kangaroo farm. He had given it such detail.

The sadness in his voice makes me want to turn to that small boy that he had been and draw him into my lap and just hold him, but I don't move. "Mom and I moved up to Wisconsin, and she filed for divorce. He'd beaten the daylights out of her one night and didn't remember it the next night. I mean, he used to hit her every once in a while, or me, or Daecus, when we got in the way, but never like this. They wired her jaw shut, and she was in the hospital for a couple days, and when she got out, we left. We lived with my grandparents, and Dad stayed here. Drinking himself into a stupor, using uppers to get through work. It was a horrible time, but at least the only person left that he could hurt was himself." We sit in silence for the longest time. His chin resting on my shoulder, his cheek against mine. I do not move or break the touch. My mind spins back through my memories, trying to place any of what he is saying. They didn't sign the papers she had filed, they worked it out and now they are perfect. I let out a long shuddering breath.

I don't remember him being gone, I don't remember his mother being in the hospital, but maybe we weren't friends yet when that all happened. "None of that seems possible. I met you when you were ten. How could I not have known any of this? I've always been so jealous of your family." I pause, realizing that I would never have admitted that to him before today. "I feel like you're talking about other people, not people we actually know."

"I know. That's how I know that it can get better, but not until the drinking is gone."

"So that's what changed it? He doesn't drink now." It's a statement made from somewhere inside of me that needs to know that even from this devastation there can be life.

"No, not now. He doesn't. But that's not all. He stopped blaming everybody else for bad choices he made or just dumb bad luck."

"So what, he just stopped?" I've stuck on the idea of him stopping, and the rest is just water off the duck's back.

"Kinda, I guess. He didn't do it alone. He still doesn't. He's been clean for seven years. He went into rehab and sobered up. He spent almost a year in residential treatment, getting out of the cycle. Even now he goes to meetings at least once a week. He's not proud about being an addict, but he is proud that he's not practicing addiction now." We sit in silence for some time, his hand resting lightly on my stomach. I do remember that I met Jake later, but I never thought anything about it.

"Do you think she is?" I ask quietly.

"Your mom an alcoholic? Yeah, Al, I do. A lot of people are. Some people never wake up from it."

"Do you think she can change?"

"Only if she wants to." His lips brush against my ear, and electricity pulses through me. Was that just an accident?

"So what do I do?" My voice flutters, and he adjusts his head away from my cheek and to the top of my head. His finger slips along the inside of my wrist, making me tingle where he touches me.

"Make sure you're safe. Stay out of her way. Don't ride in cars with her. Don't blame yourself."

"I mean, how do I make her stop?" This is the real question, the one that I must find an answer to.

"You can't. Not really. It's something she'll have to decide to do. Until then, if she is an alcoholic, she'll be sick. They always talk about rock bottom. Who knows what that will be?"

It makes my small spit of anger flare again, calling her sick. Seems that losing her job and Mitch should be enough of a rock bottom. She isn't sick, she just likes her vodka more than she likes me or anything else.

I pull out of his arms, shifting, breaking our connection. He lets me go, dropping his leg to the ground, his hand resting on the bench on either sides of his legs, leaning forward. "I remember when I saw Jake after he sobered up. He didn't even look the same. He came up to me and squatted down. He put out his hand and said, 'Hi, I'm Jake and I'm an addict.' That's when I started calling him Jake." I sit closer to him and put my hand over his, he flexes his fingers and draws mine between his, entwined. I lean into him, wishing I hadn't pulled away, missing the solidness of him around me. "That's how I think of him now. I don't see him as the same person. He's just Jake, an addict." His chin rests on my shoulder and I turn my head slightly, feeling his cheek against mine. "Just know, that if you ever need to get away, you can always come down the road." The mist begins to burn off and in the heat, the birds fall silent, the horses shuffle their feet.

CHAPTER 12

I am sitting on the couch reading The Prince of Tides, a book Vaude loaned me when she finished it. She is an avid reader and often passes books that she enjoyed on to me. I am waiting for Mom to come out of her room. I know she's awake because I woke her up. She has her interview this morning. The last one she had she was late for and probably didn't get the job because of it. She is none too excited about working in housekeeping, clearly not her strong suit, but Mitch has made it pretty clear that she needs to find something, because he isn't paying our way.

She comes out. I hear the door click, and the knob smacks into the hallway wall. "Do I look okay?" she asks, and I assure her that she does. She's dressed in black pants and a cream-colored oxford that really accentuates her hair. Her eyes have shadow, and she has used a light coral color of lipstick.

"You look great." I set my book aside.

She lets out a heavy sigh, and I hope she hasn't started drinking already. I can't smell it, but sometimes I can't unless I've been away for a bit.

"Would you mind if I rode in with you? I've got some laundry to do. I could wait for you, and maybe we could go to lunch afterwards, to celebrate."

"I don't have the job yet." She laughs. "But that would be nice."

"Great." I run down the hall to grab the bag I've already set up to take. I hate to admit that the clothes are just a ploy, a way to ensure that she doesn't drink before the interview. She needs this job. I need her to have this job.

Out in the bright sunlight, it feels like we've been set to broil and it isn't even nine o'clock. We drive with the windows down, our hair whipping around our heads. The air conditioner hasn't worked in the car since the middle of last summer, and since air conditioning is a luxury, Mitch, who can fix almost anything, hasn't bothered to fix it.

She pulls into the parking lot, and I tell her to go get 'em as I shoulder my pack and make the two-block walk to the laundromat. She is sweating and looks a little shaky. Maybe it would have been better if she'd had a drink.

My clothes are finishing in the wash, and I keep looking out the window, waiting for her to pull in, anxious to hear how it went, but when the clothes are finished spinning, she still isn't back. I load the wet clothes into my backpack and make my way back down to the nursing home. Her car is gone. I've kept an eye out, looking for her on the short walk, but she didn't pass me, I am sure of it. I wonder if somebody would bother to steal the car, but can't imagine it. I open the door to the nursing home and step inside. A fan circulates in the entryway, and I stop at the front desk.

"Did Alice Hayes have an interview this morning?" I ask. The woman looks at me for a second.

"Housekeeping?" she asks, and I nod. She picks up a phone and pushes a couple of buttons. "Did Ms. Hayes already leave?" She listens; I listen, but can't hear the voice on the other end. She hangs up the phone and gives me a smile. "She's already gone."

"Hm," I say, drawing my brow together. "Did she do the interview?"

The woman nods. I want to ask her if she got the job, but I feel a little crazy, like a stalker or something. "Did she happen to say where she was going from here?" The look that crosses her face makes me add, "I thought she was going to pick me up when she was done."

"She didn't say. But she was pretty happy when she left."

"Good." That could mean one of two things: either she got the job and she was happy about it, or she decided she didn't want the job and told them to shove it. Both would make sense coming from my mother. "Okay, well thanks." I go back out into the heat and stand, baking on the sidewalk, looking from one direction down the road to the other. I could just start walking, I suppose. Fuck. I shoulder my pack, now soaked through and actually kind of nice and cool against my back, and head down the street to the north. If I walk one mile every sixteen minutes, it will only take me an hour and twenty minutes to get home.

I walk, and as I walk, I get more and more angry. What the hell? How could she forget to pick me up? I wonder if I will find her happily settled in when I finally get there. I've walked about twenty minutes or so, just over a mile, past the square and just a couple of blocks from the road that will take me to our house, when I pass by Northside Package and Ice Chest, where I see her car. I stop and just stare at it for the longest time, my head overheating with the sun beating down on me. Sweat is pooling along my waistband and under my breasts. I have a momentary vision of beating the headlights and windshield with a baseball bat. It's kind of a lovely image, but I trail my hand over the hot metal as I make my way toward the door. It takes a minute for my eyes to adjust from the sun outside to the cool dark inside. The windows are tinted so dark that the world outside looks like dusk.

When my eyes finally adjust, I see her, leaning in toward the bartender, her hand holding a glass, empty but for ice. The barkeep fills it up, and she never even sets it on the counter. She is smiling. He is smiling. They look like old friends. I sidle in and sit next to her, letting the soppy bag fall from my shoulders. I set it on the floor. She looks at me, and it actually takes a second for recognition to dawn. She jerks her head back as if I have struck her, her eyes fluttering at my sudden appearance. "Alison!" she says, smiling. "What are you doing here?"

"I'm on my way home and saw the car."

"Oh." Her forehead puckers, and then her eyes fly wide. "Oh shit! I was supposed to pick you up, wasn't I?"

I nod.

"Damn. I completely forgot." She starts to laugh, a leg-slapping, mouth-gaping laugh that echoes around me. I am pissed. Beyond pissed, and for a split second, I have another one of those visions, and in this one, I shove her off her barstool. The vision fades as soon as it appears, and I just stand, my backpack hanging from my hand, my back wet where my clothes have soaked through. She taps me on the shoulder, her bony fingers squeezing me, holding me. "I'm sorry. Don't be mad. Come on, Alison. Don't be mad." She leans close to me. "I got the job." As if this should make everything okay. It doesn't, but it does help.

"When do you start?" I ask, trying to lay my irritation down.

"Tomorrow."

"Great." I say, cooling off. The bartender brings me a water with ice, and I empty the glass in short order. He refills it, and I am grateful. Someday this is going to be one of those great family stories—the day my mom forgot to pick me up at the laundromat and I found her in the bar. It will be funny someday, but right now it's just so much of the same crap that she does every day. I hate her sometimes, and then I feel so guilty about hating her.

I sit with her for a few minutes and then get up, gathering my backpack. "Where you going?" she asks,

"Home."

"I ain't leaving yet."

"I know. Dylan's picking me up." He isn't, of course, but I keep hearing him tell me not to ride in cars with her, and I'm getting sick from the smoke anyway. She thanks me for coming with her, but I wave it away, no big deal, and set out to walk the next hour toward home.

CHAPTER 13

I t's been a pretty good couple of weeks. Mom is working at the nursing home, and believe it or not, she actually likes the old folks. She still drinks but never seems to pass from that good phase of the buzz. She is easygoing and maybe even happy. Even she and Mitch are hitting on all the right cylinders, and I doubt he is seeing Theresa at all. Summer is stretching out long and lazy, and the conversation with Dylan about how terrible things were seems overblown and dramatic. She's not an alcoholic. She's nothing like Jake was. It was just a bad patch, and now things are better. I feel guilty about having talked to him about her like that.

Mom has already gone to work, and I've had a slow start, lounging in my bed, feeling lazy in the sultry heat of this rainless summer. My mornings are all like this, slow and lazy, since I don't go to work until two. Mom is sometimes home when I go in, but not always. In my unhurried way, I'm waiting for my toast to come up out of the toaster when I catch sight of Mitch in the front yard, leaning into the passenger window of a car. I step to the window to see who he is talking to. I squint, narrowing my eyes to see inside the dark interior. Then I recognize the car, and all my peaceful calm happy evaporates in a flash. Before I even know I have moved, I am standing on our rickety front deck, glaring hard at the back of Mitch's head. Glaring hard and hateful at the car puttering on the bubbling black-oil-and-rock road.

He turns, either because he feels the heat of me radiating toward him or because she has told him. He cuts his eyes over his shoulders to look at me, straightens, taps his palm on the inside of the car, and it begins moving again. His eyes lock on mine, and I try to freeze my face and not look away. "Who was that?" I ask when he is about halfway through the ankle-deep lawn.

A small grin quirks at the edge of his lips, and he says, "Aw. Hell. You know who that was." He shoves a hand up into his lank hair and pushes it back from his high forehead. It flops down, making him look boyish.

"You still fuckin her?" I demand. His charm isn't going to work on me. Not today. Not when she is doing so well.

"You watch your mouth." He comes to me, standing at the base of the deck, below me, looking up. "You don't need to be talking like that."

"Well, are you?"

"It's not like that, Alison." He squints into the light; he is handsome and shiny with a sheen of sweat making his skin glisten.

"Just answer me." I cross my arms over my breasts but become aware of the way they get pushed up, spilling over the top of my bra. I shift and tug my tank higher on my chest, bowing my shoulders forward, trying to diminish my breasts at his eye level. He sees all of this with an amused glint in his eyes.

"You want to talk?" he asks and settles himself on one of the steps, patting the other, with his black, oil-stained fingers, for me to come and sit beside. I go down but don't sit; instead I stand, leaning against the hot tin of the trailer. "You want the truth?" he asks.

"Yes," I hiss. Finally somebody is going to say something true.

"Well, then sit down here beside me, and we'll talk." Two beats pass, then I push myself off the tin and settle on the step next to him.

"You know I love your mama." I blow air out of my nose. Whatever. "I do. You may not think so, but I really do. We been together, what, four years? I love her, but a man needs something more."

"That's such bullshit." I spit, but I'm not really angry, I know it's kind of true. "She needs you. She's been really good lately," I say.

He shakes his head, looking out across the tangled lawn. "No, I thought I could help her, but she's beyond me. I tried. Damn, you know I tried." I don't really know anything of the sort, and I give him a look that says as much. "Come on, Al. You know how she is. Good this week, happy, easy, but next week she won't be."

"But she's trying."

"Is she?" he asks, glancing back to me, then away.

"Of course she is." She has to be trying, doesn't she?

"Really?" he asks, but what he means is, "You know that's not true." I shrug. "I mean, hell, I like a good party and to mix it up, but not all the time. I want her to lay off the booze but she won't." "Won't" comes out as two syllables, his Southern Illinois accent shining through.

"Have you talked to her about it?" I ask, reaching down, plucking a blade of grass and beginning to shred it.

"Talk to her about it as much as she will listen."

"You think she's an alcoholic?" I ask.

"Hell. Sure she is." He leans back. "I just can't keep doing this. I've tried with her, I mean really tried to make it work. She's a good woman. I love her and all, but damn. I never know who she's gonna be when I come in the door. I piss her off more than anything." True. He does piss her off.

"Only 'cause she knows you're sleeping around."

"That's not true. Come on, Alison. You're a smart girl, and you ain't a baby anymore. If we're gonna be honest, let's be honest," he says, and I nod. "I didn't cheat on your mother for the first three years we were together. She accused me a lot, but I swear I never cheated." He shifts beside me and leans forward with his elbows on his knees.

"What about when I was in the sixth grade?" I ask. "That was what she said happened then."

"No. There was no other woman then. I just didn't know she had so much shit, you know, in her head when we got together. She just scared me off for a bit."

"So why'd you start?" I ask, ready to go to bat for my mother.

"I'm real sorry. But I want to be with someone who knows I'm there, who wants me to be there, doesn't just need me. Sure as hell doesn't feel like she needs me either. She doesn't want a damn thing to do with me most times."

"Well, then you should just go so we can move on." A lump rises in my throat, but I push around it to speak.

"I will. Soon. I'm sorry." He sounds like maybe he has a lump in his throat, too. "She's got a good heart, you know. She's just so messed up. That ain't no kind of life." I nod. She is broken. "I wish I knew what had broken her, maybe then we could figure out how to heal her."

I nod, splitting a blade of grass. "Can I ask you something?"

"Sure."

"Do you know who my daddy is?"

"Nope. She never mentioned it." We sit for a bit longer, him staring out at the road, me staring down at the grass in my hand. "We done here?" he asks when I don't say anything but just continue shredding one blade of grass after another. I nod, and he stands up, ruffling my hair, and goes out back to get the lawnmower and attack the yard.

I sit. When did it happen? I really do remember her being different when I was little. She couldn't be room mom if I were in kindergarten now. What happened to her? When? Who? Was it Ed? Did he hurt her like he hurt me? Was he the evil in her nights? Was it when he left? Because she was good, even when we moved here, wasn't she? That's the problem; I don't know anything about my mother. She is a mystery and always has been. I have no history from her, no story of parents, brothers or sisters, or even where she came from, and for the most part I've never asked. When I was little, I remember asking her about my grandparents, and she had only answered, "We don't have people, little bug. It's just you and me." Hearing her voice in memory, saying the little love name she had given me when I was small, makes me suddenly weepy. It made me feel then like we were of the fairy folk when other kids were having grandparents into the classroom to look at their work. She was so good then, making me feel like we were special. She told me when I was little that I was a moon fairy who slept on the moon at night. I believed her for a long time, in that secret part of me where all children want to believe.

I sit until Mitch has finished mowing the back and made his way toward the front. He sees me still sitting and stops the mower, sweat pouring down his face. "You okay?"

"Do you know anything about her?" I look up but can't see him clearly, just a haloed silhouette.

"What do you mean?" he asks, rocking back on his heels and squatting there in front of me.

"Do you know where she grew up? Did she have brothers or sisters?"

He shrugs. Clearly I am not the only one she has locked out. "She's always been real private."

"Secretive" is the word I would use. Have we just never asked? Have I never asked her who she was outside of myself? I know I haven't.

"Did she ever tell you anything about Ed?" I ask.

"That the fellow who bought you this land?" I nod. "She never told me much more than that. I thought maybe he was your daddy?" I shake my head. I don't know who my daddy is, but I know Daddy Eddy was not him.

"How did you meet her?" I ask, thinking to gather some piece of her history for myself.

"At the Uptowner. Drinkin'." I should have known. I drop my grass and turn to go back inside before he starts mowing on the front.

CHAPTER 14

For months I've had a chip on my shoulder, but here we are, with Mitch still here and my mother still working, and I feel like the chip is melting with my high spirits and easiness of the summer. As summer begins to wan, drawing the high, dry heat in cracked and parched fields with withered wheat and browned corn stalks, I feel myself lightening, and I even begin to feel optimistic. The earth around me has shifted, and I begin to hope for something, although I am not sure what, but I feel hopeful for the first time in maybe years.

These are my thoughts as I sit in the passenger side of my mother's car one Saturday as we head to the grocery store. It feels a little like old times; she is happy, talkative even. "Mrs. Goodwin, whose daddy owned the five-and-dime when she was little, was telling me about the little one-room school house she went to. Can you imagine being in one room from first on through till you graduate? With all the other grades right there with you?"

"No," I answer. "That would be odd. Do you think the big kids picked on the little kids?" I don't really care; I'm just enjoying her talking.

"Probably." She laughs, a low chuckle, and turns left onto Elm.

"What was it like when you went to school?" I ask and glance at her, surreptitiously, hoping I didn't just blow it by getting personal.

"Same as it is for you, I suppose. It wasn't that long ago." She smiles over at me, looking young and beautiful, her hair loose around her face. I sigh and look out the window. Not so long ago. She was having me when she was not much older than I am. Pregnant when she was exactly my age.

"I guess it wasn't," I say. I bite my tongue to keep from asking if that's where she knew my father from, because I know that would end the happy tone in her voice, and I would be stuck until she decided to dump me at home. "Did you like school?" I ask, hoping that, at least, is safe.

She shrugs, "Do you?"

"No," I answer, then I add, "I don't not like school. I like the classes and some of the teachers."

"I was just the opposite. I didn't care about the classes or the teachers, but I loved the kids. I loved the sports and the games and the parties." She says it: par-tays.

"You liked sports?" This is new information. I've never thought of my mother as any type of athlete before. "What did you play?"

She laughs, a hooting ha-ha that makes me look over at her. "I didn't play sports. I just liked the boys who played sports." I'm disappointed, but nod because really that makes more sense. She always did like the boys. The car slows to a stop, its brakes squealing. I've not been paying attention as we've driven, but suddenly I am aware that we are not at the grocery at all, but rather we have parked in front of the Goodwill on the square. I groan.

"What are we doing?" I ask.

"You need new clothes," she says, already swinging her door open and putting her leg out the door.

"Really, Mom, I don't. I'm good for school, really." School is starting in just a few weeks, and we've always made a trip to this store at the end of summer, but I thought we would skip it this year since I've taken to wearing nothing but men's V-neck t-shirts, and those are cheap. Mom, apparently, has a different plan.

I hate the Goodwill store. It always smells faintly of urine and mildew. Two years ago, I found a pretty sweater and picked it out, only to wear it to school and have Shelby Dycus say, "I had a sweater just like that last year. I think I threw it out, though." That was before she started dating Dylan. I never wore it again, and ever since, I only pick out the most basic, nondescript clothes. Basic button-down, basic jeans. This year I am only looking for a new pair of jeans or two. I insist to her that I only need jeans. I don't much care that I wear the same basic clothes every day. Less chance of somebody noticing me.

I feel all of my sunshine and our easy conversation from earlier slipping, and my old chip is coming back onto my shoulder. Goodwill trips always piss me off. I understand that we don't have a lot, but it seems that maybe we could have a little more or better if we spent less of our money on alcohol.

I am about halfway down the line of jeans, hunting out Levi's without any extra bling, when the bell from the door chimes, and I glance up to see Mrs. Bancroft coming through the door. I duck back, behind the row of jeans, hoping she won't see me. Then, to my horror, Kelci trails in behind her mother, and her eyes sweep through the room, locking on mine. I shift and duck back, thinking maybe she will ignore me and move. What the hell are they doing here anyway?

"We have some clothes." Mrs. Bancroft says in a very singsong way, and I can tell by the look on Kelci's face that she is likewise embarrassed, either by seeing me here, or by the smug tone of her mother's voice announcing that they have a surplus. They are philanthropists; everybody bow.

"Alison, isn't that your friend Kelci?" my mother says too loudly, then she is waving in a "woo-hoo, over here" way.

"Mom," I hiss, grabbing her arm and trying to draw her down. "We are not friends." But the damage has been done. She has attracted Mrs. Bancroft's attention, and now Kelci is answering a question, shaking her head.

Oh shit. They are coming this way. "Why, hello, is that you, Alison?

We haven't seen you in such a long time," Mrs. Bancroft says. Kelci is trailing behind her, looking like she would like to be swallowed by the floor, much as I would.

"Hi, Mrs. Bancroft. Nice to see you. It has been a while." I step out from my crouch but don't move forward, "Hi Kelci." I nod to my mom, "You remember my mom, Alice?"

"Of course. Hi, Alice. You are looking well."

"Thank you." My mom is oblivious and actually thinks this is a truth, which clearly it is not. She does not return the compliment, is not even aware that she has a social obligation.

"Are you shopping?" Mrs. Bancroft asks. A small little smile parting her lips.

"No, just killing time," I say hurriedly. Please leave, please leave, please leave.

"Just picking up a few things for school," Mom says. I cringe. She says it like we are in a regular store, in Macy's or Dillard's.

"Well, aren't we in luck," Mrs. Bancroft says. "We have a few things we were donating. I'd much rather give them to a friend. Wouldn't you, Kelci?"

"Well, isn't that nice," Mom says, and Kelci turns away, looking out the front window. I can see the flush rising in her face; such a fair complexion as hers shows embarrassment almost as much as my ruddier one. Can this be any worse? Is there any way this can possibly get worse?

Yes, it can and it does as we follow Mrs. Bancroft out to the parking lot where her car is parked, her shiny Mercedes at that, and she hands over two large bags, which I am expected to say thank you for. I do, although I can feel my throat constricting on the words as they come out. Kelci has already climbed back into the car, looking away from me, a small kindness that I very much appreciate.

When we get in the car I feel hot tears stinging in my eyes all the way home while my mother talks about what nice people the Bancrofts are, asking me, "Why don't you invite Kelci over for a playdate?" I bite hard on the inside of my lip until I taste metal to keep from crying or screaming. Bitch. Bitch. Bitch. I hate her so much. Life is so unfair.

"Mom, we're sixteen. We don't have playdates anymore." Mitch is home, mowing the front yard when we pull up. It has been so dry that he peels up a wake of dust as he creeps along, over grass that has mostly gone to brown in the dry heat. I help my mother carry the clothes into the house, and she is giddy to get into them. "Lucky we can wear the same clothes," she says and starts pulling sweaters and jeans out of the bags and trying on things she likes. I hope she likes it all, because I swear that I will never, ever put a single stitch of Kelci's mother's charity on my back.

I make my way out the back door and into the woods, heading toward Dylan's but thankful that it is only the horses I will see. Dylan is at football camp this week, hanging out with the rest of the Haves.

The horses greet me as I come through the pasture, their muzzles tickling against my hands in search of carrots or apples. I have brought nothing except my sad, pathetic self, and when I am halfway toward the barn, I stop walking and Chessa stops with me, her neck arching and bringing her big, brown eyes low and close to my own. I rub the plane of her face, her cheeks, and up behind her ears. Her breath puffs out across my face, warm and grassy. Peaceful.

The tears that I held back all the way to the house are rolling down my cheeks, dripping to patters in the dusty ground. I wrap my arms around her neck and bury my face in the sleek muscles. She is the only one I could ever do this with, and I swear she leans into me, her head over my shoulder, hugging me back. Chessa has heard my stories all too often. She knows my pathetic murmuring probably by heart, all my little broken-heart jealousies, all my woe-is-me-isms. She knows them all, and yet she never tells me to suck it up. She just wraps her neck over me and lets me melt into her. How I wish I were somebody else. Anybody else.

Horses, I think, are the best confidants in the world.

CHAPTER 15

The last few days of summer swelter past. Haze blankets the sky, and dust devils spin out of control in litter-strewn corners. I hate the idea of starting another school year after the way I ended the last.

Mitch moved out the day of our Goodwill trip, although I didn't realize it until later. I hadn't thought anything about him going out shortly after we got home, while Mom was trying on her haul. I don't think Mom thought anything about it either. Mom realized he was gone when she went to put the things she claimed out of the bags into her closet and found that his clothes were gone. She came tearing out of their room and ran out the door, intent on finding him. I was in bed, feeling guilty that maybe I should have told her about the day Theresa stopped in front of the house, when I heard her come in, stumbling over the doorjamb, falling with a thud and a "Goddamn Mother Fucker!" She was pulling herself upright, trying to put her feet back under her legs, and I gave her my hand. The scent of vodka rolled off of her in waves and I averted my face a bit.

"Let's get you to bed," I say, trying to calm her. She is muttering and cursing just under her breath, and her eyes are rolling wild in their orbits.

"Don ever trusht a man." Her breath fogs over me. It is such a rare thing for her to slur that I am immediately worried. I steady her and guide her down the hall. I don't ask her what is going on. I don't want to start it. If I ask, then she will tell me, and I will be forced to listen and listen because she will tell it in rolling circles. I can guess, based on the recent conversations with Mitch, that he has moved on, as was his plan. He has left her. He has left us. "Why doesn't anybody love me?" she asks, and it is clear as day, not a stutter or a missed consonant.

"I love you," I say, my heart just a little broken for her. Her bottom lip puckers, and one big tear wells in her eyes and drops down her cheek. I fold her in my arms, and I let her cry into me, rocking with her sobs. He left us, and a little of my broken heart is for myself. He was the best of the men we've had, and now he has given up on us, too.

Mom missed work for three days in a row, saying she had the flu, and when she finally went back, it was with cold sweats and a sour stomach. I'm surprised she didn't get fired.

Billups had been such a good escape through the summer. The little bag of cash that I have been hiding in the vent is heavier every week, and every time I put another week's pay in, I feel a little less trapped. There may be hope for me yet. Not that I'll be going to college like Dylan and Kelci, but at least I will be able to leave, although I have to admit there is an uncomfortable feeling about going when I think about Mom being alone.

***

I see Mitch, two weeks after he left, the day before school was set to start. I was working a Sunday shift and had gone to pick up lunch at the Roadside Café for Rob and Mr. Billups, who aren't interested in the peanut butter and jelly sandwiches that I eat every day. He is sitting at one of the tables with his back toward the door, across from Theresa Calverson. I turn my face away from him and hope he doesn't turn around. I reach the counter, and while I am waiting for our order to be up, I feel him. I try not to turn, but I can't stop, and when I glance at the table where he had been, he is gone, but Theresa is there, staring straight at me. She offers a small smile and a wave. I nod, trying to pull on the same smile, but my eyes continue around the room, and there he is, standing behind me, his hand up in his hair. He lets out a long breath, dropping his hand out of his hair, which flops over his forehead like a forelock.

"How are you?" he asks, and before I even know what is happening, he is giving me an awkward side-armed hug.

"I'm good." I pat his chest with my hand as I regain my footing. "How are you?"

"Okay." He nods his head. We are so awkward. This is so awkward. We lived in the same house for years, and now we don't even know how to speak. "Your mom?" There it is, the pink elephant.

"She's good. Really good." I can't hold his eyes while I lie, but thank God my order is ready, so I make my polite goodbyes, pay, and get the hell out of the Roadside Café. I give him a small wave through the window as I walk away. I won't tell Mom that I saw him. I'm afraid it will kill her.

Mom isn't home when I get there after work, so I take the chance to go past and see if Dylan might actually be home. It was a good risk because I find Dylan and Jake up in the loft throwing in new alfalfa. The air was thick with the alfalfa dust, and Dylan and Jake are both covered by the sweat and dirt. A smear runs across Dylan's forehead where he has used the back of his arm to wipe away sweat. Jake's face is lined by running sweat, from his forehead to his chin. With the lifting of each bale of hay, air forces out from their lungs in a low "humph" as they toss the bale to the pile.

"Hey, Al," Dylan says between bales when he sees my head poking up from the ladder.

"Hey. Need some help?" I ask, even knowing that there's not much I can do. I don't have the strength to toss one of the bales the way they are.

"Nah. Almost done."

"Good timing then, huh?" I joke.

"How's your Mom?" Jake's voice is casual, but my eyes snap to him, checking to see why he asked and what he knows.

"She's okay." I try to let my voice sound casual, too. Jake stops as he's getting ready to pick up the last bale and looks at me. But he doesn't say anything. Instead he sits down on the bale, and I have to drop my eyes. I have never seen such intensity in his look before. I continue talking to break the connection between his clear blue eyes and me. "She's fine, you know. There are days, but she's okay."

"Yeah, Alison, I understand," Jake says. I feel like a bug pinned to a science project and want to escape back down the ladder and into the sun, but his eyes hold mine. I know that he knows. I know that he knows that I know about him. Suddenly I feel that I have violated him, that it's something too private. But we all know. "I ran into her a couple days ago, over at the market. She looked like maybe she had been a bit under the weather." The pit of my stomach turns slightly sour. I know that she wasn't there shopping for groceries. "So, how often does she drink?" he asks, point blank, matter of fact.

His manner is that of a doctor asking about symptoms, and I don't even hesitate. I shrug, not quite ready to turn traitor.

"Daily?" I nod. "Mornings? Night?" I nod to both. "How are things with Mitch?"

"Okay." I don't want to tell him that Mitch has left and is probably living with Theresa Calverson.

"Does he drink, too?"

"A little, I guess, but not like that." I pause. "Mitch doesn't live with us anymore." No sense in trying to skirt it. He probably already knows anyway.

"Oh," he says, as if that makes something very clear and everything suddenly makes more sense. "You, know, Alison, it took me an awful long time to admit that I needed help. I lost everything that mattered to me before I was ready to stop." His eyes move toward Dylan as he settles his last bale. "Luckily, I was able to rebuild some of what I'd lost. She's going to have to hit that point. Until she does, it's probably going to get worse and not better." I nod my head dumbly. I think of Daecus and wonder that losing his son wasn't enough. Dylan reaches his hand out to me to draw me the rest of the way up the ladder. Jake continues, "Most people have to bottom out. For me, I had to lose my family, their respect." I feel guilty, like I shouldn't be talking about this. I feel like I'm betraying her. I say that things have gotten better. Maybe Mitch being gone will be a good thing. I tell myself that the problems were all his fault, because he was seeing somebody else. But I know, even as I think it, what the truth is, that he was seeing somebody because of all the problems at home. He was a cheater; he had a history. So did we. We have a history, which is one of the reasons we moved here. Things were supposed to get better here. It was a new life and all of that.

Jake lets me off of the science board and throws the bale on top.

"Doesn't she see what it's doing? Why won't she just stop?" I ask in a soft voice.

"She probably can't. The drinking's all she can think about. That's part of the addiction, and her drinking is the only thing she thinks is getting her through." He begins to retreat down the ladder but pauses and looks at me once again, "It can be better. When you come out the other side, it can be so much better." He gives me his most beautiful, salesman smile, and I know there is equal parts sadness and grace in it. I feel for a moment like I'm a character in an after-school special and have to check myself from laughing, I'm so tense. He leaves us in the loft. Dylan touches my nose with his fingertip and goes to close the hay door. "I ran into Mitch yesterday. He asked me how you were. He was leaving the courthouse."

"I just ran into him at the Roadside." I shrug.

"So how are things really, Al?"

I just shake my head, trying to control the puckering of my chin.

PART THREE: FALL

CHAPTER 16

School starts back on maybe the hottest day of the summer. It is well into the nineties and nearing in on one hundred. There is not a cloud in the sky, and all the windows are open at school, trying to air out the staleness from a closed-up summer. It was such a dry summer that the crops are dead on their stalks and unharvested. All the rain we had in the spring did little good for the crops. The corn rows are wilted and brown, the fields of beans just shriveled, dying. Dust rises from the chapped fields as farmers return to glean their livelihood, or at least turn under the sad reminder of their failed attempts.

I am now a sophomore, Dylan's a senior. I go back to my original four hours a night three days a weeks at Billups. Dylan was voted president of the student council. Mr. Billups lets me use the computer in the office when I have papers to type, so I sometimes stay after everybody else has gone, working in the quiet store until the darkness has long settled in the streets, and then I ride my bike the five miles to our little spot in the world. I stay away from home as much as possible, a coward, but I don't know how to help her, and it's so overwhelming. Especially after she heard that Mitch and Teresa Calverson had gotten married in September. It isn't he who is scared of commitment like Mom always says; it is that my mom is not a person worthy of commitment.

She's already seeing somebody new. She never likes being alone. He is nothing like Mitch. Nothing like Ed, either. His name is Cal Robinson, and I've heard a lot of rumors about things he is into. I know without a doubt that he supplies pot and crack to a couple of kids at school. Donnie Barton and Eric Shores are both stoners who stand along the grassy area at the edge of the school property, along the far reaches of the circle drive, smoking and flipping off the buses when they pass. There are more of them, but those are the two I have actually seen Cal with at different times around town. He is tattooed on the sleeves of both arms, convoluted, dark tattoos, skulls and snakes. He wears his long, black hair tied in a ponytail at the base of his neck. His skin is so light it is nearly translucent, very vampire-esque. He creeps me out, like he wants to suck my blood. When he's around, I lock my bedroom door. How she could go from a normal, working-man kind of guy like Mitch to this vertical snake is beyond comprehension.

Mom is mostly gone in the nights, and there are weeks when I don't even see her. When she does come home, she sleeps for what seems like days on end. I don't know even if she still has a job. If she does, I know she's missing a ton of work. She sleeps sometimes, like she's in a coma, and then other times I'll find her flying through the house, in what I guess is supposed to be a fit of cleaning, a whirlwind flight to move things from one spot to another and then back again. I have never seen such intense energy from her; she is so frenetic. She has lost weight and has taken to wearing tight clothes that show off her breasts.

More than once I came home to find her in a mad search for something, which she never manages to find, and I often hear her riffling through papers and opening drawers long after I crawled into bed. She doesn't mention Mitch, as if he had never been. She now talks about Cal. Cal this and Cal that and Cal says this or that. When she is there, he is there, a permanent fixture on the sofa. But more often than not, no one is there, except me. I know she's drugging, but at least she isn't always drunk. I'm not sure it is an improvement. The puffiness that filled her face before Mitch left has been replaced by dark hollows under her eyes and the sharp jutting of her cheekbones. She now likes loud music and everything young. More than once she has reminded me that she is only thirty-two years old, and way too young to be old.

Sometimes there is food in the house, and sometimes there isn't. I keep bread and peanut butter at Billups anyway. The electricity was shut off twice through the fall, and the last time I took money from my vent to get it turned back on. It's getting too cold to not have heat in the trailer. She says she just forgot to send the check, but I know she's using all her money for other stuff, and it makes me angry. It just makes me hate her more.

Dylan encourages me always to turn her in, pushes me to get her into rehab, to intervene, but what he doesn't understand is that she scares me when she is on this new thing. She gets a wildness in her eyes, and I don't want to cross her. He offers to put together an intervention himself, but nothing ever materializes, and I assume that he realizes, like I do, that there is nobody she cares about and vice versa. I feel myself walling up. I don't talk to him about it. I try to act like everything is okay. Even though he thinks he understands, he doesn't, and I can't even begin to drag him into it. He's so busy with his big-man senior life that he doesn't have much time to worry about it.

It begins to rain in October, and the rain the crops craved all summer long deluges us for weeks. The leaves have fallen to the ground and never had a chance to rattle in the breeze. They are soggy and sluice down the streets, making ugly, sludgy piles along the drain grates. The temperatures hover in the low forties, and the rain falls, all day on most days, and the sun never peaks from behind the clouds. It is the strangest weather, and it suits my mood perfectly.

By the time the first snow falls, I have been riding to school again with Dylan for two weeks, unwilling to ride my bike with the cold wind going against me from every direction. I hadn't seen Mom the entire time I was riding to school with him. Those entire two weeks, she was just gone. And as suddenly as she went, she came back. One night she came home, and Cal came along, and then all his friends . . . their friends started coming, and the trailer was busting with people, and the fridge was once again filled with beer. There are always rocks, powder, and alcohol present, and the glazed stupor I sometimes find her in now has a frightening urgency to it. They always seems to be in some stage of stoned or buzzed or high. It is exhausting.

CHAPTER 17

November dawns with the first sun in nearly a month, and I wake with it bright on my face. With the dispersing clouds, the temperature dropped a solid ten degrees overnight. The sodden ground cracks against the soles of my shoes, where crystalline blades of grass bend and break. The frosted earth shimmers in the sunlight, and when my feet break through the crust, dirty water sluices around my shoes, seeping in to freeze my feet. My hair whips in a spiral around my head when I open the passenger door to Dylan's truck, causing a vortex around me. The cab of the truck is warm with the blowing heat vents wide open. "Good morning, Sunshine," he says, and I laugh.

"Good morning, Sunshine," I repeat raising my arms out to the beautiful sky, clear and bright through the windshield. He pulls away from the drive, and we listen to the engine and blowing heat.

"Can you come by tonight? Vaude wants to talk to you about house sitting." It's already been agreed that I will stay at their house when they go away at Thanksgiving, but I'm sure there are details Vaude wants to give me personally.

"I have work, but I can come after that."

"I have football till seven thirty. You get off at eight?" I nod. "Great. I'll just pick you up, and we can grab a bite to eat."

True to his word, as he is always true to his word, Dylan is waiting for me in the parking lot when I get off work. I climb into the cab and am delighted by the smell of burgers wafting through the car. He stopped and bought them on his way to me. We eat while he drives us the five miles to our part of the world. Around mouthfuls, he tells me about Jimmy Peterson's broken leg and how his folks are pissed because it puts him out for most of the season and he will miss out on the college recruiters.

"Will he even play again?" From my limited understanding, it seems that injuries end careers all the time. Does a broken leg ever heal to be as strong as before?

"Oh yeah. He'll play. His is a clean break without any damage to muscles or tendons. May take him a bit to get back up to speed."

"Well, that's good."

We are quiet for a minute, then he asks what he always asks. "How's your mom?"

"Strung out," I say without any emotion. I can see him nod, and I don't elaborate. They were gone for three nights last week, and when she came back, she fell into her bed and slept for hours. Cal hasn't been around this week, so I'm hopeful they are done.

Vaude holds the door open to us, and we come into the Gingerbread House. "What do you think of this weather?"

"It's better than the rain," I say at the same time Dylan says, "It's better than the rain." And we both laugh. We haven't done that in a while, but we used to, every now and then, say the exact same thing at the exact same time. We shed our jackets and leave our shoes by the door.

"Now, you sure it's fine with your mom?"

"Sure." Mom doesn't know, but she isn't going to care. It's not like she knows whether I am around or not most of the time. "She's fine with it."

"Good. I'll just feel so much better if somebody is in the house while we're gone. It's just better not to be empty over the holidays." She goes on, pulling the calendar from the fridge and spreading it open on the table, indicating that they will leave on the Saturday morning before Thanksgiving and return Sunday evening after Thanksgiving. They are visiting Jake's brother in San Diego for the holiday, a first in many years. Tom and Mary have four kids; I met them all when they visited maybe five years ago. Mary, with her wispy, blond hair, had taken over the gene pool, and all of the kids were the spit of her.

Dylan and I stop at the barn, and he runs me quickly through the feed routine, although I know it by heart. I am only partially listening as I rub sweet Chessa's forelock. My round-bellied Chessa. She puffs out her oaty breath into my face, her nostrils quivering, and I put my face along the plane of her cheek. I love this horse. I love everything about her, but mostly I love the way she always comes to me for a scratch or a treat.

It is some time before I realize that Dylan has stopped talking and is just watching me. When I become aware, my eyes spring open to see him studying me, the most peculiar expression on his face, his pale eyes nearly glowing from the hollows of his sockets. His tongue darts out over his lips. He blinks and looks quickly away from me. What was that?

"Dylan?" My voice is high and giggly. "What's wrong?"

"Nothing, Al. Nothing at all." He laughs, putting his arm over my shoulder and steering me out of the barn.

He likes me. I mean he likes me. Not like a friend. That's what I have just read on his face, that quick darting of his tongue over suddenly dry lips. My stomach plummets and twists in on itself, and I am not sure if the thought makes me happy or nervous or both. I've seen that hungry look before. I know what that look means. Does he want something more? How do we go from being friends and buddies to dating? How do we make that step? I don't know, and apparently he doesn't either. I'm a little relieved that neither of us do.

I sit in our trailer, my hands over my mouth and nose, enjoying the scent of Chessa, remembering the look on Dylan's face. My stomach is still churning, nervous, excited. I am sitting at the kitchen table, staring out the window in the general direction of Dylan's house when headlights bounce through the windows as my mother pulls into the drive. A second set follows after the first, and I start to gather my homework from the table. I don't care to be caught, and I make my way quickly down the hall to my room, where I lock the door before they make it into the house. I do not turn on the light in my bedroom, but instead grab my small flashlight and sit on the other side of my bed, so the light won't bounce under the door, and go back to reading Lord of the Flies.

CHAPTER 18

The last week in November is bitter cold. The ground is a frozen crust, and every morning when I go out to the horse trough, I have to bust through the ice with the rusted ax that Dylan keeps inside the barn. It feels good, to heft the ax, let my hands slip the length of the shaft as it settles over my shoulder before bringing it forward and down to crunch against the ice, breaking it apart to float like burgs awaiting the Titanic. I love, absolutely love being in their home. I spend hours perusing the books in the study, more hours curled in Dylan's bed, wrapped in this bathrobe, absorbed in the scent of him, reading.

When I was younger I used to imagine that Dylan was my brother and Jake and Vaude were my parents. Of course, back then I didn't know they had ever struggled with anything; they just seemed to be the perfect family. But now, as an almost adult, I am so glad that Dylan is not my brother because I am going to marry him. I'm still not sure how we move from here to there, but I know we will. Dylan and Alison. Al and Dyl. My sketchbooks are full of our names written over and over in hearts, arrow-shot hearts. I will gladly forsake my monosyllable Hayes for his duo syllable Winthrop. Winthrop. It's such a good name. Hayes is just what we are, dirty and gritty and base. Winthrop aspires to great things.

I am about knee deep in my fantastical future, sitting with a book well past forgotten on my knee, when there is the sudden chime of the doorbell bing-bonging through the house. I lurch off the sofa, leaving my book behind, and rush toward the door, trying to glimpse into the driveway as I go. Oh shit, I think when I see my mother and Cal standing on the steps. Oh shit. It is closing in on the evening of Thanksgiving Day, and this is the first time I have seen them all week. It has been really nice. I didn't really hide that I was house sitting, but I thought our conversation about it was deep enough in the vodka bottle to have evaporated. When I headed out of the trailer, she asked me why I was packed. "You running away?" she had asked. "Trust me, that doesn't turn out good." And then she had laughed at some joke that maybe I should have understood but didn't. So I told her I was going to Dylan's to house sit. I should have just said I was going to go do laundry, I realize now.

I crack the door and peer at them, not wanting to open the door as an invitation, not wanting them to track through Vaude's nice clean house. "Hi, Mom. What's up?"

She snorts out a puff and glances up at Cal slightly behind her. Her jawline is traced by small sores, an outbreak of acne gone bad. She pushes the door with a small "ooph," and it opens against me, pushing me out of the way. She strides into the room. Her black pupils have nearly overwhelmed the green of her irises, and she holds my eyes. "Aren't we fancy?" She says in a very la-tee-da voice. "Cal, aren't we so fancy?" She reaches out and fingers the threads of Dylan's sweater, which I have been cozied up in all day. "Look at you, in your boyfriend's sweater." She purses her lips and flips her hair out behind her.

For a split second I feel I owe her an explanation while my cheeks flush with embarrassment at being caught out, but I bite my tongue. "Why are you here?" I ask, trying not to sound bitchy, feeling very on edge. Cal has brushed past me, running his hand along my shoulder and sending roaches skittering down my spine.

"Can't I come to see my daughter on Thanksgiving?"

"Sure. I mean I'm not really supposed to have people over. Vaude asked me not to. You know."

"Vaude asked me not to." She mocks me, throwing her voice to Cal, who has made his way into the kitchen, his hand trailing the counters. "Aren't we fancy, playing house?" She narrows her eyes at me and goes to catch up to Cal who is standing in front of the wide-open fridge. It is essentially empty except for the few things I bought to eat this week. Mostly I live on peanut butter and jelly, so a jar of jelly sits alone on one of the shelves. He lets the door fall shut and starts perusing the cabinets. I just hate him.

"What do you want, Mom?" I try to sound solid, grown up, equal to her and unafraid. I don't think I quite succeed.

"Oh. Nothing, really. Just thought I'd visit. Isn't that okay?"

"Sure." She is not here to visit me. She is not here for me. She is here because there is something she wants. "Do you want some water?" I ask. If I have to get through this charade of a visit, I might as well move it forward. Cal is making his way out of the kitchen, and I try to keep him in my line of sight, but he turns the corner and is gone.

"So," she says, meandering toward brass tacks, "how much are they paying you?"

"Not much." At least now I know what they want. Money. "How much do you need?"

"How much do you have?"

I am so nervous about Cal being in the other room, free to take or destroy anything. People don't do that, I tell myself; surely he wouldn't take anything. I try to convince myself, but I back away and open one of the canisters on the counter. It's where Vaude left "necessary money" for me just in case. There is sixty dollars. I peel the bills flat and offer them to my mother. Anything to get them out of here. She takes the money and tucks it into her pocket. Instead of calling Cal and heading out, she moves deeper into the house. I trail behind, snatching things from their hands and replacing them on the shelves. I try to settle myself, knowing that I am only making it worse. They are enjoying my discomfort. They are laughing at me as I spin from one item to another.

"You can't be here," I say. "Vaude doesn't want anybody else in the house while they are gone." I try again, but know that they don't care.

Finally I stop when I realize that I am acting like an idiot. Cal is holding things above my head, and I am bounding up at him like a trained poodle for a treat. "Fuck you," I say, mostly under my breath, as I turn away and into my mother who is standing behind me, so it sounds like I have said it to her.

Her huge, dilated pupils stare directly into me, her rancid breath pouring out from her parted lips like steam from a pipe. I close my mouth and stop breathing, holding her eyes as best I can. Then her hand reaches up and shoves my shoulder, knocking me back into Cal, who drops the vase he has been holding. It crashes to the floor, shattering into a shards and dust. I hear it fall, I hear it shatter, but I am so shocked that my mother has shoved me that I just stand there staring, aghast.

"You think you're so much fucking better than me, in that preppy sweater. You think you're better than me sitting here in this fancy house like you are something." She is moving closer, pushing me more into Cal, who doesn't move. His hands land on my shoulders, and he shoves me off of him, back into my mother who is ready with a hearty push. I lose my footing and crash to the floor, Cal's black-booted foot under my ankles. "You think this boy is going to marry you? You think they think you are one of them? You ain't. You're just the white-trash kid from down the street that makes them feel good about doing charity." She leans low and into my face, spittle falling from her lips. "You ain't nothing to them." She narrows her eyes. "Everybody knows except you. Everybody is laughing at you fawning all over this Winthrop kid. I'm embarrassed of you." Her spittle sprays across my face, and my eyelids close and open then close again against the assault. "I may have problems," she says, "but at least I know what I am."

She straightens when I have no response, and she and Cal move back out the door, knocking off the lamp from the end table as they go. I watch, horrified, as it shatters to the floor.

The door stutters in their wake, and I draw my knees up to my chest and rock. I feel assaulted. I feel beaten. I feel completely undone. She is right, me sitting here wearing Dylan's clothes, pretending to be his future wife. I am a joke. I am such a joke.

CHAPTER 19

L ucky for me, Friday dawns clear, and the wind has finally died down. I am none too excited about riding my bike into town and hunting for the replacement lamp that I have to find. I do a quick sketch of the remaining lamp and tuck it into my backpack, which is otherwise empty. I have my money that I have been saving from Billups, which I was smart enough not to leave in my vent when I came down the road to stay at the Winthrop's. I took it mostly because I was afraid my mother would find it, and it would all be gone when I came back, and since I have not really told her I am working, it's probably best if she doesn't find my wad of cash.

My mind hovers in dark places, hearing the words my mother spat out at me, hearing again her saying in her la-tee-da voice that I am nothing to Dylan, that I will never be anything to Dylan. I am their charity case. No matter how I spin these thoughts, her words, there is a certain ring of truth to them. An honesty that I have not often associated with my mother. How I hate her for telling me this truth, but in my heart I always knew.

My fingers are cramped and frozen from the ride, and I feel like my nose may snap clean off. I spend several minutes, after coming into the warmth of the furniture store, blowing into my hands, cupping my mouth and nose, until I finally start to have some normal feeling in my fingers and the tip of my nose starts to feel less chilled. I walk the lines of furniture, the pseudo rooms, looking for the lamp that I need. My fingers trail along the leathers and fabrics until I catch sight of myself in a bureau mirror. I am all angles and bones, with my hair flying loose around my head like fire, my fingers on the fine wood. A reflection of Calvin fingering Vaude's kitchen ratchets through my mind, and I draw my hand back as if the veneer has burned me. I walk on, my hands clasped behind my back, leaving no prints or evidence of my passing.

I owe Vaude a lamp, and a vase, but the vase I know has been a part of the house since well before I met them and is probably an antique. I cannot replace it. I can't even try. My only hope is that it is such the fabric of their daily lives that they no longer really see it. It makes me sick, remembering it crashing to the floor and knowing that it is my fault.

The lamps are scattered throughout the warehouse, mingled amongst the living room groupings, and after about twenty minutes of slowly strolling, a sales woman comes up to me, dressed to the nines in a black sweater dress and porcelain skin. Her hair is straight and long down her back, glossy blond. Her smile is edged in red, precisely drawn and friendly. I know she has picked the short straw when I glance behind her and see two others standing in a small pod, waiting for the Black Friday Sales to draw in the customers. I do see several other people, mostly couples, strolling the warehouse, debating the benefits of sleigh bed over pedestal maybe. That would be something normal people would discuss. "Can I help you find something?" she asks, and my hand is already digging in my pocket, ready to move on, even if it is a very cold and unpleasant journey back to the farm.

"Yes. I'm looking to replace a lamp." I show her the drawing I made and bite my tongue to keep from making excuses, spilling my guilty soul onto her clickety-click shoes.

She glances at the drawing and then back to me. Her eyebrows raised. "I think we have this set. Come with me." We make our way past her fellow salespeople, and I hear the chime of the front door again.

We find the lamps two rooms back, and I am so relieved that my knees feel a little weak. "Great," I say. "I need one."

Her chin juts out to the side in a quirk, and a small smile spreads her lips. "They come as a pair."

"Oh. You can't split them up?" I ask, trying not to sound wheedling.

"I'm afraid not. They are each individually painted, no two sets are alike.

"Oh." So had I bought the one and gotten it back to the farm, I would have then seen some minute difference, or worse, Vaude would. It's better to buy the set, the matching set and take the unbroken one from the farm to my own home. Does that qualify as stealing, me taking Vaude's lamp and replacing it with the set?

I am sick to my stomach as I pay for the lamps. Only one lamp will fit in my backpack at a time. I shoulder the one and make my frozen way back to the farm, warming up and then heading back for the other. When I finally finish all my riding, I am exhausted and chilled to the bone. I take a long shower, thinking the heat will warm me, but when I get out, my teeth are still chattering. I sit in the kitchen, my hands around a mug of hot tea, my peanut butter and jelly uneaten.

I make my way out a little later to crack the ice on the water trough, almost more than I can handle. I manage to break the ice, but only because I broke it this morning, and it is just a thin layer refrozen. I fill the feed pails and leave the horses for the house, where I spend the next two hours curled on the couch waiting for night to fall so I can go up to bed. I've rechecked the locks several times throughout the afternoon, but check again before I go up. They should be home tomorrow. I'll have to take the lamp from the broken set home before they get here. I dread going to the trailer and only hope that my mother will not be there. If she is, I can only hope she is passed out and drunk. I never thought I would wish for such a thing.

CHAPTER 20

I t has already been a long five days since we got out for Christmas break, and I am more than anxious for the whole holiday to be over and done. Billups cut my hours over the break, saying that it's always slow the last two weeks of the year. I am missing my job and even school, just for the reason to leave. It's so cold out, though, I am grateful I am not trying to figure out how to get to and from. It's probably for the best that I don't have anywhere to go.

We didn't put up a Christmas tree or bring out any of the decorations. Christmas falls on Thursday, and the house is unusually crowded with tattooed men and women. I count fifteen when I emerge from my bedroom to go to the bathroom during the height of the evening. The cigarette smoke is thick in the hall, and from the din in the living room and kitchen, I can tell that the party is in full swing.

When I open the door to leave the bathroom, Cal is waiting. A bottle of beer in his hand and a cocky grin on his face. My skin creeps over my bones in an effort to remove itself from his presence. He doesn't ever look me in the eyes; he looks at my mouth or my breasts. He makes me feel naked. I try to shoulder past him and return to my room, but he steps away from the wall and blocks me. "Alice wants to see you."

"She knows where I am," I say, clipped, not quite rude. He scares me a bit, more than a bit, and I am not quite brave enough to be openly rude.

"You don't like me?"

I don't say anything; there is nothing I can say that will make him go away. His hand reaches out and touches my hair, his eyes on my mouth. I jerk back. His fingers close into a fist, and my hair tangles in his grip. I open my mouth to scream but nothing comes out as he draws my head back and down. I grab his hand and bend my knees to go down. Panic rises, and for a split second I think he is going to take me. Then his hand is gone, almost before I realize what has happened, and he turns from me and strides down the hall, back to the party. I stare after him, fear rising in my stomach, until I pull myself up from my knees. He just showed me how weak I am. I turn back to my room, and I sit on my bed, my knees drawn up, rocking slightly, staring out the window at lightly falling snow, listening for the handle of my bedroom door to jiggle. Not again is all that runs the circuit in my mind. Not him.

"Alison, honey, come out here." My mother's voice wafts through my door, and I stop rocking. I stand up and remove the chair, opening the door so I can see her. "Come here. I want you to meet my friends."

"I have met your friends." I am still chilled from Cal's fist wrapping my hair. "It's Christmas. I want them to leave."

"That's right. It's Christmas, and we're having a Christmas party. Come join the fun." Her voice is singsongy, punctuated by small giggles. I have a split second memory of her the day she came to Dylan's and broke the lamp. I have no idea what she was on that day, but I will take this version of her over that any day—at least when she drinks I know essentially what to expect. That other person is foreign, not my mother.

"No thank you." Please leave, please leave, please leave.

She pushes the door open, and her eyes settle for a split second on the lamp from Dylan's sitting on my dresser without a shade. I'd had to leave that there with the new set. Who would think that fancy furniture stores sell the lampshades separate from the lamps? I had no idea. Her eyes come back to me—her normal green-rimmed pupils with the lids shadowed by purple, fringed by black-mascaraed lashes.

"I'm sorry," she says, and I am shocked. Apologies are not part of my mother's répertoire. "I know this isn't the life you want, Alison, but it's the one you've got. You can either make the best of it or make the worst of it. Either way you are going to live this life." I stare at her, slack-jawed. Is this advice? Is this motherly advice? It is the first time she has ever given me any reason to think that she understands what my life feels like to me. The look in her eyes is soft, and for an instant, I remember her from years ago, before she and I seemed always to be at odds. I long for that person, and my vision suddenly blurs with the almost remembered sense of mother.

"Come on." Her hand takes mine, and in my moment of being sentimental, she draws me out of the room. "Life is hard. Make the best of it."

So I follow her out into the throng of her Christmas party. This is a small concession. This is not a day I want to fight, and this is not a fight I think I will win. I am seriously outnumbered. We stop in the middle of the living room. There are five men and three women besides my mom. "Isn't she a beauty?" Mom says in a very warped rendition of the proud mother. I do a quick scan of the people and realize that there are only two besides mom and Cal whom I have met. A low whistle emanates from one of the men, but I can't tell which. And the connection I had felt a moment ago evaporates, and I feel like I'm on the auction block, to go to the highest bidder. I think I'm going to be sick. "Look at that hair." She takes a handful, and it slips through her fingers. I shake my hair out of her hands. What the fuck with my hair today? Cal is watching me through lowered lids. I pull myself away from my mother and glance at her before I stomp down the hall to my room. I slam the door to a resounding chorus of laughter and stand with my back to it. My breath coming in staccato gasps, I suddenly think I might cry. I don't want to make the best of it. I want a different life. Why can't I get a do-over?

There are hoots from the living room, and I hear my mother saying something. I am so angry. I am angry all the time. I am angry at her for drawing attention to me like that. I am angry at whatever idiot man thought it was okay to whistle like that. I am angry at Cal for looking at me like that, for touching me the way he did. I am angry that it is Christmas, and this is what my family has become. I am angry because I miss Mitch . . . because even though it wasn't great, he never once touched me. I long for those Christmases so long ago when Ed was with us and we'd put up a tree and the three of us would share our gifts on Christmas morning, regardless of how meager they were. I am disgusted because he was a bad man and he did bad things to me when I was so young that I didn't even know anything was bad. I hate him, but I hate him less than I hate my current life. Even that time was better than this. He could have kept fucking me if he could have stopped what our life has become. I gasp. Drawing my hands up over my face, horrified at what I just thought. Oh God. What is wrong with me?

I step away from the door and put the chair back in place. I sit on the bed and draw, angry dark lines dropping on the page. The charcoal crumbling with the pressure. Tears are streaming down my face, plopping into pools on my art pad. I have a flashback memory of walking home from school when Mom walked with me, before we moved here. She was at school a lot when I was in kindergarten; she was my room mom. When she came to help out, we would walk home together, and sometimes we would stop at the five-and-dime and she would buy me a package of Milk Duds. I stop drawing and let the sketchpad fall to the floor. I roll into my pillow and cry for that long lost woman. I can't help but think that it was something I did that made her pull away from me. When I am cried out, I push myself up and wipe the tears and snot off of my face, pushing my pathetic self away.

If Dylan didn't have a house full of people, I would sneak over there. I wonder if I could just get to the barn without being seen. I know his grandparents from Wisconsin are here along with at least one uncle and his family. That's too many for me to risk, especially since I've been lying low from him since they returned after Thanksgiving. I haven't seen him except at school and haven't seen Jake and Vaude at all since the afternoon they came home. That was all fine. They didn't seem to notice the changed lamps, and I am still hoping they haven't noticed the missing vase. I even put the sixty dollars Mom took back in the jar from my own money because I couldn't bear the idea of taking it from Vaude. I didn't want her thinking I needed her charity. House sitting for them ended up costing me just under forty-four dollars after they paid me.

The snow outside begins to stick, and I pace my room as the hours of Christmas evening slip to night. I pull my hair into a braid to keep it from hanging in my face. I chew my fingernails, listening to the laughter coming down the hall. Dusk is fully settled when I hear steps heading down the hall. The rhythm is not my mom's, and not Cal's. I'm surprised when a soft knock lands on the door. I don't say anything—the bathroom is just before my room, and I figure that is the intended destination. The knock comes again, soft.

CHAPTER 21

"**A**lison." My name is whispered on the other side of the door, between knocks, and the hairs on my arms stand up like electricity has just arced across me.

"Who is it?" I ask, not leaving my perch on the bed.

"Won't you come out?" The voice is soft. "I'm the ninth wheel out here." He laughs a little, and I hear him slide down my door, and I figure he has turned to sit with his back against the door. Down the hall somebody calls for "shots," and I hear the head on the other side of the door bounce against it. "Can I come in?" There is such a pleading sound to it that I want to let him in. I imagine the speaker wants to not be here either, but feels compelled.

I don't respond, and a few seconds pass before another bounce of his head knocks on the hollow wood. I draw the chair away and open the door. He looks up at me, his hair mussed, his eyes dark and shadowed in his face. He contorts his body and hops through the door as he is coming to his feet. He is certainly more boy than man. He is certainly more of the Cal variety than the Mitch variety. A small metal stud pierces his left eyebrow, and his arms are inked, skulls and snakes, like Cal. I recognize him as one of the people who had been in the living room, but I hadn't really given him a glance then. He has dark blue eyes and black hair. His cheeks are smooth, and his lips are red. He would be a wonderful art subject. His bottom lip pulls into his mouth and comes out with a sheen of saliva covering it. I notice all of these things in an instant, but feel that I've been gazing at him for a bit too long when he finally speaks again. "Warren."

"What?"

"That's my name. Warren. Can I come in?" His voice is deeper than I would have thought, rusty from a cold or too many cigarettes. Without waiting for an answer, he is sitting on my bed beside me, leaving the door to fall shut of its own accord.

"I guess you already are." This is not good. This is not good at all. There is an intensity in his presence that makes me feel small. Why did I open the door? Why did I open the door? The question runs on a loop inside my head. Slack-jawed and stupid, I gape at him. I can't seem to stop staring . . . at his shoulders under his black sweater, loose around his collar showing some very nice hollows, at the way his hair stands up slightly away from his forehead.

"What's this?" He leans down and picks up my sketchpad from where it has fallen to the floor and looks at the angry lines on the page, the spreading puckered circles from where I cried.

"Nothing." I reach for the pad, but he doesn't release it.

"Can I see?" His voice is so soft; his eyes are so open and deep, deep enough for me to fall into.

"I guess." I let him look. I watch him looking. Strange as it is, I want him to be impressed, and he is. He pauses at a sketch of Dylan and asks who he is.

"A friend."

"Boyfriend?" he asks, and for whatever reason, I feel myself blush as I deny any possibility. "Good." He smiles, his full lips parting over straight, white teeth. He finishes looking through the pages, pausing for a long time at a sketch of the three horses. "These are amazing." I blush again and take the sketches as he extends them out to me. I stash the book on my dresser, out of reach.

"How do you know my mom?"

"Cal's my brother." He shrugs. "Well, half-brother." I don't know where to sit, not wanting to sit on the bed next to him, so I finally slide down the door and sit with my back against it.

"I guess that makes sense." I don't know what to say. The room feels electrified since he stepped into it. My stomach is fluttering like a butterfly when he looks at me, with those thunderstorm-blue eyes.

"Why don't you come out? These people aren't that bad. I know you're mom would appreciate it."

"It's Christmas," I say, as if that should explain everything.

"Yeah, a good day to celebrate." He smiles, his full lips stretching and drawing my eyes.

"Not like this." I'm not sure what makes this party so much different than the Friday Fires, which I loved, but it is different.

"Because your dad's not here?" He makes an effort, but seriously he is so far off the beam I almost feel sorry for him. I'm so far past missing a father I never knew that I almost smile at his naïveté.

"Well, just everything."

"Like what?" He has a quiet way about him that makes me feel safe, or at least not threatened.

"I mean everything, it's just not right." I pause, not really sure why I'm talking to this guy, like he's somebody I know and trust, but I am. "It's just Christmas. It's Christmas. There should be something more."

"Like a Christmas tree or lights or something? Like presents?"

"Yeah." I smile. "I guess like that." Not really what I had in mind, but since I had nothing in mind, I latch on to this, because clearly there is no tree, no lights, and certainly no presents. Santa stopped coming to my house many years ago.

"So if you had a tree, would you come out?"

"No, probably not." A small laugh escapes my body, and I draw my hand up to cover my mouth.

"Why not?"

"Because I don't belong." I don't belong anywhere, not just here. I never fit. "I'm just feeling sorry for myself."

He winks at me, "You belong wherever you make yourself comfortable." Then he reaches out and grabs my hand, "Come with me." He draws me up from the floor and swings wide my bedroom door. I'm padding down the hall behind him, even as I'm thinking that I don't want to. His hand is warm, electric, and comforting after this long day of solitude. We reach the kitchen, and they are milling around, filling drinks and eating from a tray of cheese and vegetables. There is a football game on the TV, and several people adjust so we don't interrupt their view on our way past. Otherwise, nobody notices us. Warren is talking about my coat and shoes, but I can't really hear him to understand. The men at the TV erupt in cheers as one team scores.

We reach the kitchen, and he is grabbing his leather jacket from the couch, shouldering it, telling me to grab my coat. I tell him, "I don't want to go anywhere," nervous about being spun out of my room and ushered from whatever vague safety there is behind my locked door.

His laughter is low and bemused. "I'm not stealing you. I just want to show you something. Come on." So I grab my jacket and put on my shoes. I follow him out the front door and nearly slip in the moist snow, but his hand wraps around my upper arm and steadies me. We are moving down the driveway to a car parked in the back. He pushes his hand into his pockets and comes out with keys. We pass by the doors, and he stops at the trunk, which he opens and begins riffling through the tightly packed contents, and I wonder if he lives out of his car. He pilfers through blankets and plastic bags and clothes until he finally finds that which he is searching for. A single strand of Christmas lights. He turns back to me, the smile of a mischievous imp parting his lips. "Voila." He says it: wall-ah. He leads me around the trailer and pauses at the evergreen that stands just beyond my window.

It comes clear to me his intention, and I hear myself laughing with the craziness of it. We zigzag the strand of lights across the front of the tree, laughing and helping each other as our fingers grow cold and damp from the snow melting at our touch. Our breath fogs the air, and our laughter reaches the others in the house. Heads poke out the back door, and somebody delivers us an extension cord. Soon we are all crowded around the tree, blowing on our hands, laughing. I am part of this for the first time in years, my mother standing next to me, Cal behind her, Warren on my other side. I reach out and slip my hand into my mother's, and she squeezes my fingers and lets me.

The snow begins to fall with more force, and one of the women begins to sing Silent Night. Her voice is soft and clear. Other voices join in, and I find myself leaning into Warren, the savior of my day, singing quietly, off key, my hand still clasped in my mother's. Our rendition of Silent Night is fully out of tune, with some of us humming through parts that we aren't quite sure of the words, until the whole group collapses in laughter, and we retreat to the relative warmth of the trailer for the rest of the festivities. When Mom lets go of my hand, it feels suddenly cold and lonely. She catches my eyes as she turns and smiles, her face lit up, flushed with the cold, beautiful. We leave the extension cord closed in the back door, running to our twinkling beacon through the night.

When we tumble into the living room, Warren hands me a drink. I have drank before, not often, because I don't like feeling out of control, but I don't want to go back to my room. I don't want to be alone anymore. One is no big deal, and I probably won't even finish it. The impromptu tree lighting and concert have made me feel better, maybe. I take the drink he offers and sip it. I have not eaten all day. My stomach feels raw from the inside out, and the liquid is burning as it moves through my body. I feel flushed; my hair is suddenly hot against my head. I eat a few chips, bumping into Warren as we stand together, still close, still giddy with the gift he has given me. There is dancing to the radio, and I fall into Warren, heady with the drink and the change from cold to hot. We are neither of us good dancers, but we laugh and he keeps me on my feet until my head is spinning, and then he takes me to my room. Nobody seems to notice our going. I'm not even sure I notice us going.

We trip into my room, and I stumble over my own feet. His arms are there, catching me, drawing me against his body until I can feel his heat. I can feel his breath coming from his slightly parted lips, those lush lips that I can't seem to take my eyes off of. Then he is lowering me onto my bed, his warm red lips on mine. The sounds from the rest of the house are muffled by the door and by the sudden rush of our breathing.

Outside, the snow continues to fall, covering the slowly blinking lights outside my window. He is on my bed with me, his hands cupping my face, kissing me, electricity jolting through my nerves at the sensation his touch brings. My head feels so heavy; my body feels so heavy. Then he is drawing back, dropping a last kiss on my forehead before walking to the door, turning the knob to lock it before he draws it closed. I slide under the deep layer of the alcohol, thinking how alcohol never made me feel like this before. I didn't drink much tonight. There is no reason I should feel so numb, so unable to move. I know I've drank more at the Friday Fires, so why is this so different? I didn't want him to leave, but was already drifting beyond language when he went.

I can hear him, just outside my door, his voice rising, falling, another voice. Something crashes against my door, and I try to respond, but I am unable to move. What is wrong with me?

CHAPTER 22

I rock under the water, my arms crossed over my stomach until the water runs cold and my teeth begin to chatter. I vaguely remember the night. The darkness in my room and the feeling of his hands touching my body. It's like a dream. I feel nervous, and my mind feels fuzzy. I vaguely remember him leaving my room, but I know I woke up under my blankets with my clothes piled on the floor by the bed. I know I had my clothes on when he left. I feel achy, sore in ways and places I've not felt in a long time. I feel dirty, gritty, and no amount of soaping seems to help. There are a series of bruises on my hips, and I barely remember feeling his hands tighten there. The muscles of my thighs ache. It's not just external. I have been entered, and I remember nothing at all about it. I don't know how much of what I feel is the residual of alcohol in my system or residual of him in my system. I reach up and turn off the water. He left, though. I remember: he left and I still had my clothes on. Think. Think. Think.

What have I done? It wasn't supposed to be like that. I can't believe I let that happen. I am so angry at myself. I should never have opened my door, no matter how nice he seemed, no matter how sweet he was. After pulling on my boots and jacket, I slip out into the lightly falling snow and make my way through the woods and finally arrive at the back gate to Dylan's pasture. I pull my coat more tightly around me, my hair has frozen in crystals around my head. People like Dylan don't get into situations like that. I can guarantee Kelci wouldn't have gotten into a situation like that. Is that what makes us different, some moral boundary, some ability to avoid bad things?

I don't know what I should do. I'm not stupid about things, and I know that having sex with Warren was stupid. Stupid. Did he use protection? I don't know. I don't know. I don't even remember. But he left my room . . . the small niggling part of me that remembers something pushes forward . . . he left my room and locked the door and then . . . what? He locked the door when he left my room, and I had all of my clothes on. Maybe nothing happened. Maybe I'm wrong. I try to convince myself that I'm wrong. I want so badly to be wrong. Unfortunately I know all too well what the day after feels like, and I am definitely having a day after.

My skin is crawling, and I dig my nails into the flesh at the base of my wrist, scratching until the skin is hot and moist, red and inflamed. God knows that I know nothing about Warren. I could be pregnant. I could have any number of diseases. What a mess that would that make my life. What about all of my dreams? What about college and my art studio someday? Who am I kidding? I'm not going to college. I've never been going to college. I will work at Billups as long as they will have me and then move on to one of the factories. That is the shape of what my life, my defective life, is going to be. Is this how my mom felt, when she was just a little younger than I am now, realizing that I was on the way? Is this what made her the way she is? Me? Coming too soon for her to have any dreams of her own? I destroyed her life.

My head throbs in the cold, and I sneak into the barn and up the ladder. It's too early to knock on their door. I dig at the red patch on my wrist until it actually hurts, and then I dig some more. I'm not sure why I've come here anyway. God knows I don't want to talk about what happened, definitely not with Dylan. The wind bats against the side of the barn, and I huddle on a bale of alfalfa, trying to think. Slowly my hair begins to thaw, and I pull it back to a braid to keep it from touching my face, cold and wet. My body begins to shiver, and I fold in on myself trying to keep my teeth from chattering

The door to the back of the barn opens, and footsteps echo through the building. A whistle breaks the air, and I know the horses will soon be here. I hold my breath, listening to the feed bin opening then closing. Corn and oats rustling into their buckets. I wait, my eyes closed, for the door to open and close again and for me to be alone in the barn.

Once I am sure he has gone, I creep back down the ladder and out into the drifting snow. I make my way back through the woods, following the path I had blazed earlier. When I come out into the clearing that is our backyard, I see the faint glimmer of lights flashing through the newly fallen snow on the branches of the evergreen. I remember suddenly . . . the warm feeling of my mother's hand and of Warren's shoulder as I leaned into him, singing Silent Night, surrounded by my mother and her friends. The warmth of that moment is separate from the rest. I blow air into my hands and make my way back to the trailer. I am not the person I thought I was.

PART FOUR: WINTER

CHAPTER 23

spend the rest of Christmas break with a nasty cough and a low-grade fever. Mom makes chicken noodle soup from a can and brings it to me where I sit huddled on the sofa in the living room. I watch her, studying her, in a way that I never have before. I wonder about what her life really is and who she is inside. She is still a very pretty woman, thin and busty, her dyed auburn hair thick, falling to her shoulders.

She nurses her drink while I nurse my soup. We sit in silence. I would like to ask her questions, but I don't know how to start, so we sit, isolated and alone together, the low-level hum from the TV filling the air.

The news is on, a picture of a young, blond-haired girl comes on the screen. She's been missing since Christmas Eve, and I strain to see if this is just the same report or if there has been a change. She is five years old.

"You were such a pretty little girl," Mom says, her hand lazily reaching toward me. I see her hand and reach out to touch her fingers, without fully looking at her.

"Do you remember when I was in kindergarten?" I ask. I can see her nodding and go on. "I loved Mrs. Kimball. She was so kind."

"Was it Kimball?" I nod. "I don't really remember her," she says.

"Do you remember," I blow out a low laugh, "how on Fridays we could bring in our favorite thing for show and tell?" I look straight at her, for maybe the first time all afternoon. Her mouth spreads wide, and she laughs. She knows what I am thinking. She is still a beautiful woman when she smiles, when she is at peace. It is so nice to see that I almost forget what I was telling.

She picks up my story where I left off. "I remember you took me one day."

"I was so proud of you," I say. And I was. She was so good and kind, so beautiful. All of my friends had little crushes on her back then. Everybody wanted to hold my mom's hand when we walked down the hall. Everybody was jealous that I had the most beautiful mom.

"What happened, huh?" she asks, her voice full of irony. A wistful expression in her eyes. This is the closest we have been in months, years maybe. She looks suddenly into her drink, which is empty, and gets up to get another. Yep, I think, that's exactly what happened. She continues talking as the bottle clinks on her glass. "Do you remember Ed?"

I nod, then answer out loud because she is not looking at me. "I do."

"I always wonder how much you remember about earlier. I don't really have any solid memories before I was ten or so."

"Really?" I've heard the story of my mother's life in stuttered starts and stops, and this is new. I want to draw her out, I want to learn who she was, to maybe understand what has made her so private, so broken.

"Almost nothing. I remember my grandmother's funeral, and that would have been when I was seven maybe, but almost nothing other than that."

"I remember living in the white house where we had the big garden. You remember the ledge going up the stairs that I used to sit in and color?"

"You hid all over the place in that house."

"I remember that." I do not say that most of the time I was hiding from Ed. That would be saying too much. I do glance quickly at her, gauging whether she realizes that or not. She is not looking at me, but down into her glass, the clear liquid heaving over the ice, melding.

"I kind of loved that house." She heaves a deep sigh. "Too bad Ed was such a dick." She laughs self-consciously, and her eyes catch mine. Does she know?

"Yeah. I didn't like him a whole lot myself." What difference does it make? He's been gone for so long he barely exists in my memory, except for the touch of his hands, his hairy body. I close my eyes and crack my neck. Just the thought of him makes my stomach crawl up against my backbone to hide.

She takes a long drink, and I say quickly, "Well, I guess that's enough about that." I stand up and change the channel to America's Funniest Videos. Seriously, who doesn't feel better after watching complete strangers getting minor injuries because of their own stupid choices? It makes the rest of us feel somewhat less idiotic. "I sure did love that year when you were room mom, though."

———

She is sobbing. I can hear her down the hall in her room. The TV has gone to static, and I think she must have just left the living room. Is that what woke me up? I lurch off of the sofa and rocket down the hall and nearly smack into her as she's coming back out of her room. Her face is sloppy and tear stained, all the many drinks of her day showing in the fluid under her skin.

"Are you okay?" I ask. I was feeling so close to her this afternoon.

Talking about the time before we moved here, remembering her before, thinking about how her choices were robbed from her by a pregnancy she wasn't prepared for, me. I wonder why she didn't get rid of me or give me up for adoption. She had options. I didn't have to be the thing that stole her dreams. She could have given me away. I could have had a family, with a mom and a dad and maybe even brothers or sisters. She could have found her dreams. It could have been so much better.

"Ohh." It's a long shuddering sound. "I was just missing him."

I'm confused. "Cal?"

"No." She shudders, much as I do when he crosses my mind. "Mitch. He was such a good man." She smiles a soggy smile at me and leans into my shoulder. I stroke her hair. "What is wrong me? Why can't anybody ever just love me?" she asks, and I can't answer. "Why am I never enough?" Is this it, the feeling of incompetence, that has broken her? Is it the failure in love that has destroyed the person she could have been, or is she just one more person suffering the consequences of stupid choices?

"You're enough," I say.

"Then why won't anybody ever stay?" She slides right down the wall, and I slide down to join her on the floor. Pity party for one, or two. "I still look good, don't I?"

"Mom, you're beautiful." Not right now of course, but how could I say otherwise.

"I wish he had stayed." Her accent has grown long-voweled and slow, very Southern, and I wonder where she grew up. All the little things I don't know about my mother.

"I do, too." I hold her hand. "But we don't need him."

"You know he married that bitch." The word "married" takes her nearly thirty seconds to complete, and she spits the last word out and onto the floor. "He should have married me. I could have made him happy." But she couldn't have, she can't even be happy herself. I know better than to comment but just say small encouraging things while she rants about Mitch leaving her and how unfair it all is and that bitch, spit, out onto the floor. When her rant subsides and she leans against me, I am surprised to realize she has fallen asleep, right here on the floor of the hall. I maneuver myself out from under her and head toward my own room, turning off the static-ridden TV as I go.

On the last day before returning to school, I get my period. Hallelujah.

CHAPTER 24

The bruises on my hips have faded but are still visible, a green-yellow smudge over my bones, but the tenderness is gone. I haven't seen Warren again, although Mom and Cal have had people over a couple of times. I don't know whether I want to see him or not, but I know that when I hear voices in the living room, my stomach jumps, either hoping he is there or hoping he is not. The whole thing is very confusing. What does it say about me if I do want him to be there? After everything that happened?

I am in gym, changing into my red and yellow gym suit, noticing the green bruises, realizing that if it weren't for those bruises, I would believe it had all been a dream, of sorts. For a second I remember the heat from his mouth covering mine, and I bring my fingers up to touch my lips. When I glance up, I can see myself in the mirror, and my cheeks are flushed with the memory. I turn away. Ashamed that the whole experience confuses me. I liked kissing him, anyway.

I join the other girls going into the gym, and Anna catches up to me. Anna is small with curly, brown hair that she tries to tame and only succeeds in making it big, fuzzy. She has a limp and thick glasses. We team up in gym because we're kind of the oddballs out. Kelci and the popular crew make up five of the girls in class. Toni Britton, bad-ass

Toni, and her four friends make up the rebels in the class, and Anna and I just try to get through it. Anna's mother is a writer of romance novels, and they live in a huge house south of town. Her father runs the bank. If anybody in town should have had a free pass into Kelci's clique it was Anna, but she is a little too quirky and badly put together to fit. So we suffer through kickball and softball, and together, we don't care so much about not fitting.

Today we play volleyball. We have four teams and two nets going. Mr. Spintz calls the teams, and today I have the misfortune of being on Kelci's team, with two of her girls. I'm not a talented volleyball player and, quite honestly, don't like any team sports. My lack of confidence makes me hesitant, and when other people are counting on me to do well, my lack of coordination combines with the confidence thing and I just want to not be there. Gym is a nightmare always because I can't be invisible here. I am all geared up for jeering and groans, but my stars must be aligned because when the ball comes to me, I make contact and it goes where I hoped. Kelci smacks me on the back as we head to the locker room. We won both games. "Good job, Ali." She walks beside me, and I crowd the wall, wondering what she wants.

"Thanks. You, too." We're going down the hall and are about ten feet from the door into the locker room. Our silence is awkward.

"How was your Christmas?" she finally says. "I saw you had some people over." Which means she was past my house at some point, most likely on her way to share gifts with the Winthrops.

I nod. "It was good. How 'bout yours?"

"It was all right. We went to my grandparents. Ugh." She rolls her eyes and reaches out to open the door, laughing as we pass through the door, and I realize there is something else she wants to say. "I didn't know you knew Warren." I'm stunned and stop short. My face, I can tell, is flushing.

"I didn't. Not until then, anyway. I don't really. Know him, I mean." This is the closest I've gotten to talking about my mixed-up feelings, and I want to know something about him. More than what I do already.

"Isn't he gorgeous?" We've reached the edge of the row of lockers. "He works with my brother." She laughs, explaining how she knows him, and we part to shower. This sudden friendliness makes me very nervous. Why would she mention him to me, out of the blue like that? I'm suddenly sick to my stomach and afraid that I may faint. I sit down on the bench and wait for the nausea and thin-headedness to pass. I feel naked, from the soul out—everybody can see what I've done, what happened. When the wave of dizziness finally passes, I slip out of my clothes and wrap my towel around me to head to the shower. I wrap my hair into a knot as I walk. Steam rises from the showers, and I cut through to a back corner, facing the wall and soaping quickly. Girls are talking and laughing as the water runs down. I rinse and turn my water off. I wrap the towel back around my body, escaping from the showers with my eyes on the tile floor. Back in the locker room, I dress, still damp. I stop in front of the mirror and let my hair down.

A movement behind me makes me spin.

"Hey, um, can I talk to you about something?" Tammy Bridges is standing there, already dressed. She's one of the Toni crew, but not quite as rough as the others, maybe.

"I guess." I straighten and return her gaze. She glances away from me. Twice in one day, to be approached by people who normally don't seem to know I exist, is really too much, but twice in fifteen minutes is simply overload.

"You ready to go?" she asks, clearly not wanting to talk here.

"Sure." We leave the locker room together, me carrying my books, her carrying nothing.

"Look, Alison, this isn't any of my business or anything, but I overheard some things and thought you should know."

"What?"

"Well, it doesn't matter who, and if you ever say it was me that said anything..." Her words drift off with an upraised eyebrow, suggesting that perhaps I should not tell anybody about this conversation. I nod emphatically, feeling very mafioso, curious about what she might have to say. "Well, anyway, couple of days ago I overheard something. I know it's none of my business, but I thought you should know. Like I said . . ." Clearly she has a speech planned out. I'm surprised that she has given any thought at all to what I should or should not know, let alone spent effort on composing something to say to me. Suddenly I am feeling distinctly not invisible after a lifetime of trying to blend to grey. Her attention is making me uncomfortable, and I'm afraid that she, too, is going to say something about Warren, and I know my face is red again.

"Okay," I say to move her along.

"Look, you know Cal Robinson, don't you?" I'm surprised and relieved. I can cope with that conversation. Of course I know Cal Robinson.

"Why?" I ask, hesitant.

"You know him, right?" she demands.

"I do."

"Yeah, I know." I stop walking and look at her. She turns. "He's bad news, ya know?" I nod my head. "I mean serious bad news." Her voice drops low and becomes conspiratorial. "Drugs and other stuff, too. You should really tell your mom to stay away from him."

"Yeah, well, she doesn't really ask my opinion."

She drops her voice lower. "She needs to watch herself. He should be in jail, but some evidence got contaminated."

"What are you talking about?"

"His last old lady." She glances around. She slashes her hand across her throat, sticking her tongue out, lolling her head in a grotesque pantomime for dead. "He's a loose cannon." She tells me he's been arrested a couple times, the last time for attempted murder. "Shot in the head, should have killed her, but she ended up in some institution. She's all messed up in the head, like an invalid, ya know?" It strikes me that she says that word "invalid" just like my mother has, as two distinct words and not one. "She can't feed herself or go to the bathroom or anything." She waits for a couple of kids to pass us by. "They couldn't prove he did it, but you know he did. He's just really not a nice guy."

"Who did they say did it if it wasn't him?"

"Said she did, self-inflicted, suicide attempt." She glances behind us, as if checking to see if anybody can hear. "I'd hate to see anything happen to your mom. I mean, she was always a nice lady."

"Me, too," I say, mulling over the possibility of telling my mother any of this. "Well, thanks for letting me know." The class bell rings, and kids start coming out of classes. She stops and turns back to me. Her black eyes look deep, like chasms in the night.

"Just know, they're watching where he's staying. I'd hate to see anything happen to you, too." She is gone, making her way down the hall amongst other students. I turn and go the opposite direction to my civics class. What exactly am I supposed to do about that?

CHAPTER 25

I try to talk to my mom a couple of times after Tammy's warning, but each time she is either in a frenzy or a near stupor, and she honestly does not want to talk to me. She hasn't been to work for a week, saying she has the flu. I find her in the living room today, sitting on the sofa watching TV. It's a new big screen TV. A gift from Cal, I assume. She looks very much like she could be in the throes of a major virus, possibly Ebola. "I need to talk to you about what's going on with you." I pause, and she begins to look impatient. I know already that I've put her on the defensive; I've started out all wrong. "Look, I'm worried. I don't know exactly what he's into, but I'm hearing that there are 'people' watching Cal. I'm afraid you're going to get caught up in it." I try to look small, young.

She narrows her eyes at me, staring at me with a smoldering anger. "What are you saying?"

I take a deep breath, forcing myself not to break eye contact. "I don't like him hanging around here. You know he tried to kill his last girlfriend."

"Well," she leans back, looking away from me, her jaw flexing as she presses her teeth together, "I like him hanging around here." She lets loose a rampage about exactly what she thinks of the "pigs." She completely ignores my comment about the former girlfriend.

"I just want you to be careful."

"Nobody asked you." I think she is defensive because she knows I am right.

"How deep are you in it, Mom?"

"I don't know what you're talking about." But her eyes flash to the pillow at the end of the couch, and I know that she has something hidden.

"I hear things, and I see people talking. I see you. You look like hell, and I know you're doing stuff." She doesn't deny it, but her eyes begin to get more narrow. "Is it meth? Mom, are you doing crystal?" She is sizing me up, trying to find out what sort of threat I hold for her. I try to tone my voice low, non-threatening, the way Jake did that first day he talked to me about all of this. "Cal's been in all sorts of trouble." I mention his last girlfriend again, and this time she reacts.

"That's not true. She was a crazy crank-whore." Which is exactly what she looks like at the moment, with her jaws cranking together, chewing something that isn't there.

"Mom, I'm worried about you. This guy is trouble. I don't like him."

"Well, you don't pay the bills, do you? I like him. He's likes me. He loves me." Which I know is not true. People who love you don't give you drugs that make you crazy and destroyed.

"Mom, it's not just him." My voice is quiet. I'm scared that she'll get mad and not listen. "I mean, Jake says that there's a place you can go in town that can help you clean up. They can help you."

"What the hell are you talking about?" Her voice is beginning to rise, and a splotch of red appears on her chin as her jaws churn and churn.

"I think you need help. I think you may be addicted to whatever you're using now."

"You been talking to Jake about me?" She spits his name out at me. "You been sitting down there with your fancy boyfriend talking about what a fuck-up your mother is? Is that what you been doing?" The veins pop on her neck, and she glares at me with so much darkness in her eyes that I begin to get scared.

"No. Mom. I'm not talking about you to anybody. I'm just worried about you."

"I am fine." Her voice becomes light and airy, like a breeze coming through the window, and I know that what she says is what she wants to believe. "I'm having fun. I mean, don't you think I deserve to have any fun? I never got to do any of that when I was your age. I was pregnant when I was as old as you."

"I just think you're gonna get hurt."

"You just don't want me to have any fun. You want me to sit around here like an old woman and take care of you. You are so fucking needy. You've always been sucking the life out of me. Suck, suck, suck. Want me to walk around on eggshells and bend over backward for whatever you want me to do. Well, now I've got somebody that takes care of me, do you understand?" I don't. I don't understand anything, but her anger is coming back.

"I just want you to be well." I use my smallest voice, but I'm angling toward the cushion at the end of the couch, where her stash is hidden.

"Just leave me alone. Stop nagging at me all the time." Her hand has edged under the cushion, and she draws her fist out. I reach out and lift the cushion. A small mirror lays there, filmed with white powder, a single-edge razor blade on the side. I grab her wrist and force the vial of white powder out of her bony hand. The vial is over an inch long, clear glass with a black screw-on top.

"What is this?" I ask, and she grabs it back from me, shoving me. I trip, falling backward over the coffee table. The door flies open, forced by the wind, and the rain roars.

"Get out of my house." She is screaming, standing over me, her hair flying in the wind. I scramble to my feet and escape out into the rain. Was that crystal? Cocaine? What?

I find him, sitting in the solarium, playing guitar. I can hear the strings as I come up behind the house. I stand just beyond the circle of light emanating from the room and watch He is wearing jeans and a burgundy sweater, leaning back with the guitar resting on his stomach, his fingers moving across the frets, fingering the strings, so softly it's barely a pause before glancing off to other parts to touch down. I've wanted those hands on me so many times. All of my nerves are frayed and raw, and my skin prickles under my clothes. Just to feel the way he feels the music. Who is he, this boy turning to man, and who will he be?

My teeth are chattering, my body pulling all my muscles together to quake, I can't force myself into the light as the water pours down my face, dripping in rivulets from my hair, plastering my clothes to my body. Sometimes, like now, I catch a glimpse of the man he will be, and it makes my breath stop. A broadening and thickening out around his eyes, a strength that lights along his jawline. I make my way to the glass door and tap. He jumps, startled, then he sees me through the window and lays the guitar aside, opening the door.

"What are you doing here?" Concern hangs in his voice, seeing the weakness in me, seeing my need. "You're soaked!"

"You know," I laugh lightly, my teeth clacking together, "I haven't heard you play in a while." He leaves me just inside the door and is gone from the room for a moment. I stand dripping, my mind whirling as I hear him stepping down the halls and finally returning to me. He brings towels and a bathrobe, large and worn, his, the one I snuggled in when I was staying here over Thanksgiving. He hands me the things, and I repeat that I haven't heard him play in a while.

"I haven't played." He motions me to the bathroom, where I am presumably meant to dry myself. For a moment I contemplate stepping out of my clothes and returning to him bare, but my teeth are chattering so noisily and my muscles are so tense that my movements jerk and start as I try to remove my soaked garments. My seduction plot is thrown out in favor of the warmth and comfort of his bathrobe wrapped tied around me, enveloping me in his scent. I could drown in him.

He is sitting again when I return to him. I am listening for sounds in the rest of the house, but it is quiet, uncommonly so. I stand in front of him, looking down for a moment, my hair wrapped up in a towel like a turban. I put my hands on his knees, lowering myself to the floor in front of him, my muscles still moving in hitches and spasms. I sit on my feet and fold my elbows across his thighs. I want to love this man. I do love this man. I want him to love me. I know how to make him love me, his flesh against mine. I take in a heavy breath and let it out, before I meet his eyes.

CHAPTER 26

"**S**he threw me out." She hasn't, I know, really thrown me out, but I want him to tell me to stay with him. It's why I came, but not why I'm here. I tell him the story of the night, inflating the crazy as much as I dare.

"Does she think she needs help?" I shake my head. This is not what I want to talk about. I don't want him to try to fix her; I want him to try to fix me.

"No. But this guy is such bad news." I have a split second where I think about telling him about Christmas, about how he grabbed my hair and took me to my knees, but I'm afraid that if I say anything about that night, everything will come out, and then he would never want me. That would be too much. It would seem too much like me begging for his sympathy. It's not like I was hurt. He didn't hurt me. I wasn't hurt. Liar.

Dylan's hand reaches out to brush my hair, a damp strand I missed when I wrapped it, away from my face. I turn my head and kiss his fingers. I hear the sharp intake of his breath, but I do not look at him. I close my eyes. I have never kissed him before. "What would I do without you?" My voice is quiet, just air passing my lips. I kiss his fingers again and lean my head onto my arm. The towel untwists from my hair, and it all falls free. His hand tangles in my hair. "I tried to talk to her again. It's no use. She doesn't see anything." A shuddering sigh mingles with a shiver, and my body quakes for a second. "You should have heard her. She's insane."

"I bet." His fingers move over the base of my skull, at the nape of my neck, fingers on guitar strings. He isn't thinking about her, about my life. He is thinking about my closeness, maybe my nakedness under his robe. I can hear it in the shallowness of his breathing.

"I don't think she's going to quit." I look finally back at him, and his eyes meet mine. "I don't know who she is. You know. God, I remember when I was little, and we'd go for picnics at the park and play frisbee. She loved me. I mean, we'd do normal things. Then everything just went wrong. I mean, everything. Now, I don't even know where she is half the time. Then this . . . I mean, it's unreal. It's not a life. This is not what life is supposed to be." I keep talking because I don't want him to realize that something has shifted and that his hands are caressing my neck under my hair and my whole body has gone electric.

"No, it's not." His hand slides down toward my jaw. He nods his head toward the house, "Let's go in." I follow him into the darkened hall, where he leaves me standing in the kitchen. I can feel the press of my breasts against the fabric of his robe, and I know he is struggling with the watching of me. I hand him the towel which I have been patting my hair with as we walked, and I am relatively dry now. He leads me into the living room and onto the couch. We sit in darkness, with the glow from the security light filtering through the streaming rain, making a wavering patch of light on the floor. He holds me in front of him, one leg on either side of me, my back against his chest. His arms wrap around me, and our fingers entwine. He rests his chin on my shoulder, and his breath whispers past my ear. "I don't think you should go back there." His hold on me tightens, then relaxes. I melt into him, this boy who has always been like the half of my soul I lost along the way.

"Where else am I going to go?"

"I don't know. We'll figure something out." His breath brushes my ear. "We'll talk to my folks, see what they think."

I turn my face toward him and adjust myself so I am facing him, our eyes barely inches apart. I glance from his eyes to his lips, then back. He would keep me safe. Always.

The first touch of lips, light against his, draws his hand up to my cheek, makes my breath stop. His lips are soft, gently drawing mine open, his tongue lightly touching them. For so long I have wanted to feel this, to feel his arms holding me, his hands sliding under my hair along my neck. This is the way it is supposed to be. Then he is pulling back, his eyes boring into mine.

A smile flickers across my lips, still sensitive from his touch. "We've never done that."

"No. We've never done that." His voice catches in his throat, and then his lips are on mine again, hungry, his mouth exploring mine until we pull away, our breath ragged.

"I've always wanted to," I say, his forehead leaning against mine. I feel like I am lying to him, leading him to believe I am a better person than I am. My throat is choked. Even as his lips touch mine, I am thinking, a mile down the road, seeing us, together, living my lie. My mind is whirling, thinking that if he loves me then nothing else matters. His family could be my family. He would make me safe, always. The heat is rising from my skin, and I long for his hands to touch me. The belt of his robe has loosened, and my shoulder is bare in the relative cool of the living room. His hand is suddenly on me, sliding inside the curve of the robe where it has shifted, over my shoulder, drawing me even closer until I feel that my bones will turn to liquid and meld with him.

We shift when we must breathe, and he settles me again, my back against his chest, his fingertips running light along my collarbone. I can feel his breath near my ear, and I so want to turn back to him, back to those lips, to taste him in my mouth, to feel the heat of him inside of me. I can feel the hardness of him, low against my hip where I lean into him.

"What do you want, Al?" And I'm confused, baffled by his words against my ear. It seems it would be quite obvious what I want. A low chuckle comes from my throat, almost a gasp.

"You." I turn into him again and our lips collide, our breath mingling and his tongue touching mine. Our motions, my turning has loosened the robe, and when his arms move inside the fabric, a groan escapes his throat. He tightens his arms around me, his left arm inside of the robe, next to my flesh, his finger splaying across my lower back. He tilts his head up, and I kiss his throat. "Make love to me," I say, breathless. I have never wanted anything the way I want him, clear headed and with every ounce of my body. I feel his hips press against me and his arms tighten and he is kissing me again, his hands feeling my body, realizing how completely naked I am beneath his robe.

"I can't." His voice catches, turning "can't" into a two-syllable word. "We can't."

"Why not? I love you, Dylan. I always have." I am more bare than just my body, and my face glows with the heat of my admission. I expect him to say that he loves me, too—isn't that the way it's supposed to go? But he doesn't; he just holds me slightly away from him, his eyes intent on mine, an expression on his face that I do not understand.

The clock in the hall begins to chime, bong, bong, bong, and he is drawing away. Standing up, running his hands through his hair, physically pulling himself together. I draw the robe around me when he turns on the light. I feel disoriented. "Um. We need to get you some clothes." He runs from the room, and I follow, wanting to get back to where we were. The clock in the hall chimes its ninth bong as we enter his room. He offers me a sweatshirt, boxers, and sweats. "Jake and Vaude will be here—" Before he can finish the sentence, lights flash across the ceiling, and I know they have pulled into the drive. The garage door begins to ratchet up, and we are both caught in laughter at the nervous realization that we had nearly been caught with his hands all inside his robe, all over me. I drop the robe, turning my back slightly to him and draw on the sweatshirt, which is luckily baggy enough to keep my nipples from showing through. I draw on the boxers, the sweats, rolling the waist down to help them stay up. Dylan has left me, and I hear him descending the steps, two at a time from the sounds of it. I wonder where he has run to. I stay sheltered in his room, dressed in his much-too-big clothes, still feeling the pressure of his fingertips.

My whole body hums with the memory of his touch.

CHAPTER 27

I
t is some time later, when my blood pressure has come back to something resembling normal, when I hear the three of them downstairs, their voices rising and falling in slow rhythms. I should go down, but I have stopped at the top of the stairs, where their voices come clear to me.

". . . That's all I'm saying, Dyl. Be careful. I know you care about her, but you really have to think about your future." Jake's voice is pitched low, but it still carries up the steps to me.

"I know," Dylan says, his voice quiet, reassuring. "It's not like we are dating. She's just a friend. It's just that her life is so messed up."

"Yes. Very. People who come from that repeat it. It's what they know." My face flushes hot, and I step back into his room. My stomach in knots. That was Vaude. I feel so betrayed. It's what they know? I repeat the words and sit on the edge of his bed, trying to put myself in check. Maybe I misunderstood. Maybe it wasn't about me. But it was. It was them telling him not to love me. I am just rising, stealing myself for the inevitable facing up, when I hear pounding on the front door. I am at the top of the stairs before I hear my mother's voice, shrill and angry. "Is she here?" she demands, and I duck back inside Dylan's room, leaving the door cracked to hear what transpires. I hear Jake assuring her that he hasn't seen me, and then I hear him stepping outside. "I don't need you filling her head with shit," she yells, her voice ricocheting. "She wasn't born with a silver spoon like your son." I'm not positive those are her exact words, but I am humiliated that there are any words like that. Dirty. The word bounces through my head, chased by its companion, trashy. Not sick, not broken, not sad. Their voices rise and fall for a few minutes before I hear her car backing down the drive. I make my way down to join them in the living room, for whatever conversation there may be, plastering a quiet face over the inner confusion and anger that is roiling against them all.

<hr />

We are sitting on the sofa with a fire raging and hot chocolates waiting to cool on the coffee table. I reach out and wrap my hands around my mug, enjoying the warmth of the ceramic on my hands. It is still too hot to drink, but the aroma is delightful.

"No, I mean, really, what do you want in your life? What do you want to be when you grow up?" It's the second time he has asked me this, and I know he expects a better answer than "survival," which was my first response. It's a question I remember from my childhood, and it's one that I haven't thought of in a long time.

"I want to be an artist." It is so easy, saying those words. It's what I have always said when asked this question. "Maybe an art teacher," I add because I'm really not good enough to be an "artist." I definitely need something more down to earth. But college is required for teaching, and that is out of the question, so maybe what I should have said is that I want to work the line at the factory or I want to walk the streets as a prostitute—at least those would be more realistic. But really I don't want to be anything. I just want to live from today until tomorrow without any chaos. I just want to sit somewhere and not move for days on end and watch the world go from light to dark on a repeating loop. I don't want much of life, I see that suddenly, very clearly, and I've never looked at it so honestly. The art thing is just a thing, something I do that I'm tolerably good at, maybe not even as much as that. I haven't thought of it in months; it just seems that it's a dream, and not even one that I am much willing to strive for. It takes so much energy just to breathe in and breathe out every day that I can't focus on anything more. I look suddenly down the road on my life and wonder if it will always be this strange mix of people coming and going, fighting and drinking and sexing. It's all so futile. Just breathe. Just breathe. None of the rest matters anyway.

"Then that's what you should be," Jake says very matter of fact, and it takes me a second to refocus, to return to the conversation at hand. I nod as if I can be anything I want to. "You just have to remember that is where you're going and don't let yourself go down any other path." I nod and smile at him, fucking hypocrite. I heard what you had to say about me.

I am thinking of my mother and the shambles her life has been. Did she ever have a dream, a place she wanted to get to, something she wanted to be? It haunts me thinking about her and her dreams, because I know I had to be the reason she lost them. Thinking of my father, wondering where he is, who he is. Thinking of Warren, thinking that the night with him made me less than the person I had thought I was. I drop my face into my hands suddenly. Is that what my mother had with my father? One night that created me and destroyed whatever hopes she may have had for the future? I'm ashamed. I'm ashamed because I know they are right to warn him. I am trash. I come from trash, and that is all I will ever be.

I look at Dylan where he stands by the fireplace, and I know that he is where I was going. He has always been where I was going. The shame is not strong enough to supplant the desire to touch him, to be touched by him, and to be part of "his." It's a shame that has enveloped me for so long that I didn't even know it was there. The shame of knowing that I would have drawn Dylan into my quicksand, and I will yet, and taken him down with me had the clock not struck and drawn him to his senses. Then I would have killed his dreams, too. Killer. Vaude is sitting on one side of me, holding my hand, and Dylan is standing next to the fireplace, his eyes not meeting mine. Jake is my interrogator, sitting across the coffee table from the two of us, leaning forward with his elbows on his knees, his fingers forming a diamond where they come together. It is a Dylan pose.

It is some time later still when it is decided that I will sleep in the guestroom tonight, and tomorrow we will figure out the next step. Dylan is sitting on the edge of the bed, looking down at me, and I ask him the question his father asked me. His finger slides lightly across my forehead, brushing my nearly dry hair from my face. "What do you want to be? When you grow up?" I ask. We smile, and air rushes out of us to meet in the space between.

"I don't know. I'm still testing the water." We place our hands together, palms touching, and he folds his finger down over mine. "We have a whole life out there, just waiting for us to get to it. I'm not in a hurry." He is so much smarter than I am, so much older in all the ways that really matter.

"I am." I laugh slightly, trying to make it all sound light and easy. I feel guilty that I thought I could make him mine, make his family mine, make them all keep me safe from my own life. Of course they don't want me, but I want some future life now, anything other than my present one.

"That's because of the way things are for you. They won't always be like that." He looks at me for a long moment. "Everybody makes mistakes." For a split second I think he is talking about my mistakes, and I look quickly away from him, afraid that the reality of my dark self is plain on my face. "I learned that from Jake."

"We all repeat what we know," I say, my voice low, telling him without telling him that I heard them talking about me as if I were the local gutter rat. He doesn't catch on, doesn't realize what I am saying.

"Lots of mistakes were made in this house. I just watched." He laughs quietly, and his fingers slip between mine, closing around me. "And lots of counseling." He leans forward and kisses my forehead.

"Stay with me," I say, holding his hand as he starts to go.

"I can't," he says, his brows furrowing.

"Please?"

He shakes his head. "I can't. Jake and Vaude are just down the hall. I can't." He runs his hands through his hair, making it stand up in spikes, then he turns and leaves, flicking off the light as he goes. I lay in the crisp, fresh sheets of the Winthrop guestroom, frustrated and unsleeping. I can still hear small voices, low, speaking in other parts of the house. If I can't love him, will I hate him?

CHAPTER 28

The next step, it turns out, is for me to quietly return to the trailer. I come through the back door and go straight to my room. It is cluttered. Clothes are strewn across the floor and books lie on every surface. Dylan doesn't live like this. I gather my dirty clothes and pile them on the bed. I gather cups and bowls and return them to the kitchen. I make my way down to my mother's room and find her sleeping. She is alone. I wash the dishes in the sink and sit them in the strainer to dry, careful not to let the dishes clink. I am not ready to see my mother awake. Back in my room, I toss the pile of clothes onto the floor, and I draw the sheets and blankets up into place. I empty my school pack and reload it with my clothes and pull up the vent to reach the wad of money I've stashed there. For a moment the vent is empty, and I panic, then my fingers touch the edge of the envelope, and I draw it out, clasping it to my chest until the flutter of my heart subsides. Money makes everything possible. Jake is well now because he makes money. Mom is always worse because she doesn't. Money may not buy happiness, but it certainly is a good down payment.

There are two laundromats in town. I won't wash at the trailer because the water has rust in it and turns all my clothes a dingy yellow. I ride to the nearest one, next to the grocery store instead of the better one by the Dairy Queen. My fingers are frozen, and my face feels like silly putty that has been stretched too far. The grocery is more practical. I load my clothes to wash, using the individual packets out of the vending machine for soap, and when they are safely churning, I stroll down the sidewalk to the grocery. Nobody would bother stealing my bike, so I leave it leaning against the wall. It's a hodgepodge mash of parts, and if somebody needs to steal it, they must need it more than I do, which is almost unimaginable. I buy two apples and an egg-salad sandwich from the deli, which at least looks like it was made today. Back at the laundry I eat, pacing from one end of the room to the other. I'm just polishing off the last apple when my mother's car swings into the parking lot, landing at an angle in front of my bike. My feet shift me to the back of the laundry, moving toward the bathroom with its door and its lock, not sure which version of my mother is going to walk through the door. Through the window she looks frantic, her hair tumbled on top of her head in a messy bun.

The door flies open on the car, and she barely manages to swing it closed before she is running toward the front of the laundry. She shoves into the laundry, and the two other people here turn to the jerked open door to see the wild woman standing there. Her eyes catch me, and for a second I am not sure what I am seeing. Then her lips part, and she says my name in a deep, shuddering gasp. She rushes to me, and I stand as tall as I can, waiting for the concoction of booze, drugs, and maybe vomit to hit me, which it does, but in a day-old sort of fashion. "I thought you were dead," she says, thankfully moderating her voice so as not to let the others know all my shit.

"No. Not dead." I try to hold her eyes but can't, and my own flit toward the window.

"Where did you go?" She asks, and her hand is touching my shoulder, brushing my hair off my cheek.

"I just went." She is not drunk. She is not high. She is not cranked.

She is just a mom, worried about her kid. Tears well up in my eyes, and I blink them back, trying to remove myself. "I don't want to live like this, Mom."

"I know." She is contrite, accepting of blame. I've seen it many times since I was small. Next comes words about how she will do better. She will be better. This time will be different, just wait and see. Then she says something I wasn't expecting. "I've told him to leave. I told him to get out." She's never gotten rid of someone for me. It gives me a glimpse of hope.

PART FIVE: SPRING

CHAPTER 29

The snow began to fall on Tuesday, and by Wednesday morning we are sitting under four inches. The snowplows started early, and all of the roads were clean by the time the buses rolled. I ran out to the bus as it slowed in front of the trailer. I hated not having my bike for later, but the thought of riding in this crisp, frigid morning is more than I can handle. I walked from school to work, where I am working the register in the last twenty minutes of the day. Rob is out closing the buildings, and Mr. Billups is in his office, finishing up a deposit that he'll leave at the bank drop on his way home. The door jingles, and a man comes through the door. He shakes his head and a spray of water spreads away from him. We are back to rain, frozen, slushy rain. Air catches in my throat, and my stomach clenches when I realize that there stands Warren, in all his glory. He doesn't notice me and passes by me without even looking, heading into the store for whatever he needs.

He brings about two feet of plastic tubing to the counter for me to ring up. "Hey." He smiles. His full lips spreading over neat teeth. Teeth that braces probably graced in times gone by.

"Hey." I am stunned and startled by the current of electricity that is coursing through my body as he moves closer. "How are you?" I put aside my calculations and try not to meet his eyes.

"Wet." He smiles more broadly. I let my eyes meet his, and there is nothing there, absolutely no recognition, nothing to tell me he ever met me. It's been five, six weeks, and every day he has pounded into my mind, leaving me confused and embarrassed because of the way that he haunts me.

"How's your Mom?" So he does recognize me. I am more confused than before, but then I don't know what I had expected when I should see him again.

"She's fine, doing good. How 'bout you?"

"Good. Been real busy." I can see that he's older than I first thought, probably in his late twenties, early thirties.

"I'm sure." He is looking around the store. "You here alone?"

"No, there's a couple of us left." I indicate the one-way glass that lines the top of the building. Mr. Billups is up there, with the files, and I hope he is not watching this. I just want Warren to pay and be gone.

"You know, I've thought about calling you a couple of times, but didn't know if I should." His eyes soften, and he glances away, pulling bills from his jeans. I don't bother to tell him he couldn't have called because we don't have a phone anymore. "About Christmas . . . I didn't know he put something in that drink." His voice drops to a hushed whisper, and his finger traces a small, freshly healed scar above his left eye. He's trying to explain something, but I can't seem to wrap my mind around it. My lips part to speak, but close again, dumb, not knowing what to say. I know that my cheeks are burning, the red creeping under my skin.

"You okay?"

"Yes. What are you talking about?" I look at his lips, then back to those storm-cloud eyes.

"Maybe I'm wrong. You just went down so quick I thought . . ." His voice trails off.

"What happened?" I remember the aching, the bruises on my hips, and the sore, bruised flesh between my legs. I had assumed that Warren was the cause of it all, that his were the hands I remembered running over my body. A sudden jolt of memory shows my hand being held at the wrist by a strong, tattooed arm, the black ink wrapping around the thumb. I glance down at Warren's hands; his arms are un-inked to at least where the cuff of his shirt drops just below his elbow. A gorge of bile rises in my throat, and I cover my mouth with the sudden impulse. It's not Warren who has tattooed hands; it is Cal. Oh God. I know my face has drained of color, and I feel small pricks of sweat under my hair all across my scalp. "Something in my drink?" I ask, keeping my voice steady.

"Yeah, like a ruffie, you know." He smiles, nervous, almost whispering the word. "I had no idea, but you just went out so quickly, I didn't think a drink would do that."

"A ruffie?" I ask. My mouth falling slack. "It wasn't you?" My voice is slow, controlled.

"God no. I don't use that shit. If a girl doesn't want to be with me, why would I want her?" That's not really the question I was asking. But the back door breezes open, and Rob's bulky frame wrestles through it. It's the interruption I need to get my face under control, and I find my voice as Warren hands me the money. I don't take my eyes off of his lips as I say coldly, "I have no idea what you are talking about."

"Good," He says, real relief on his face. "I was worried, you know." His finger draws along the scar above his eye.

"How'd you get that?"

He blows a puff of air from his nose, a laugh, a snort. "Oh, he was waiting for me when I locked you in. Knocked me cold, man. He may not look like he's much, but he's got a mean hook."

"He hit you?"

"Yeah. A couple of times." He nods. "Then he picked my ass up and threw me out of the house." He isn't too proud to say this, and I like him a little more for it.

"Wow," I say.

"He's a tough bastard." Now it is his turn to shift uncomfortably as Rob passes the register. "Maybe I'm wrong. I'm wrong. I just assumed, you know. Why else would he kick my ass like that?" He sighs, still looking worried, confused.

"Yeah. I just slept. You know, I don't drink, and I hadn't eaten much that day. It must have just hit me hard."

Warren lets loose a deep breath, and the relief that etches across his face is stark. "I'm so glad." He reaches out and touches my hand, letting out another deep breath. I hand him his change, and he steps back from the counter. Running his hand through his wet hair. "See you around, Alison?" I nod, and he nods, then turns and heads to the front door.

"Damn, it's getting cold out there." Rob shakes his head, much like Warren had when he came in. Warren is passing through the door, and a whoosh of air races through the building until the front and the back doors both fall shut. A nervous, out of control laugh breaks from me, and I hold the counter for support. I must make some sound, and laughing is better than crying, and crying is better than screaming, which is what I really want to do. "What's so funny?" Rob asks, still shaking his head, water dripping from his chin.

"Nothing, just a joke. Such a joke." I pull myself together before I fall into a full bout of hysteria, the bile churning in my stomach. How can I go back there? How can I go back to my home and risk seeing him again? How can I ever look at my mother again? She has kicked him out; he's gone, I remind myself but feel no better. Does she know? Sudden flashes of memory flood me, the words outside my door, the banging against it—that would be Warren falling into it when Cal attacked him. I close my eyes and see a vision of Cal's hand holding my wrist, then a single word hissed into my ear. "Whore." I lean over the trash can and vomit into it.

CHAPTER 30

I am not alone in the house. Rob has just dropped me off after I threw up in the trash can at work. I held myself together until I got out of his truck, waving back to him as I unlock the trailer door. She is here. He is here. They both look up at me when I come in, but neither of them speak. I let my eyes pass over them like oil over a pan, like vodka over ice, and make a straight line to my bedroom. I prop my chair under the doorknob and scan my room. I need something.

The word is too much. His voice hissing into my ear, "whore, whore, whore" in rhythm to his movements. I have to get it out. I have to get the word out of me. Something sharp. Something sharp. Something sharp.

My eyes light on the picture I did for my final art project last year, the three horses caught in the storm. It is hanging by four pushpins on the paneling. I pull one pin out, testing the point by scraping it along the pad of my thumb. It doesn't bleed. I need it to bleed. I trace the line again, faster and with more downward force, two more times, and am rewarded with a small wheel of blood. It is not enough. It is not enough. My mind rings, and I throw myself across my bed. I almost cry out but hold it back. The surging tumble of knowledge is more than I can handle. The pushpin is closed in my fist, and I slide off the other side of the bed, sitting cross-legged like I did when I was in kindergarten. Criss-cross applesauce. I kick my shoes off and peel off my socks. Whore, whore, whore. Dirty.

I scratch in the space between my ankle bone and my heel the word that has followed me all of my life, blocky, bloody, sharp, and angled. Dirty. It isn't enough. I go for my other foot and down goes the other word, the one that he gave me as a gift on Christmas. Isn't it true? My mother has said it often enough. I've known it was true all my life. I am not crying. I am cutting, scratching ugly jagged lines in my flesh, and with each scratch the tension in my head diminishes, the pressure in my chest wanes. Scratch, wipe, scratch, wipe. The sock I am wiping the blood with is dotted with sharp, red smears. The release is like a small pop in my head, and suddenly everything is calm. Scratch, wipe, scratch, wipe. One letter done, two letters, three, four then five, and when the furious scratching is done, I stare down at the wad of my bloodied sock.

I don't have to live this life. There is power in that knowledge. I sit for a very long time with the thumbtack poised over my wrist, sweat sliding in rivulets down my spine, pooling at the waist of my jeans. I hover over my wrist, watching the tip of the tack tracing the blue vein beneath, and finally fold my hand back over it, standing up and replacing the tack in the corner of my picture. My fury is spent, and for now, my two ugly words are enough. It is with the strangest sense of peace that I feel the small tugging of the shallow cuts on my feet as I walk. I would shower but don't want to risk leaving my room, so I change my clothes and open the bottom drawer of my dresser where I have a jar of peanut butter stashed. I dig my finger in and eat it all by itself. Soon enough I am not hungry, and for the first time in days, my mind is quiet when I go to get in bed.

There are blades in the art room. There are blades at Billups. I can't wait to go in to work tomorrow. I can't believe I never thought of it before. I don't have to do this. I don't have to do any of this.

Dusk is wrapping tight around the room when I close my eyes and sleep like the dead.

CHAPTER 31

It's Thursday. I am at Billups, finishing up the midweek filing. It's been slow today because the weather turned bad around noon with ice and hail clacking against the glass. I will take snow over cold rain any day. The wind is whistling through the cracks around the door. Around seven thirty, sirens wail somewhere out in the night. I stop my filing and look up, through the large plate-glass window, into the murky gloom lit only by the gleam of the streetlights. The sleet slashes across the road, almost horizontal. It is one of those rare spring storms that throws us right back into the depths of winter. Just this morning I was noticing new buds on a few of the trees. I almost didn't even wear a jacket. It's been such strange weather this year, and this sudden ice storm certainly tops it all.

Off in the distance, I can still hear wailing sirens, but they are finally lost to the wind and I turn back to my filing. Mr. Billups is checking the doors to lock up. There is no sense in staying open until nine like normal; nobody is getting out in this weather.

We leave together, Mr. Billups and I. When the weather is bad, he often gives me a ride home, even though it's a good five miles out of his way. He's a good man, a decent man. Wish my mother could have found just one of them along the way, but decent isn't what works for her. The headlights of his pickup barely grace the iced road, and the murk seems to invade the interior of the cab. He squints through the flapping wipers into the gloom as the heater pumps out tepid warmth onto my hands.

***

The trailer is dark when Mr. Billups stops to let me out, and it does not seem odd that my mother isn't here. She's probably with Cal. She has been around less and less these last few weeks, and I've been mostly glad when she is elsewhere. Even more glad that her absence makes it less likely that I will see him. Her promises of being better, of drinking less, of being "mother" were broken and forgotten within hours it seems, and I barely even care. She is who she is and will be who she will be. I'm angrier about him.

The house stays cleaner anyway, and I don't have to deal with the tension. I turn and wave to Mr. Billups as I step into the doorway and flip on the porch light. He backs slowly out of the drive and turns toward the way he came. I flip on lights as I move through the house, my eyes scanning for evidence. The pillows on the sofa are set askew, so I know she's been home since I last was. The kitchen counter has a single glass sitting out, residuals of some drink filming the bottom. I can smell the vodka as I pass through, on my way to my room. I stop in the bathroom and brush my teeth. I know it's early for bed, but I suddenly feel tired to the bone and want nothing more than to settle under my quilt and let the world disappear.

My room is black as pitch when I open my eyes some time later, the reverberation of someone pounding on the front door ricocheting down the hall to me. I debate for a moment on whether to crawl out of bed and admit whomever it is or just stay where I am and let them pound. Then I remember that I locked the door, and depending on her state, Mom may not be able to get it unlocked. Sometimes it sticks, especially when it's damp out.

Something is wrong, very wrong. I know as soon as I open my bedroom door. The kitchen and living room glow red, and the pounding on the door suddenly seems very businesslike. I turn on the light and open the door. There, standing on the porch, with ice in his mustache, is a policeman, nearly frozen.

The thoughts in my head run the gamete from her being arrested for some drug or another, to her being in the hospital because the crazy bastard hit her over the head with a two-by-four. "Alison Hayes?"

"Yes, what's happened?" The creeping panic rises up my spine.

"There's been an accident. Please come with me." He leads me to the car and opens the passenger door for me to slide into the front seat.

"What's happened?" I ask, convinced that the two-by-four is the most likely scenario.

"Well, ma'am, your mother's been in an accident." He hesitates, and I notice that he is so young. He has the look of a deer in headlights, with wide, adrenaline-wide, eyes. This is probably one of the first big things that has happened since he has been with the force. I turn and watch out the window. A mixture of rain and ice pelt the glass and distort the world outside. My mind frames the image of my mother with her head crushed. It's a horrible, disturbing image but one with which I can cope. What kind of accident?

"Is she alive?" I ask, my voice sounding strange and calm outside of my own head.

"Yes, yes, ma'am, she is." I can feel him shift on the seat, looking at me, probably wondering how much he should tell me. I hope he can't see how disappointed I am that she lives. I can't make myself speak, and the dread of whatever comes next makes me shake. I am a horrible person. He doesn't speak again, and neither do I.

We move slowly through the sleet-slicked roads, passing under the misted glow of street lamps. The rotation of the light on top the car should allow us swifter passage, but we move at a snail's pace, and I feel trapped. A lone snowplow creeps along, spreading salt as it goes; otherwise, we are alone out in this night. My stomach churns as we ease into the hospital emergency lot. The officer is out of the car and to my side before I even have my feet settled under me, his hand firmly under my elbow, steering me toward the sliding doors of the emergency bay, moving in double time after our slow progression to the hospital.

The glare of the lights reflecting off the walls and tiled floors shocks my eyes and forces me to squint against the intensity. I'm glad for the policeman's hand under my elbow, steering me, guiding me, holding me up, since for half a minute or more I am blinded.

"Sit here," he says and steps away from me, leaving me and my eyes to adjust. The acrid smell of hospital antiseptic and the bright lights flashing off of the white tiles makes my head hurt. A few minutes pass, and I sit, unsure of what to do, where to look, whom to ask for details, and finally the young officer, Officer F. Jones according to his name tag, comes back and sits beside me.

"Okay, Alison, the doctor is going to be out to talk with you as soon as he can. She's still in surgery." He pauses, unsure of how to handle the situation.

"Can you tell me what happened?" It is not that strange, calm voice from the ride over. It is something shriller, closer to off-kilter, ricocheting through my inner walls, echoing too loudly now in the subdued waiting room. Officer Jones glances around the room then back to me. I follow the direction of his eyes, as if that's going to provide me an answer. There's only one other person in the room, a young man, sitting along the opposite wall, his head lowered, pressed into his splayed hands.

"She had an accident." His voice is low, almost a whisper. I don't want him to whisper. I want him to talk loudly and clearly and tell me exactly what has happened. "Apparently she slid through a stoplight and ran into another car. That's really all the information I have right now." So the two-by-four theory is shot.

"Was she drunk?"

He looks startled. "I don't have that information, ma'am. I was just told to go pick you up. The roads are terribly slick."

I can tell I've made him uncomfortable, so I change my tack. "Who else was hurt?" I ask, my eyes spinning back to the young man sitting alone in the corner.

"I don't have that information." Which is apparently officer speak for "I plead the fifth" or whatever. I can feel him shifting, uncomfortable, and a slow, red anger starts to bubble in my stomach. I know he knows more but won't say. "The doctor will be out as soon as she's out of surgery." He pauses. My eyes glue on the young man, who suddenly stands and moves in halted jerks through the room, crossing in front of us, stepping through the bay doors and out into the frigid night. "Can I get you anything?" I shake my head, and he reaches out and touches my shoulder. "Is there anybody you want to call?"

I want Dylan to be here with me. "Yeah, I'd like to call someone." My voice has gone back to the oddly calm, disconnected tone. "You don't have to wait with me. I'll be fine. Thank you for coming to get me." I put my hand out to shake his, and an odd look crosses his face. He takes my hand in both of his and squeezes.

"I'll be back to check on you after my shift." Finally he releases my hand and turns away from me. I do not watch him leave. I feel like I could start to cry, and I really don't want to do that. Not here. Not now.

I call Dylan from the phone in the waiting room and go to the corner farthest from the spot where the man has now returned. He is sitting again with his head in hands. His shoulders rock slightly, and his body sways back and forth, slowly. I turn and look out the window into the ice covered night.

CHAPTER 32

The registration nurse peers from her little cubbyhole, her eyes moving between the two of us, the man and me. Time passes, crawling, the second hand clicks from one second to the next, but the minutes never march forward. Twice the man rises and paces the floor, his hands rumpling through his hair, making it stand in spikes and cowlicks. He stares at the doors without blinking, and after several minutes he jerks to his feet and goes out into the night, like a person who just remembered they had an appointment elsewhere. Time passes, and I am alone in the waiting area, listening to the silence of the walls. When the bay doors open again, Dylan blows through, his eyes scanning, adjusting to the brightness. He catches sight of me on a third blink and rushes my way. Through the doors I can see the man, pacing in the cold night in front of the entrance.

"What happened?" He kneels in front of me.

"Not sure, nobody has talked to me. She's in surgery." He settles next to me, drawing me close to him, and we wait. Time passes, click click click go the seconds. The woman at the desk continues to pass her eyes from us to the young man who has come in again. After noticing her glance several times, it suddenly dawns on me that after she looks at us, Dylan and me, her head turns away and moves slowly from side to side. That pity movement. The word dirty hums on my left foot. After seeing her do this three times over the next two hours, I push free of Dylan and walk to her. She looks up at me, standing on the other side of her counter, her painted-on eyebrows raised in question, as if she doesn't know what I might want to say to her. Before I manage to summon a single word, the door leading to the emergency room springs open, and a white-collared pastor steps out into the waiting area, going directly to the young man, who peels himself from his seat and stands.

The words are spoken quietly, almost whispered, "Please come with me, Mr. Dollman." His words are normal, but the impact is extraordinary. The man crumples, as if the bones of his back and legs have turned to liquid. The preacher collects the man, who looks small and broken, his body shaking, as if wracked by tears, but his eyes and face are dry. He is cried out. The pastor does not look away from the man, and what seems like a lifetime later, he helps him to his feet and they move past me into the recesses of the hospital. Dylan has come to my side, and I feel his arms around my shoulders. I turn back to him, leaving the counter without ever asking my questions. The slow sinking that had quickened in my stomach when the preacher came out has moved to my knees, and I make it about halfway across the room before I realize I am crying. The crumpling of the man has somehow hit me, and in his crumpling, I know the truth. She has not killed herself; she has killed somebody else. A preacher wouldn't come instead of a doctor if there was anything left to be done for the body. She's killed somebody. She's killed somebody's somebody. There is no other reason for a man of God to come instead of a doctor.

"Miss Hayes?" comes a voice from behind me, and we turn together, Dylan and I, his hand on my elbow as we meet Dr. Connard, who looks like he's been awake for days, looks like he hasn't slept much in all of his fifty-odd years. His hair is thinning, and there are dark circles and bags under his eyes. He is dressed in blue scrubs. I feel so guilty for thinking that it would be better if the preacher came for me and the doctor for the other man. Wouldn't the world be just a little better? I close my eyes and squeeze them tight. What is wrong with me? Who thinks something like that?

"Yes?" I sniff and wipe tears from my cheeks and onto my hands.

"I'm Dr. Connard. Your mother is in recovery. You'll be able to go in to see her once she is moved to her room."

"Can you tell me what happened?"

He begins listing details about her physical condition—she has a steel pin in her right leg, a concussion—and then he explains about the rehabilitation, and, yes, she will be able to walk again. But what I want to know about is the accident and how it came to be. Nothing seems to matter until that information can be filled, and he is not the man to provide that detail.

She is sleeping when I enter the room, so I stand there, beside her bed, watching her. Her chest rises and falls slowly. Her thin arms are covered by bruises and sores, and an IV drips into her hand. I'd known she was doing drugs, but until now I had not known that she was doing intravenous drugs. That's a whole new story. How am I supposed to think of her now? This is so totally not what MOTHER is supposed to be. In her neck I can see her pulse beating, fluttering like the wings of a hummingbird. The tendons in her neck and the bones of her skull are covered by flesh that looks like rice paper. What would happen if I unplugged all the beeping machines? Are they keeping her alive or only monitoring her as she lives?

The blue-tinged lids of her eyes flutter open, and her unfocused gaze looks through me, somewhere past me. "Mom." I take her hand, although I don't want to touch her. I don't want to look at her. I want her to be dead. Her eyes widen, and the air catches in her throat, and she begins to cough. Spittle sprays from her mouth, speckling my arm where I am reaching toward her. I force myself not to recoil. The rhythmic beeping of the heart monitor speeds up, and a nurse comes in, pushing me away from the bed. I stand in the corner, wiping spit from my forearm discreetly on my jeans and shirt, watching as the nurse tries to calm her.

She begins to yell, my mother does, in a small, frightened voice. She begins to yell that the devil is here trying to take her soul. I am rushed out into the hall, where Dylan is waiting for me, and I would laugh except for the tragedy of that young man's somebody being gone. I would laugh because that heinous bitch, that Satan, that evil, selfish, insane woman lying in that bed thinks I am the devil. That thing that stole my mother from me thinks I am the devil. The cold stone in the pit of my stomach shifts, and I swear by the life taken today that that woman will never forget what she has done. "That's right, Bitch. I am your Devil."

"What?" Dylan asks, but I just shake my head and tell him nothing, and he puts his arm over my shoulder and draws me to him.

CHAPTER 33

Once we arrive at Dylan's we find Jake and Vaude huddled together in front of the fireplace where a hearty blaze licks up around the logs. The house is completely dark, except the glow cast by the fire. The sleet has snapped a power line somewhere, and it vaguely occurs to me that it was a very dark ride to their front door. What a horrible day.

Vaude leaps to her feet and comes to draw me into a motherly hug. I love her. She is so kind and good, even if she does think I'm trash. I let her fold around me, and I rest my cheeks on her chest. I accept her charity, but only for tonight—on such a horrible night a little charity is a good thing. Her chin on my head, "Darling," she says, and I fear I will completely come apart. She smells of the cold and of the smoke from the logs before it drew out of the flue. She is warm and strong and reassuring. My anger begins to ebb in her arms. It held me rigid all the way back to their house, in the silent car, where Dylan drove slow and cautious, still keeping half an eye trained on me, waiting for me to melt. I held it together; I always hold it together . . . until this mother, this wonderful, kind, loving version of mother holds me, and I am sucking for breath, and my body ratchets against her. We fold together onto the floor, and she rocks me. Dylan at my back touching my shoulder, so unsure of what to do, how to help. I sob. I sob as I don't believe I have ever sobbed before. I try to speak but only wail in my agony. She killed her. That nice young man's somebody special. That good woman who was full of light and hope.

Vaude rocks with me until I am cried out, exhausted, my face slick with tears and snot. I drag my sleeve under my nose and over my eyes. Vaude keeps her arm around me, and I become aware that she is talking, low and quiet.

"She killed her," I say, and my stomach jerks and my body convulses again. "Oh Vaude. She killed his somebody. Oh God." I gasp and draw myself up to look at her in the flickering firelight. We are alone, I realize. Jake and Dylan have left the room. In the firelight I see the flickering trails of her own tears. Her own sadness in her life that she holds close to her heart. He had killed someone, too—Jake had. He killed Vaude's somebody, her son, her eldest son. How has she not been poisoned against him? How has she not murdered him in his sleep? She is a better person than I am. Because that's what I want to do. That's what kept me silent all the way from the hospital. Planning her end. A pillow over her snorting, snoring, drink-addled head. A knife slid between her ribs and into her heart. A carefully placed burning cigarette in her bed while she is incoherent. It would be so easy. So easy to rid the world of this horrible excuse for humanity. The knife wouldn't be easy; I remove it from my list. But the others are simply accidents waiting to happen. It is amazing that it hasn't happened already. How I wish it had, a million times over, before she killed this somebody. Even if it had taken me, too, that would be better than this. It's not like I'm doing such great things in the world myself. Trash. Dirty. Whore.

Vaude strokes my hair, and I lean slightly into her shoulder. "I wish she was dead. It should have been her. Instead of that woman." I am haunted by the young man from the hospital, the way he never once looked at me. The way he crumpled to the floor, completely void of strength when the priest came for him. I am devastated by him.

Where did he go afterward? I hope he is not alone.

Jake pokes his head in the door, and I feel Vaude nod, and the two of them come quietly into the room. Jake offers us both a hand up, and we come stiffly off the floor to settle around the fire. Vaude sits on the arm of Jake's chair, and he rests his hand on her thigh, leaving the small sofa for Dylan and me. He draws me close to him. Tucking a blanket over my legs, which are folded beneath me. I lean into him. Exhausted from the events of the day. We sit, the four of us, staring into the fire, each lost in our own thoughts.

Surely this is rock bottom. Surely it can't get any worse than this.

Sometime later I wake and find that I am alone on the sofa, stretched out, tucked neatly under blankets with my head on a pillow. The fire has burnt down, and only embers and one charred log continue to flicker. I lift my head and look around the room. Dylan is sleeping in the recliner, his feet up, his face turned toward me. The memory of the night, the memory of all that happened since the knocking on the trailer door floods back, and I draw in on myself, shuddering. I am drained of emotion and drift back into a stupor with the embers glowing in the crease of my eyelids.

The storm blows itself out through the night, and we wake to a world that is crystalline. Thick, clear ice coats the fence lines and blades of grass alike. I walk alongside Dylan as we slip and slide our way to the barn to check on the horses. The entire barn is coated in ice, and I'm impressed that Dylan came prepared with a hammer to crack the ice from around the door. Once inside we are welcomed by nickers and snorts and the warm smell of horses huddled together. We mix their corn and oats and give them each a quick nuzzle before leaving them to snooze the day away in their darkened barn.

I keep feeling Dylan's eyes on me, and I know he is worried. I accidentally bounce into him as we get back out into the cold. He slides and teeters but holds his footing, and I burst out laughing.

He smiles and settles next to me again. "Thanks for coming yesterday," I say as we walk along the drive back to the house.

"Of course." He drops his arm over my shoulder. The sky is still dark with heavy clouds, but they are beginning to break open, and sun sparkles across the ice covering the encapsulated buds on the trees, teardrops at the edge of a lash. There is no place to go today, and no way to get there if there were.

CHAPTER 34

T hree days later my mother comes home from the hospital, Cal in tow. He apparently has not actually left our lives. The storm that blew through the night of her accident has left nothing in its wake. The ice has melted, and the buds on the trees are still growing, and the many shades of spring green are visible all through woods behind the house. I haven't seen her since our brief encounter in the hospital, and I am not prepared for her to come home. I don't know what I expected. Where else would she go? She is walking with crutches, and her cast comes above her knee. She looks at me with a mixture of emotions marching across her face. I recognize disappointment, hurt, irritation, amongst a few others I am not quite able to place, but I'm pretty sure the abject terror I saw in the hospital is not present. I jump up from where I am having a bowl of cereal at the table to help them in the door.

"Welcome home." I try to sound enthusiastic, but my voice sounds thin and guarded. Cal gives me a cold look, and it may well be the first time I have seen him look me in the eye rather than at my mouth or my boobs. My mother shoulders past me, huffing with the effort of moving with her extra appendages.

"So nice of you to come see me while I was in the hospital." Oh. I see, she's angry because I didn't come see her.

"I was there," I say, defensive. "I was," I repeat against the look she gives me. "It's not like I have a car." Her eyes snap to me, and I know she knows I said that to remind her of what she did. My stab has slipped right past Cal, who is moving into the kitchen, putting vials and bottles of medicine into the refrigerator. "Can I help you?" I drop my tone and offer my hand under her elbow, and she allows me to help her settle on the couch. Only now do I notice the metal rods sticking out from the cast. I do feel a little guilty that I never even asked about the extent of her injuries, but then the image of that young man crumpling to the floor flashes through my mind. She lives, which is more than she deserves.

After several conversations start and falter I excuse myself back to my room where I prop the chair under the doorknob and count the money in my vent. How much would I need to just disappear? I hear Cal's car leaving the yard, so I stuff my money back in the vent and get up and make my way to the living room. She is awake, staring vacantly at the TV. Funny videos are running, one after another, stupid human tricks, dangerous human tricks, painful human tricks. Surely some of the videos had ended in serious injury, and here we laugh and chortle at the tragedies of others. Even worse, all of these videos were submitted by someone displaying their stupidity for a chance to win ten grand, the price of dignity. I sit down on the chair next to the couch, where my mother reclines, her leg propped on a pillow.

"Can I do anything for you?" I ask quietly, trying to gauge her mood.

"What? Like get me arrested?" She says the words very calmly, but there is an edge, and I glance quickly away, unsure of this turn.

"No. What does that mean?" I hear the rise in my voice, that wheedling "I didn't do it" tone. She gives me a very level, cold look. I have a sick feeling that she has somehow discovered the anonymous tips I have called in on her and Cal over the last several months.

She puffs air out between her dry lips and looks at me with very icy eyes. "Frank told me what you said." She is pissed. I see it now, seriously angry at me.

"What did 'Frank' tell you?" I don't know anybody named Frank and can't even imagine what she is talking about.

"It was slick," she spits out and turns back to the TV.

"Okay." I let the word draw out, still trying to figure out what this conversation is really about. She snorts again and rocks back, shifting her leg which causes her to suck her breath between her teeth. I wait. I'm not going to beg her to tell me why she is angry.

Then she says something that makes my jaw drop open, and I stare at her while she very pointedly does not look at me. She says, "You are just like your father." I don't know my father. I have never met my father, and she has never, ever been willing to talk about my father. Ever. When I was little, I thought Ed was my dad, but she told me he wasn't, and looking back, I have a vague sense that there was somebody before him, but I can't remember him at all.

Finally I drag my jaw up off the floor and turn to face the TV, "Well, I wouldn't know would I?" We sit in hostile silence for a few minutes before I say, "What was his name?"

She looks at me then, her eyes still cold but half lidded. She snorts out a small laugh, looking away from me again.

"Why did you bring him up?" I ask.

She smiles, and I know she did it just because she could. She did it so I would want something from her that she could refuse. She did it to take the power back. Bitch.

"You know what? I don't fucking care. He couldn't have been worth much if he hooked up with you." Her eyes snap to me, fully open now, and I repeat her snorting laugh, holding her eyes.

"Look at you, big girl," she sneers. "Using all your big-girl words. I know what you said to Frank, and I will never forgive you."

"Who the hell is Frank?" I say, using my big-girl words again.

"Frank is the cop. The one you told I was drunk."

"Oh." I did ask the cop who picked me up if she was drunk.

"Yeah, 'oh.' Good thing Frank and I are friends. You could have caused me trouble." She looks so smug.

"You and Frank are friends?" I am incredulous. Why would a cop, a young, good-looking, decent-seeming cop be friends with my mother, and what does that even mean? I shake my head. "I don't even care. I didn't tell him you were drunk, I asked him if you were drunk, as part of the accident, as any normal person would ask considering how seldom you are not drunk."

"Ooh," she says, "more big-girl words." I'm not sure what she means, but she is looking at me like Kelci looked at me when she told me that she was in junior high now and everything was different, like I just don't get it. And I don't get it.

"You killed somebody." My voice whines, I feel nauseous.

"It wasn't my fault," she says, "God killed somebody. Mother Nature killed somebody. It's not like I didn't get hurt, too." She motions toward her injured leg, and I am stunned.

"Well, somebody died," I say, quiet, not sure how far I can take this.

"And you just assume it was my fault?"

"You ran a red light," I say, exasperated.

"I slid! It was slick." She pauses, and I close my mouth, tightening my lips over my teeth. "It doesn't matter what I do, you only see the bad." I start to call bullshit. If you only do bad, how can I see anything else? How can she turn this into something about us? I start to tell her about the man, crumpling to the floor when the preacher came to see him, but I keep my mouth closed. There is a strange, wounded look in her eyes, and for a second, I doubt myself: do I do that? "I can never do anything right for you. I've never been able to do anything right for you. Just like your father."

"What?" My father again? Shit, that word hasn't come out of her mouth so many times in years. She just shakes her head and waves her hand toward me, done with the conversation.

"I'm tired." Her voice is suddenly drained of energy. "I'd like to rest. Leave me alone."

I stand there for a moment, but she closes her eyes and turns her face away from me. I give up, frustrated, and go down the hall to my room. The word "bitch" falls out on the arch of my left foot, where I can stand on her for the rest of my life. The satisfaction of the tiny blade cutting through the flesh on my arch makes all the ugly in my head leak out through my sole.

CHAPTER 35

T he next morning I find her still on the couch, the remains of her last cigarette in a cylinder of ash falling from the ashtray. Her bottle of painkillers sits next to her empty glass for a last-night cocktail of Percocet and vodka. Certainly not a healthy combination. I shoulder my bag and step out into what is a beautiful spring morning. It's unbelievable that three days ago the world was encased in ice. There is damage, limbs that snapped under the weight of the ice, but on the whole, the world has completely returned to spring. My mind is still unsettled, angry, restless. I just don't understand what that conversation was about last night. I don't know why she mentioned my father like that. I don't know how she can think she has no responsibility for what happened. Ever, in her life. It is always somebody else's fault. There is always somebody working against her, somebody causing her to need a drink. Causing her to mess up.

I let the brisk spring air clear my mind, and I shove all my negative energy out as the wheels of my bike hum on the road. It's the first day back to school after the ice. I know it's going to be a bad day. Everybody will be talking about the accident, and I am sure everybody will assume the same thing I did—that my mother was drunk. I'll have to get through it, survive. My little wall needs more layers, and

I am trying to formulate how I will respond to the questions that will come my way. How will I say that it was a terrible accident, caused by the weather and not by alcohol, and not just sound like I am defending my sot mother? Maybe I should just not respond. I am solidly in my thoughts when I ride into the parking lot at school. I'm in the middle of a conversation in my head, my lips moving with the imagined words I will say.

I am not paying attention, really, bicycling into the lot, standing above the seat, muscle memory from the hundreds of times I have ridden into the lot in the exact same fashion, the word "bitch" pulsating on my arch with the pressure of my foot on the pedal. Bitch. It sings, it hums, it throbs. My mind calms with the throbbing of it, and I swerve down into the lot at a pretty good clip. I don't see the truck until it roars beside me, startling me. I jerk the handlebars, trying to avoid the impact, and for a split second, my eyes lock with Derrick Jessop's, and he jerks the wheel. I slam into his passenger-side mirror, and my bike falls away. I am hung for a split second, tangled in his mirror. His brakes skid, and his wheels crunch over the front forks of my bike. I fall in slow motion away from the truck, my right arm, shoulder, and chest on fire. My head smacks down onto the blacktop, and my face falls to the side, seeing the mangled front end of my bike still caught under the back tires. The world goes black.

When I come to, Derrick is squatting beside me, his truck still running and my bike a mangled heap behind his rear tires. My shoulder burns, and I can't breathe easily. I am unable to lift my arm or sit up. My head is pounding, and my ears are roaring. "Damn, Derrick," I say between gasping breaths. "What the hell?"

"I'm sorry. It was an accident." He looks intently down at me, and others are beginning to gather around, everybody clamoring, talking. "The road must have been slick. I didn't see you." I glance at him, and just the comment of slick roads brings everything back into focus.

Was it? Was this an accident? There is no malice in his grey eyes. No anger, just a sadness and concern that makes me think I'm becoming paranoid. I let him take my left hand and help me to my feet. I stagger but right myself. "You okay?" he asks. "Not dead." There is a cold glint in his eyes, a sardonic tilt to his lip, quirked, then controlled and I don't understand the look at all, but my head is ringing and really my vision isn't great, so maybe it's just me, just me.

Derrick reaches his hand to steady me as my balance wavers and I nearly go down again. A quivering draw of breath snakes down my throat, and I nod, tears spilling over my lashes. I nod my head. I'm fine. I'm not dead. He is crumpling, that young man at the hospital, with bones turned to liquid, in my mind, and I turn from Derrick to attempt to extricate my bike from behind his truck. Then it is me, my bones turning to liquid, crumpling to the ground.

I wake and the first thought in my head is that I hurt, very badly all along my right collarbone and shoulder. My head is throbbing. The second thought in my head is of the young man at the hospital and of the somebody he lost. I test my fingers and they move. I try to raise my arm, and although it causes the pain to shoot out in sparks, I can lift it. "Careful," a voice says to me from my left, and I turn my head to see Nurse Janet. She's a small, round woman, with small, round glasses glinting in the florescent lights. She has been the school nurse for years. "How are you dear?"

I try to speak but only croak, so I clear my throat and try again. "I'm okay."

"You took a nasty tumble, dear." She is now standing over me, looking down at me. "I think you should be looked at. That's quite a bang you have on your shoulder." She smiles down at me. "Can you tell me what happened?" I try to remember, and I can't. I remember riding into the parking lot, standing on my pedals, then . . . nothing. I shake my head. "I'd like to take you to the hospital for some x-rays.

I don't believe anything is broken, but we should probably make sure."

I shake my head again. I can't afford x-rays. "No, I'm fine. I'll go this evening, after school."

"You're going to stay for school?" It hadn't occurred to me to do otherwise, what with my mode of transportation destroyed and my only alternate place filled with my mother and probably Cal. She helps me to stand when I am ready and guides to me to the door. "They'll want to see you in the office." I make my way there, and on the way, I pass Derrick, who again stops to ensure I am okay and even turns to walk with me back to the office.

As he opens the door for me, he again says "I'm really sorry, Alison." I nod.

"I know, Derrick. It was probably my fault, I wasn't really paying attention. I'm okay. Don't worry."

"I can give you a ride home tonight, if you'd like." I smile at his being so nice.

"Thanks. But I'm okay." I'm thrown a bit by his kindness, his concern. I touch his arm with my left hand before going into the office. "Seriously. I'm okay." I pass through the door that he holds open for me, and I'm touched when I glance behind me and see him still standing on the other side of the door as it closes behind me, his face an odd expression that I don't know how to read.

On the counter in the office is a copy of the day's newspaper. I notice it, but don't have a chance to really look at it before I am ushered straight back to Principal Tucker's office where he is sitting at his desk, staring out the window. My head is still roaring, throbbing. He stands when I come in and greets me. "How are you, Alison?" It seems like a much heavier question than what my current situation warrants. But really, doesn't my current situation warrant exactly that? I've been run over in the school parking lot.

I reassure him that I am fine, although I don't really remember what happened. "Derrick said you swerved on your bike, and he didn't see you until it was too late."

I nod, and pain shoots behind my eyes. "Probably." I don't remember. "I wasn't really paying attention, I'm sure." I look at my hands and realize there are scratches across my knuckles, where I must have hit his truck. "It was just an accident."

I feel so broken. My head is throbbing, and I surreptitiously lift my hand to the back of my head where a very large mound is forming. There are crusts of blood in my hair. Very efficient, Nurse Janet. I wonder if she even noticed. I feel like I may be sick and lean forward, putting my head between my knees and drawing in breaths. I can see on the floor between the legs of his desk another copy of the newspaper. I can't miss the headline. I can't miss the pictures. I reach out and gather it to me, sitting up, drawing the paper with me, feeling dizzy with my rapid upswing. I hear the intake of breath from across the desk, but I do not look up.

There is a picture of a beautiful woman and a little boy—he's probably five—and a headline that says "Slick Conditions Claim Lives." Below the bend is a picture of the mangled vehicles, my mother's and the crumpled wreck of a small, grey sedan. How fast was she going? People died . . . this isn't a fender bender, this is a crash. How fast do you have to go to make two cars look like that? "Claims Lives." I am rising to my feet. I hear Mr. Tucker pushing back from his desk, coming toward me. I put up my hand toward him, never taking my eyes from the page. I back toward the door then spin, opening it and escaping through the front office as he calls out behind me. I read as I weave down the hall. When I stumble against the row of lockers, I stop and lean against them before slowly sliding to the floor. The article reads:

> Slick road conditions were cited as the cause of the double fatality, two-vehicle crash Tuesday evening on the intersection of highways 130 and 34 east of Charleston. Lydia Dollman, 27, and her young son, Terry, 5, of

Charleston were both killed when their vehicle was struck by the vehicle of Alice Hayes, 32, also of Charleston, when her vehicle crossed into the intersection against a red light, causing her vehicle to impact Mrs. Dollman's. Slick road conditions have been cited as the cause of the accident. Ms. Hayes sustained injuries as well and was treated at Charleston Hospital.

Services are pending for Mrs. Dollman and her son, who are survived by her husband, Jonathan Dollman, her parents, Mick and Marsha Jessop, and one brother, Derrick Jessop.

I feel the dark edges of my vision narrowing, and I see what's left of the tunnel. Lydia and Terry Dollman, Jonathan Dollman, Mick and Marsha Jessop, and Derrick, who has just run me over in the parking lot. I close my eyes and force the darkness back, and when I open them, there are shooting sparks, but I can see. Did he swerve toward me? I see the flash of memory, but it is just as quickly gone. I fold the paper and tuck it into my backpack.

I leave the school, struggling with the pain in my shoulder but manage, shouldering my pack on my good side and setting out for the long walk home.

CHAPTER 36

make it back to the trailer and am thankful that Cal's car is not here. I wake my mother and remind her to take her medicine. I bring her a glass of water to wash it down. I have been stewing in my throbbing head all the way home. I take her other glass, the vodka glass, and refill it for her. I hand it to her and she looks at me with stupefied eyes but takes it, graciously thanking me. "I think maybe you are right, Mom. Maybe I do only see the bad." I take one of her Percocets for my own aches and wash it down with a glass of water from the tap. The water tastes like rust.

"What are you talking about?" she asks.

"Remember saying that to me last night?" She looks blearily at me, and I know she doesn't. "Oh anyway. It doesn't matter. Just I'm sorry if you feel like I am not nice to you." Her lower lip puckers out a bit, and I turn away because I want to slap her.

I go to my room and empty my backpack. I put in a sketchbook, three pairs of jeans, four shirts, underwear, bras. A light jacket. I grab my money from my vent and tuck that into my pack as well. I crumple papers that are on my desk and leave them strewn through the house. I close my bedroom window.

She has finished her drink when I come back and is bleary eyed.

I refill it, hand it to her, leaving the bottle on the counter for easy access. She totters a little in her seat, and the liquid pools out across her chest. There is a pack of cigarettes. I take one and light it. Taking a slow draw before coughing all the smoke out of my lungs. Why do people do that? My mother laughs, a slow, inert laugh, and jostles more liquid around her. "I can't do that," I say and laugh a bit at myself. "Want it?" She purses her lips and nods slowly. Sure, why the hell not?

"Oh, Mom. Don't forget your medicine. You don't want that leg to act up." She looks puzzled, but I open the bottle and take out two pills, and I hand them to her. She still looks puzzled but the look passes, and she reaches for the pills. She washes them down with the vodka. Now there's a good mother.

She is sucking long breaths of air when I leave the trailer, her cigarette smoldering to ash in her stained fingers. The dredges of the empty bottle tipped at her side. I am never coming back. I will never come home again. I stay just down the road, crouched in some bushes, watching until I see the smoke beginning to sneak out of the cracks. There should be flames by now, but there are none.

I think about the trail I've left, and if the fucker doesn't burn to the ground, it will be so obvious what I did. I turn my face to the side and retch into the grass, causing the pain in my head to magnify and pulsate again. I sit back, wiping my mouth with the back of my hand, holding my head until the throbbing subsides enough that I can open my eyes again.

The first flame licks out from the kitchen window. Burn baby burn, but then I think of her, and I remember her smile and how much I loved her when I was small. I see her lip puckering when she thought I was being kind. What have I done? I heave my backpack and stumble, jog back down the road.

The trailer is smoldering, not so much burning as steaming. I push through the front door and instantly drop to my knees. The smoke is overwhelming. Is it true that most deaths related to fire are caused by smoke? I heard that somewhere. I think. I can see the couch. My mother is still there, asleep, breathing in the noxious air, her casted leg propped on a pillow. Her brows are furrowed in her sleep. I grab her hand and try to shake her awake, but she just bobs, and I can't tell if she is breathing or not. Then she lets out a long, wet snore, and I pull her off the couch. The trailer is hot, and when I open the door, the air licks the flames into a frenzy. Now that whole section of the living room is engulfed.

I try to lift her off the couch, but I don't have the strength in my wounded shoulder to do it, so I drag her. Her butt thumps against the floor, followed by her cast. She moans. "Wake up!" I yell into her ear, but the fire is getting so loud that my words are sucked away. What have I done? What have I done?

I drag her through the kitchen, which has not yet lit, and torturously down the hall toward my room, toward the back door. I shove the door open, and the change in wind sucks the smoke down the hall, and it roils over us out into the morning sun. I am trying to turn her body, to make the angle toward the door, and my lungs are screaming with the pain of the smoke. I close my eyes and pull her toward me. She flops to her side, and I drag her to where my feet are now standing on the step outside of the door. The door swings wide and bangs against the trailer, rebounding in the wind again and swinging to hit me in the back. "Fuck!" I scream and yank her, shoving back against the door, and she jerks forward. I wrap my arms under her chest and drag her out into the sunlight. Her poor leg bumps along the steps, and I drag her back and away from the smoldering ruin of our trailer until we are surrounded by grass and have fresh air again in our lungs. I turn her on her side and listen to her back. I can hear the slow, irregular beating of her heart, and I'm afraid it isn't going to matter. I've killed her. I try to remember how many of the pills I handed her, how many did she already have in her stomach, how much vodka went down? I don't know. I can't remember. It is a blur, confused in my memory.

Throw up. I think. She needs to throw up. I don't know what to do. I wrap my arms around her so her head is in my lap. I am crying, rocking her.

She shifts, retches, and vomit splatters into the dirt and across my leg. Her casted leg bounces against the ground as her body convulses. The flicker of red and orange scorches my face and hands, her face and hands, the yard and world surrounding us. The opened doors have given the fire the breath it needed, and it is fully lit now. Her hair clings in strands to her neck and my arm where I support her head. She convulses again.

"Good girl." The voice is clear in my head, and "girl" sounds like "gurl." I twist my head around to see who has spoken, but we are alone, my mother and I, cast in gold by the smoldering inferno of our trailer. If I weren't so consumed by the misery of what I have done, what I attempted to do, I would maybe think I was losing my mind. My mother is still retching, terrible dry heaves pulling the dregs of acid from her stomach, drawing the remains of my attempted murder from her body. I squeeze her to me when she stops and rub her hair out of her face. Tears are dropping from my chin and into her tangled, smoky hair. The wind lifts my hair, and a chill wraps around my body. I have the strangest feeling that we are not alone.

CHAPTER 37

Sirens call from the volunteer firehouse, and a few minutes later, the truck is here. Six men are connecting the hose to the hydrant and proceeding to squirt water on the ruin of our home. Several minutes later, the ambulance and paramedics arrive. "Help her," I plead, and they ease me out from under her while they begin assessing her. "I saw the smoke. I got her out, but I can't wake her up. She's on pain pills." I start to say that she drinks but hesitate. She would be so mad at me, but they need to know that she isn't just asleep. "She drinks," I scream out and one of the paramedics glances at me while the policeman begins to lead me away.

I watch them putting a mask over her face, checking pulses, checking her leg, looking in her eyes. I turn my back, glancing out into the woods. I have the strongest urge to run to Chessa. Run to the farm, but I stand still and then turn my back on the path leading to them. This is my life. Dylan can never be part of it. I can never be part of his. He has a future. People like me don't have futures. We are broken. I drop my head onto my arm and let myself cry. What have I done?

"Let them work on her," the officer says. He offers me a hand, and I let him pull me up. He leads me around to side of the trailer, out of the way of the spray of water and out of sight of the paramedics.

I stand there, numb and throbbing, and the street slowly fills with the people. "Do you live here?"

I nod, glancing at his name tag. Officer M. Daniels. He is tall and lean with just the beginnings of a paunch showing under his uniform. I try to pull myself to rights, but I can't keep my eyes off the smoldering edge of the trailer that blocks my view of the paramedics working on my mother.

"Your mother?" I nod again. He asks me my name and I tell him. "Do you know what happened here today?" I've stepped away from him, tottering, and can see them again—they are lifting her onto a stretcher, raising it, wheeling her to the waiting ambulance. I see her arm lift, and I am relieved. She wouldn't do that if she were still out, would she? She must be awake. I need to go with her. I start to move in that direction, but Officer M. Daniels stops me with a touch to my shoulder. "I'll give you a ride to the hospital. I'd like to talk to you."

He doesn't put me in the back of the car but lets me sit in the front, next to him. I glance in the backseat and see my backpack there. I groan and hope he hasn't heard. Stupid. Where did I leave it? I don't remember bringing it from the bushes, but surely they didn't find it all the way down the road. If I weren't already so fried from the day, I might have felt something more than defeat.

"Is that yours?" he asks.

"What?" Time. I need time.

"The backpack. I found it by the road. Thought it was probably yours."

I nod but don't speak. It's been a horrible, shitty day.

"Can you tell me what happened here today?"

"No. I don't know what happened." It really feels true inside my bruised brain. There are whole portions of the day that I have lost. I don't remember most of the walk home, I only remember pieces of pulling her out of the trailer. Did I really crumple papers and pour vodka through the house?

"What grade are you in?"

"I'm a sophomore."

"So why aren't you at school today?" His tone is friendly, just keeping up the conversation.

"I was. I mean, I went this morning, but I got hit by a truck, so I came home." I lean my head on the window and close my eyes.

"You got hit by a truck, you say?" I can feel his eyes on me, hot, assessing.

"I did."

"Where did that happen?"

"At school. In the parking lot. I was riding my bike into the lot, and I . . . I don't know. I don't really remember how it happened."

"Are you injured? Did you fill out a police report?"

I shrug, suddenly so tired I can't bother to answer. I lift my good hand to my collarbone and shoulder and then point to my head. My body is throbbing and pain shoots all down my arm, radiating from my shoulder, but my head is the worst. I feel myself weaving in and out of pain.

"Hit by a truck." He goes through a red light, his lights flashing behind the ambulance, with their sirens blaring in a high/low way. "Then your home catches fire, all before noon. What a day."

"Yeah," I say, opening my eyes, watching the flashing light in front of me. Trying to stay focused or to get focused.

"Can you tell me about your backpack?"

"What do you mean?" I don't move to look at him.

"Well. It looks like maybe you were going somewhere." He pauses. "Were you planning to go somewhere?"

"Yeah." Tears spill over my eyelashes and down my soot-darkened face. I don't bother wiping them away, just let them drop, one after another onto my dirty jeans.

"You want to tell me where?"

I turn and look at him. "Anywhere but here." My chin puckers, and I draw my lips together before turning again to lean on the window.

"You were going to run away?"

"Wouldn't you?"

"Well. Running away from my problems has never solved them for me." I don't give him the look that I want to give him, and he goes on. "Lucky for your mother, trailers don't burn well, being made mostly of flame-resistant materials. Has your mother ever shown suicidal tendencies before?"

"No." I pause, "I don't know, really." The words on my feet sing out, the scars of the words that define me, and I wonder if they would think I have suicidal tendencies.

"She's had a rough week?"

Week, month, year, life. "Yeah, it's been a bad week." I wish we could stop talking.

"She was involved in the accident on 130 on Thursday?" I nod.

"Was she upset about it?" I nod: of course she was. "That was a bad situation."

"Of course she was upset," I snap. Somebody died, you idiot. Lydia Dollman and her son Terry, age five. "The roads were slick," I say, defensive.

"It was a bad storm, for sure," he agrees. The ambulance pulls into the emergency entrance ahead of us, and I draw my head away from the glass. "I reckon you aren't planning to run away any time soon?"

"No. I'm not going anywhere." Ever. Stuck. Trapped.

"That's good. I think it's best if you don't leave town right away." He steps out of the car, opens the back door to retrieve my backpack. He hands it to me as I get out of the car. What does that mean? Isn't the backpack evidence? Is he telling me not to leave town because they know what I did, or is he just telling me that running isn't the answer? Do they really say that to people, to perps? I always thought that was just for the TV dramas. I don't have time, though, to consider it longer than that. They are wheeling my mother inside, and I am relieved to hear her coughing as they go.

My mother is admitted, and when I am given the once-over, they give me ice for my shoulder and arm, which are not broken, only badly bruised, and six stitches followed by an ice pack for my head. They give me some medicine to numb the pain, and when they leave me, I spit the undissolved bits into the toilet, vaguely remembering that I took something from her pill bottle earlier. I don't want to have my stomach pumped on top of everything else. I am not admitted, just outpatient, but I am permitted to stay with her. They provide me with a pair of scrubs and some mesh underpants and tell me that if I would like to shower in the bathroom I can. I look at myself for a very long time in the mirror before I strip free of my grimy clothes. There are black smudges on my cheeks and chin, and the red rim of my eyelids cut jagged edges toward my iris. I had reached through flames to get her off the couch, but there is not a single scorch mark on my flesh. The devil doesn't burn. I draw my clothes off in the sterile, antiseptic bathroom and close my eyes to the girl standing in the mirror.

I let the water run down my body, scrubbing suds through my hair, avoiding the stitches as best I can. They told me not to get them wet for twenty-four hours, but I smell like a torch. I'm not sure really that I care a whole lot if they get infected and take me out. Death by infection can't be counted as a suicidal tendency, right? I am careful with my bruised skull, but rub fiercely at the smudges on my flesh. I am sobbing again, the tears wracking my body until my legs crumple abruptly, leaving me in a pile on the tile floor. How do I go from here to any kind of life? How do I turn this horrible life into something worth living? How do I go from trying to kill my mother to doing good in the world? What I know is that I cannot rely on her. She will never change. She is trapped in her own hell, and she cannot escape it. I have two more years before I can move out, work full time, build a life. One more year I might be able to manage, but two seems like too much. But I have to. I have to do that.

When I come back into her room, the skin of my face scrubbed fresh and pink, I find my mother asleep, connected to monitors and an IV. They've cleaned her face as well, and there is only one small bandage where the fire must have licked too long at her arm. I sit down solidly in the chair beside her bed, done in, exhausted, cried out. Beep, beep, beep, beep. I let my mind slip to empty. I stare at the half moon of her fingernail, where it peeks out beyond the edge of the bedrail. I am chilled to the bone, even though I showered in the hottest water I could stand. I draw my legs forward and wrap my arms around them, feeling hollow. The throb and pain in my shoulder and across my collarbone, the soft spot on my head . . . the reminders that it was only this morning I was run over in the parking lot by the younger brother of Lydia Dollman, the woman my mother killed. I close my eyes and count down, one hundred to zero. Somewhere before reaching rock bottom, I drift off to sleep.

CHAPTER 38

We were on the evening news last night and the late night news as well. The image of our trailer smoldering, the charred shell of our dilapidated home with curls of smoke still seeping from the seams, behind the ambulance my mother was slid into, leaving me behind, talking to Officer M. Daniels. It feels completely unreal every time it comes on, and my stomach churns because "the police have not ruled out foul play."

I am sitting in one of the many "family rooms" of the hospital, drinking the cafeteria coffee that brews all night, listening to the silence of the hospital around me. A nurse shuffles past the door outside, but I have been peacefully alone tonight. I couldn't stand the beeping of the monitors when I woke up, so I made my way here. I am still dressed in the scrubs they gave me, and I feel a little like a person in costume, assuming a different identity. I could have put on my own clothes—I have my backpack—but there is something strangely comforting in the anonymous, slouchy, blue scrubs. I have a concussion, which probably explains why I am missing so much of my memory, and maybe that's why I didn't think of putting my own clothes on after I showered.

I am struggling to reconcile the parts of myself. The restless energy of my guilt for what I attempted and the sick feeling that they will figure it out, or worse yet, my mother will remember, makes it hard for me to sit still. Does it make it okay that I bite because my life has been spent chained to the doghouse? Does the fact that my mother is broken make it okay? It doesn't. I know it doesn't, and I am trying to figure out how I can live a good life when I am every bit as broken as she. What do I have to look forward to?

I scoured my mother's room before I left in search of a sharp object, a scalpel, a blade, even a paperclip. Almost anything metal would do. I have new words singing to be placed, and the skin of my right arch and my left ankle are itching with the need of it. Hopeless. Broken. I am dwelling on the dark and ominous aspect of my future when my solitude is interrupted by a young man coming in with a dolly of boxed snacks. He doesn't look at me, in my corner where I sit hunched. I catch his face in profile when he shifts to open the vending machine. Damn. My breath hitches in my throat, and it is a sound he hears, glancing back and over his shoulder, startled. Apparently he thought he was alone. It is Warren. Warren from Christmas.

"Hey!" A smile spreads on his mouth, that beautiful full mouth, and he comes around to face me. I straighten, unrolling my back a full six inches until my shoulders pop into their normal position.

"Hey." I let my smile come free. It's strangely comforting to see a friendly face tonight. He is a friendly face. Strange.

His mouth, that mouth, contorts, expressing his puzzlement at seeing me here, dressed in scrubs like one of the nurses. "Your mom?" I nod. "Yeah, I had heard she'd had an accident. She still in here?"

"No. She was home for that." I hear a small laugh escaping my chest, and I suddenly am aware that I am still unhinged. "Our house burnt down today . . . well, yesterday."

"Oh shit." He leaves the vending machine open and comes to squat down in front of me. "What happened?"

I just frown and shake my head. I feel my chin puckering, a sure sign that I am about to fall out, and the sudden welling in my eyes makes me look away. His proximity is disconcerting. I can smell him, the scent of shampoo on his hair, the tang of a cigarette smoked some time ago.

"Damn." He reaches out and wipes an escapee off my cheek. His voice is quiet, with none of the attitude that he carries around him like his clothing. "You've had a hell of a week."

"Yeah." I laugh, and another tear escapes. "And I got hit by a truck this morning . . . well, yesterday morning." He expostulates again, and I suddenly am laughing at the complete improbability of my life. He wipes another tear from where it is getting ready to drip off the end of my nose. I draw my hands up over my face for a second. Trying to pull myself together. It doesn't work, and I find that I am shuddering and tears are spilling free. I raise my hands in a "what the hell" motion and release a small, broken laugh. "Sorry," I finally manage to say, trying to set him free, but he is still kneeling in front of me, his hands resting on my knees.

"What kind of truck?" His lips quirk into a small, lopsided smile, and I am suddenly laughing. Nearly hysterical laughing, but released from the intensity of emotion that has held me all day. I laugh until my face hurts and I can feel the blood throbbing in the large knot on the back of my head. What a strange sensation.

"I don't know!" I slap against his shoulder, and he falls back, splaying across the floor, which causes my laughter to start all over again. When I finally catch my breath again, I reach out and offer him a hand up. He takes my hand and rises to his feet and draws me up after him. He wraps me in his arms for just a second, a second of my cheek pressed against his chest, his arms folding around me, a squeeze, and then he releases me. He leads me to the vending machine and slices through the tape on top of one of the boxes with a yellow box cutter, flinging the lids out and starts loading it. "So you're the vending machine guy?" I ask.

"Yep." He smiles, and I swear there is pride in his face when he says it. "I'm the Vendor Tender." I start laughing again, and he smiles at my hilarity. "Really. That's my company."

"How long have you worked there?"

An eyebrow raises above his storm-colored eyes. "About a year."

I stand up to join him where he has begun sorting treats and snack packs into the chute. I don't ask if I can, but I follow his pattern and help him fill the pretzels, honey buns, gum, and chips until all the slots are full again. "You're a natural," he says, and I smile at the praise. What is wrong with me?

"Thanks." He's repacking his dolly, and we make our way toward the door. "It was nice seeing you," I say, bumping lightly into him, like I would Dylan.

"Yes it was." He bumps me lightly back. "I'd like to do it again."

"What?"

"See you." We are through the door and into the hallway. "Again." I feel my face redden, and I look down at my feet as we walk.

"I would like that." I glance at him, but he is looking forward.

"You would? Great." He pauses a beat. "Friday?"

"Yes." I smile. "I work till eight."

"I'll pick you up there."

Just like that I have a date. What an insane, eventful, and crazy day. I feel like all the bad is just going to slip away, and that it's really all going to be okay. I slip the yellow box cutter into the inner pocket of my scrub pants and wave as he walks away.

CHAPTER 39

I don't go to school on Tuesday or Wednesday. I left the hospital at two to walk down to the square for work on Wednesday night. When Rob saw me coming through the front door, he came over from behind the counter and gave me a hug. It felt very odd to be touched like that, but not really bad. He's a good guy. I let him hug me, but I do it with my left arm crossed over the front of me. He lets me go to arms' length and put his hands on my shoulders. "Are you okay?"

I laugh a little with the intensity of his gaze. "Yes." He nods, looking relieved. "Faye came by the hospital yesterday. Mom really was glad to see her." She was, too. Actually, I was even glad to see her. She talked to my mom for a long time, and when she left, she asked me if there was anything I needed.

"She cares about your mom a lot." He nods.

"I know she does."

"She cares about you, too." I snort and tug loose from his hands. "Really, she does." I know he's probably right. I'm sure she cares, but I don't know how to respond.

"I know. She told Mom that we can stay with you until we find a place," I say. "That was real nice."

"Well, I think Mr. Billups has something better worked out for you." I raise my eyebrows to him. "Yeah, he wants to see you."

"Oh." There he is, looking very Santa Claus as he comes out of his office, his suspenders just the right shade of red.

"Alison." He nods and beckons me toward his office.

"Yes sir."

"How is your mother?" he asks, closing his office door behind me.

"She's going to be okay." I rub my hand down my thigh.

"Good. How are you?"

"I'm okay." I shrug and look down at my fingernails. He is quiet for a half a minute. There is a sour feeling in my stomach, a knot or a ball that has been with me for days, and I swallow, trying to dispel it.

"Did you really get hit by a truck?"

I laugh and all the tension drains out of me. It's crazy, and I still hurt from it, and I know it shouldn't be funny, but every time I think about being hit by a truck, I hear Warren asking me what kind of truck, and I can't stop laughing.

"I did." I contain my laughter. "It's been a really shitty week."

He takes a deep breath and says, "Well, I can make it a little better," he says and then tells me that he has a small, two bedroom apartment that he would like to let us have until we can replace the trailer or decide what to do.

"We can pay," I say, feeling the hint of charity and feeling nauseated by it.

"No. It's been empty for a while. Alison, you are a great kid. You have a lot of potential, but you've been dealt a rotten float." I don't know what that means, "float," but I don't bother to ask. I've been dealt something rotten for sure, so I get his meaning, "You're a hard worker, and I know sometimes people just need a little help. This is not costing me anything for you and your mom to stay in the apartment, so don't think of it like I'm giving you something. I like the work you do here, and it will make your life a little easier for a little while. That's all."

Mom is out of work officially now, and I know I can't get free of her, so I have to make the best of it and get through the next couple of years until I am eighteen and can leave her behind. "I can work full time," I say abruptly. I've been thinking about it all afternoon, that I will drop out of school and get a GED. I can go to work full time and take care of us.

"How are you going to do that?" he asks, his brows knitting together, almost touching.

"I'm done with school. I'm not going back." I can't go back. How can I go back and face people who hate me and hate my mother and think we are the same? How can I go back after Derrick tried to kill me? And he did . . . I know he did, even if I don't know how it all happened. Call it a moment of insanity or whatever, but he wanted me dead for that minute, just like I wanted my mother dead when I set fire to the trailer. I'm not even angry at him. I understand.

"No," he says, and my stomach drops. "Alison you can't drop out." He leans back in his chair, staring intently at me. "Can I be frank?"

"Of course." His word choice has me smiling in spite of myself. Who says that, really?

"You're that horse that can't get into the starting gate because of a bur under its saddle. You've had a rough road, especially here lately . . . God knows. But just 'cause you have a hard time getting up to that gate, you're gonna get there. If you don't get to the gate, you can't run the race."

"I understand what you're saying, but how else am I going to do this?" My voice shakes, and I feel that damn pucker in my chin.

"It's not always going to be like this. You just need a little something to get you to the gate. Take the apartment. It's been empty for months, so I am not missing anything by you being there. Say three months, time for your mom to get back on her feet, then you can move on if that's what you all want."

"I can't just take your apartment." I don't want to be pathetic. "We don't want charity."

"It isn't charity." He steeples his fingers and looks at me through them. "Think of it as an investment. I'm investing in your future."

"I can pay. How much does the apartment cost?" I start to open the pack for my wad of money. But he puts his hand out and stops me.

"Stop," he says and I look at him. His face is sad, and his hand takes mine. "Listen. Life is not easy. We all have terrible things that we have to deal with at different times. This is one of your terrible times. Let the people who care about you do this." He smiles. "I talked to your mother earlier this afternoon. It's already arranged. I'm just telling you. It's not your job to take care of this." Tears suddenly well down my cheeks, whether because of the kind words he has said, the gift he is giving, or the simple sensation of a kind hand touching mine . . . I do not know. "Your mother and I have already worked this out. You don't need to worry about it. It's settled."

"Oh." I didn't know that he had spoken with my mom. "When did you talk to her?"

"Around three. She's already getting settled in." He talked to her while I was out walking. How did he find her, how did he know how to get a hold of her?

"Are you sure?"

"Absolutely." He leans forward and adds, "But listen to me, Alison, you have got to finish high school or you will spend the rest of your life trying to get to out of the hole that somebody else dug. Understand?"

I nod. He stands, I stand, and we go back to work.

The little weave of our life has at least a few nice patterns. There are people who are good and who care about us—the Winthrops, Mr. Billups, Rob, and even though I don't like her, I have to admit that Faye is one of the good guys. Even Cal, who is definitely not one of the good guys, picked us up and dropped us at the hotel on Route 16. He's paid for our room for the week. He is probably helping her "get settled." I hope he is. I don't want her to be alone, but I couldn't stay with him there, his slick eyes moving over me like I was the mouse and he the snake. I spent the afternoon walking through town until it was time to come to work. I'm still carrying my backpack, with all my money. No way in hell I am leaving that behind. I have to admit it was a kindness that Cal picked us up when my mom called him. Dylan would have done it, but I really am done sucking him down this drain. He's had enough ugly in his life before I even knew him, and his is good now. My mom and I, we have a long way to go before we are ever good. Maybe someday, when I've done something decent in the world, I will find Dylan again, and then we can be equals, and maybe I will fall in love with him all over again.

I am taking care of the register and restocking the impulse display when in walks Warren. I pop up with about the closest thing to happy I have left. "Hi."

"Hey." He smiles that radiant, sensual smile. "How are you?"

"Good." My hand goes involuntarily up to the knot on the back of my head. It is beginning to go down, but it still hurts. "What you need today?" Feeling my cadence slip to the speech patterns I hear from the men who work here at Billups.

"Nothing." His lips quirk into a half smile.

"Nothing?" He shakes his head. He just came to check on me. Really. A small fire begins to glow beneath my skin, and I reach out to touch his arm.

"Nope, just wanted to see you," he says.

"Wow. That's . . . nice." That electricity that he draws through my body is crackling along my spine.

"Creepy?" he asks in a low-slung voice. I'm not sure why it should be creepy. Even if he is a good ten years older than I am, he doesn't seem older in any way that matters.

"No. Not at all."

"Good. We still on for Friday?"

I nod, drawing my lip into my mouth, remembering suddenly the sensation of him doing the exact same thing.

CHAPTER 40

Apparently Warren is just a huge ball of surprises. When he picks me up Friday night and takes me to a bar called Blind Billy's, I am more than a little surprised and disappointed. Irritation narrows my eyes, and my teeth set hard against one another. I had thought we would go to a movie or a restaurant for a real date. My stomach sinks realizing he has brought me to a bar. "You realize I can't go in there," I say, drawing back.

"You can. Come on." We walk up to the door, and the man standing there nods us in, giving a high-five to Warren as we pass. "You're with the band." He winks at me and mimes drumming in the air, leading me through the bar to the small stage where three other boys are already setting up. I should have said, "I don't want to go in there." But I didn't, and now I'm here.

"You're late, dick." I do a double-take when I see the man connected to these words, as he stands up from plugging in a cable. Except for the stud in Warren's eyebrow, this man is his doppelgänger. I realize that my mouth is hanging open so I close it with a sharp intake of breath. He makes eye contact with me for a very assessing second before nodding and going back to his business.

"Yeah, yeah." Warren turns to me, still holding my elbow lightly and leans into me. "That's Elliot. He's my brother." He turns and points to another man, making his way from the bar. "That's David, not my brother."

I nod, taking in the unruly, blond hair and the ink creeping up the side of his neck. "How many brothers do you have?"

He raises his eyebrows, puffing out a small laugh, "More than I know." He laughs again, probably at my shocked expression. I wonder if all the brothers have such old man names: Calvin, Warren, Elliot. Maybe there is a William, Clarence, and Millard in the wings waiting to come out.

"You hungry?" he asks. I am, somewhat, and nod. I've not eaten since breakfast and was really looking forward to a restaurant meal, a rare enough occasion in my life. So hungry, yes. Awestruck, yes. My irritation fading as I realize that he's brought me to see him play in a band. I have finally put together the thought that has been in the edge of my head.

"You're in a band?" I ask as he settles me at a table, dashing off quickly to bring back a menu. I repeat my question when he comes back.

He nods. "Elliot's Child." I must look puzzled, so he adds, "The name of the band is Elliot's Child." Recognition hits. I have seen fliers for them at school and around town.

"No way! Wow." I am sincerely impressed. I am with the boy in the band.

"Okay, now look, I have to go set up. Order anything you like, Do you want a drink?" I shake my head no. "You good then?" I nod as he starts to back away, his eyes still on mine, "Is this okay?" His sudden look of insecurity makes the rest of my irritation ebb away.

"Yes!" I call out, "This is totally okay." I watch them set up for a few minutes before I realize that I am staring at him and probably look like a lovelorn sheep, so I turn my attention to the menu he brought. Appetizers, a series of fried foods, mozzarella sticks, fried pickles, french fries, and the like. I flip the card over and find the other side has sandwiches and burgers available. I order a grilled cheese and fries, water.

He comes back to check on me once before the music starts, and his eyes land on me several times during the session. The band is good, not that I know anything really about music, but I know what feels good. Warren keeps a nice solid beat and Elliot seems very good on the guitar. David plays bass, like guitar but with four low strings. They all sing, at different times, and sometimes together. The first couple of songs draw people in, and within minutes my nearly empty side of the bar is filled with people. One group is made up of five women and two men, clean cut and smiling. The men are clearly married to two of the women, and the others are along for girls' night. The tall blonde with an open and friendly smile is the first to take her man to the dance floor, and the others soon follow, after long draws on their drinks.

The third song brings Warren out of his drum cage and to the front of the small stage where he taps the skins with his lithe fingers. He catches my eye and motions me to come to the dance floor. I do. I like to dance, I'm probably not good at it, but it is so dark that as long as I don't fall over, nobody is going to pay any attention to me. I meet him over by the bongos, and he flips his hand to me as if to offer me the skins. I feel the rhythm and try to set the beat. With less success than Warren. He joins me and soon our four hands are slapping down on the skins, and I am giddy with life. My blood is singing through my veins, and this beautiful, talented, man is my date.

I dance the night away with the cul-de-sac moms, as I've come to think of them, and think I have never felt more alive. At the end of the night Warren hands me a set of broken drumsticks, a souvenir of our date.

We finish the night as the bar closes down, sitting around a table. I know I am glowing with sweat and excitement. This is like the Friday Fires, but a million times better. Live music and a dance floor. Dang.

"You guys are good," I say for maybe the third time. They all three laugh, and Warren is suddenly wrapping me in his arms. I let him because we are all loose and feeling alive and free. Everything is good tonight. "So you liked it?" he asks, and they all burst out laughing.

"Shut up." I try halfheartedly to knock him off of me, but it only makes everybody laugh harder. I know I am gushing, like a girl with a crush, gushing.

"I think you should write press for us."

"Shut up," I say again.

David leans back in his seat, stretching his arms over his head, his eyes lowered to half mast. "Well, boys, I hate to break this up, but I have baby duty in the morning." Everybody except me around the table groans. "I know . . ." he says and pushes himself up from the table, rocking the pedestal and sloshing Elliot's beer onto the tabletop. Warren's hand rockets out and settles the table. Elliot rises from his chair and pounds David on the back, walking with him to the door.

Warren's arm comes back to rest on the back of my chair, his fingers light on my shoulder. I turn to face to him, my chin low. "I had so much fun tonight." Warren tugs me slightly closer.

"I'm glad." He quirks his lip. "Lame for a first date?"

"No. It was awesome."

Elliot comes back, dropping his hands solidly on Warren's shoulders.

"Okay, lover boy. Let's pack it up." We've already packed the van with their equipment, so this is just his farewell.

"Right behind you." We shuffle from the chairs, and the three of us weave our way to the door.

They slap hands in the parking lot, and Elliot puts his hand on my head, mussing my hair like you would a small child or a pup. "Nice to meet you, Alison." Normally I would be uncomfortable with somebody touching me like that, but for some reason, on this night there is nothing that can make me feel uncomfortable. I am so happy tonight. I am so alive. We watch him get into the van and drive away.

"Can we do it again?" Warren asks, taking my hand in his.

"I would love that." I don't want the night to end.

CHAPTER 41

I go back to school finally on Monday. I expected to have a million make-up assignments, but by third period, I only have two, and all of my teachers are treating me with a little extra tenderness. I hate being here. I have to admit that part of my plan to dump school was because I'm a coward and don't want to face all of these people again, especially Derrick Jessop. Thankfully he is not a person who is regularly in my daily rounds, so I am quite surprised when I see him standing by my locker between third and fourth period. I almost turn to go the other way and just forget about getting my text from my locker, but he sees me coming down the hall and stands up from his lean, holding my eyes. I quickly look down, hoping he will move on, but when I glance back, he is still there—actually, worse, he is moving toward me. A well of panic starts to rise, and I stop in the flow of kids and start to back away, starting to turn, going to run. He already hit me with his truck. Oh God, oh God, oh God.

"Wait," he says, seeing the panic, I am sure, as it rises in my eyes, noticing I am backing away, noticing that I am preparing for flight. Somebody knocks into the back of me, and I skid to a stop against the lockers on the other side of the hall. I close my eyes as the hallway begins to spin, and I can't catch my breath. "Gurl," a voice says, and

I shake my head. "Shhhh," the voice says, and I try to place it in my rising panic but can't.

The flow of kids past me has gone, and a hand is resting on my elbow. "You okay?" I open my eyes and Derrick Jessop stands there, his hand outstretched, tethering me. My eyes are suddenly blurred, and tears flood my vision. I bring my hand up to cover my mouth, lowering my face.

The image of Lydia Dollman and her young son Terry flash in my mind, her pretty, pretty face and her beautiful son. "I'm so sorry," I say. "I'm so sorry." I am crying for real now, shuddering gasps, and Derrick is saying something that I can't understand, and then he wraps his arms around me. I feel his own chest shudder, and I realize then that it is not only my sobs rocketing into the hallway but his as well. I wrap my arms around his waist. We are nothing to each other. We are not friends. We do not know each other. My mother killed his sister and his nephew, and he ran into me with his truck. We are nothing to each other but we are both, in this moment, completely broken by the tragedies of our lives.

The bell for fourth period rings, and the halls have emptied out. We are alone. Slowly my panic and shame come under some control, and I feel his shuddering stop. He still holds me, and I say again, "I'm so sorry," and nearly break into tears again. I feel him nod, and I start to draw back, disengaging myself from him, him from me. I do not look in his face. I can't.

"Hey." His voice is quiet, almost hoarse.

"I'm so sorry." I pause. "I didn't know exactly what happened." I knew. I knew she killed that young man's somebody, his somebodies, but I hadn't known that she was a somebody to other people, too.

"Not your fault." I can tell he is straining to speak, to say these words. "I'm sorry, too. That I hit you, I mean. I was kind of crazy."

I shake my head, refusing to accept that he owes me an apology. "No."

"Hey, look at me." I glance up but immediately drop my eyes

again. I cannot face him. "Alison. You didn't do this." He puts his hands on both sides of my face, wiping the streaks of tears from my cheeks with his thumbs. It is a very gentle, kind touch, and I almost resume my crying but bite hard on my lip to keep myself together. "I've talked to the police. I know it really was an accident, just an accident. It wasn't your mom's fault. It was just a fucking horrible accident." His voice quavers, and I bring my hands up to his.

"I don't know that," I say, and my chin puckers and I look away.

"It's true," he says. He squeezes my hands, and I just shake my head. She wasn't sober. I know she wasn't. She is never sober, never not high, never not impaired. I hate her so much. "Regardless. It was definitely not your fault." I press my lips together, trying to wring myself out.

"I'm so sorry," I say again, almost inaudible.

"I know. Me, too. But that's not why I was waiting at your locker." I nod, waiting to find out exactly why he was waiting for me at my locker. "So, I feel really bad about running into you. Are you okay from that?"

"I'm fine, Derrick. I'm fine." Is he seriously asking me if I am okay? I'm still alive. "Not dead," as he had said. Seems like that's more than his sister and nephew can say. "Can I ask you something?" He nods. "Your brother-in-law, is he okay?"

His looks away from me, down the hall, and says, "I don't know."

"I saw him at the hospital that night." I shudder. "I can't stop seeing him."

"He told me. He told me there was a girl there that night. I assumed it was you." He is pulling himself together, and another thought seems to come into his head, "I saw your house burnt. What the hell?"

I puff out air. "Yeah, that was a really bad day."

"It's been a pretty bad week. Or two."

"It's been a pretty bad life." I catch myself too late to bring the words back. "Sorry." I draw in a long breath and start pulling all my bricks back into line, rebuilding my wall from where it lays scattered.

"No. I get it. I just wanted . . ." he runs his hand through is hair, "I don't know. Damn. I just wanted to tell you I was sorry about hitting you and shit." Then, he blurts, "I bought you a new bike."

"What?" His words register, and I frown up at him. "What?"

"Yeah, well, I just felt like shit. I think I hit you on purpose, and I could have killed you like that. I mean I don't know, or maybe not. I don't know, man. I was just so fucking crazy right then. I don't know. Maybe not, but then what I said to you after. That was shitty, too." His face is red with embarrassment or frustration.

"You didn't do anything. I wasn't looking. I'm fine." I start to reach down to gather my notebook and textbooks from the floor, but he reaches them first. He hands them to me, and I turn away. This is the last person on Earth from whom I would ever accept charity.

"Alison. I'm trying to make this right." His voice is so quiet, so hurt.

I turn back to him and say from where I stand, "We can't make this right, Derrick. I can never give you back your sister and her son. This can never be right. It may have been an accident, but she is still here and they are not. She gives nothing, nothing, to the world, and they did. She is here and they are not. We can never make that right. You don't owe me anything, Derrick. It's very nice that you think you do, but what my family took from yours can never be fixed." I give him a sad, broken smile, turn, and jog down the hall.

I do not go to class. I step out into the warm spring day and leave school.

CHAPTER 42

I am such a train wreck. I walk away from the school, unnoticed, since others are leaving as well. Early lunch is after third period. I walk down the drive and make my way through town at a pretty good clip, just walking, but walking with someplace to go. I realize after I have walked for a little over an hour that I am no longer carrying my third-period textbook and notebook. I wonder where I left it. I walk down and out of town, taking the country road that leads to our trailer, our burnt-out shell of a trailer.

It is well past noon when I arrive. Walking five miles takes a good bit longer than riding a bike five miles, or even jogging five miles. I would have jogged, but my shoulder and collarbone are still tender, and the walk was more than I really felt up to. I stop at our drive and walk slowly toward the caution-taped husk of the trailer. I think I am going to go inside, but I am hesitant to break the taped seal over the door. I walk around the trailer, looking at the scarred tin and debris that litters the ground nearby. I walk past the house and out to the fire pit. I sit on the log next to the cold, dry ashes. Looking up at the building, smoke-blackened and warped, I see the memory of my mother stepping out that back door and staggering down the steps.

I'm so embarrassed. Not just by my mother but by myself as well. The replay of me sobbing into Derrick Jessop's chest makes me cringe. How am I supposed to survive here? How do people with horrible lives go on? Why do they go on?

I am staring into the ashes, watching the light reflect, not registering until it finally does, a broken shard of a bottle. It's about two inches long, curved and sharp. I dig it out of the dust, careful. I wipe it clean and stare for a long time through the distortion of it. I run my thumb along the sharp edge, and a small wheel of blood pools. Better. My focus narrows and tightens, and some string that has been wound so tightly suddenly pops, and there is the strangest sensation of less. Less pressure. Less fear, less pain.

I don't think; I just watch as the sharp-edged shard shreds along the blue line of my vein. It is deep, but strangely satisfying after the small scratching of my words. Small pops release in my head, and I watch as the drops of blood make little puffs in the ash when they fall. Ashes to ashes, dust to dust. What is that from? I run the glass up again, following the first cut, and the tension running down my back begins to lesson. Deeper, deeper, deeper, and the flood of blood pours, doesn't drip, doesn't drop. I hear a car coming down the road and am on the move again. I walk into the woods and make my way toward the little tilted building that Dylan had taken me to that day he told me about Jake, so long ago. I stop once when the flow slackens, to reopen the congealing line. I leave a blood-spattered trail and end up sitting next to the tree where Dylan had started telling his story about coming here to escape from Jake. From drunk Jake.

I feel so much better. So much better than the words scratched only a couple of layers deep on my feet. So much more satisfying. The small pain of the cut is so much easier to cope with than all the other muddled pain inside of me. Slice. I've maybe not even touched the vein, my target, but it is so satisfying. So completely satisfying.

It is late afternoon when I make my way out of the trees and slowly walk back to town. The blood dried and caked and flaked from my arm. There are a few smears on my hip, and a couple lower down, but nothing that will make anybody say that I slit my wrist today. I want to open it again, but I am hungry and need to go home instead. The shard of glass is safely in my back pocket, its curve matching nicely to my own.

The apartment is dark when I get there, and it is only after I look in her room that I realize my mother is not here. I hope she doesn't come back. I take a shower and change. I open the cut once more in the shower and watch, hypnotized as the red slips silkily down the drain. So this is what survival feels like.

I am eating a peanut butter sandwich when there is a knock on the door. I am dressed in jeans and a sweatshirt, my feet bare and my hair still wrapped in a towel. I pad through the living room and look out the peephole. Dylan. I feel like I haven't seen him in months, although it was really only a week ago since the trailer burned. I take a deep breath and open the door.

He doesn't move for a minute, just stares at me, breathing. "Can I come in?" I realize that I have been doing the same thing, staring at him, breathing.

"Sure." I open the door wide, thinking to glance at my wrist and assure myself that my new hobby does not show itself.

"You okay?" His hand brushes against my cheek, and I tilt into his palm, nodding. "What happened today?"

"Nothing. I just had to go." I shrug as if it doesn't deserve more than that.

"So, Jessop?"

"He gave me a bike." I say it as offhandedly as I can, as if it is just a kindness someone showed, as if it hasn't sent me over the edge.

"I know. He told me. He feels like shit for destroying yours."

I laugh. "He shouldn't. It was junk anyway."

He glances at me but then continues looking through the living room.

"So this is your new place?" I nod. "Nice."

"How did you know where I was?" I ask.

"Stopped and talked to Mr. Billups." I nod again. Of course, that makes sense. "Are you okay?" I nod again. I so badly want him to touch me, but I keep my distance. He has had plenty of horrible in his life, I remind myself; he does not need mine. He has a future to think about. "Derrick thought he upset you."

"You know it was his sister and nephew that she killed?" I ask

He nods. "It was an accident." I nod. Just like your brother was an accident? But I don't say it, and am worried that he has seen the thought pass through my eyes.

"They are dead, and he's giving me a bike." I close the door and follow him into the room. "That's fucked up."

"It wasn't your fault." He reaches out and takes my hand—the hand attached to my freshly sliced wrist. "It was an accident," he says again.

"Yeah, I know." I retract my hand, giving him my other one as I turn him into the kitchen. "Peanut butter and jelly?" I offer, and he shakes his head. "I appreciate the bike, really, but I just can't accept it. He doesn't owe me anything. Nobody does." I feel so clear headed. I haven't felt so stable, so non-crazy in weeks. I pick up my sandwich to take a bite but end up setting it back down. "I went out to that building, the one you showed me in the woods." He nods and I go on. "It really is a good place to think. I sat there and just thought. I thought about how I've been so upset and so angry, trying to understand what I am supposed to do, and it suddenly just came clear. I don't have to do anything. I don't have to fix my mother; I don't have to try. I don't have to care what anybody else thinks of me. That's hard because I've always cared. I am going to be away from this town someday, and I will never, ever look back. So really all I have to do is get to that point. Every day between now and then, I just have to get through." He nods, looking out the window.

"Can I help?" he asks, his voice quiet.

I shake my head. "No. You already have. This is something I have to manage on my own, or I will never be free. You can't fix my life. You can't fix me. I thought you could, that night I came to your house in the rain . . ." My voice trails off, and a fine flush rises up his neck and floods his cheeks. "I'm completely broken in ways you don't even know. I have to fix myself." He nods, but I can tell he doesn't like it, he doesn't agree.

"You know I am always here for you." He steps closer, and I can smell the scent of him, that warm, peaceful scent that is only him.

"I do." I wrap my arms around his waist, and his arms encircle me, his chin resting on my head, his breath rustling my hair. "You are my best friend. You are always my best friend."

"I really care about you."

"I know." And I love you, I think, but do not say it. I hear his voice telling his dad that we are "just friends" that night in the rain, and I hate him a little bit as well. I have to push you away, push you on with your life, push you out of mine. "I just need some time to get myself together. It's just something I have to work through on my own."

"What do you mean?"

"I mean you can't do it for me. You're a great friend, and you've always been there for me." I hear the clip on the word friend, and a shadow passes his face. I wonder what that means. "I can't keep seeing the beauty of your life and not having any of my own. I have to figure this out on my own."

"No. You don't. You shouldn't." I start to disengage from him. He lets me go. "You really don't have to do this alone."

"But I do. I've tried doing it with you, with your family, but it just gets so confusing. I just need to focus on my shit and work it out. You know." He looks at me for a long time, and I can almost see him dredging up his own memories of how he dealt back in the day, after his brother died, when Jake was still drinking.

"You don't." He runs his hand over his chin and mouth, a motion I have seen Jake use when he is deep in thought. "But if that's what you think you need, I'll give you space. I'll do whatever you need me to do."

"I think I need space," I say, the sharp pain hitting my wrist when I spin, rubbing the wound against my cuff.

"Is that what you want?"

"That's what I need." I know this is what has to happen, whether I want it or not. God knows I don't want him to walk out that door, but a few minutes later, I am closing the door behind him with the strangest mix of relief and pain warring in my chest.

CHAPTER 43

I have been sitting for over an hour, not moving, just staring at the flickering light of the TV. I haven't even registered what is playing; it's just noise and light and distraction. There is banging coming up the stairs and the low voices of conversation. The banging clop, clop, rest, clop, clop of my mother's ascent draws me up from in front of the TV, turning it off, moving toward the kitchen, Her key is in the lock, and the door springs open. I am putting a pan on the stove with water to heat for pasta when I hear them fully in the living room.

I poke my head around the corner seeing Cal settling her on the sofa. She is flushed and smiling, a happy place in her medication. "Hi," I say and wave. "How are you feeling?"

"Well, I didn't expect to have you home?" she questions.

"Yeah, well . . ." I have no place else to be. "I'm making spaghetti for dinner."

"Garlic bread?" she asks. I nod, and we share a smile. "Stay for dinner?" She smiles her best "love me" smile up at Cal, who laughs and turns his head away.

I look at him, seeing where his bones and Warren's bones are similar and where they are not. They are both tall and dark haired. They are both angular in their facial features, although Cal's are sharper, and maybe longer. Yes, definitely longer, especially his sharp, angled chin. I wonder if that is his age or the roughness of his life that has etched him so sharply. The eyes are different. Warren's are that beautiful storm-cloud blue, with exquisite arching brows above, long lashed and pretty. Cal's brows are flat across, even slightly drawn together, and his eyes are brown. I think. I try to close my mind to the fact that it was Cal on Christmas, as revolting as that is to know. "There will be plenty," I say and dip back into the kitchen. I can hear them, talking, laughing, then the TV comes on, and their voices are overshadowed.

When everything is ready, I make up their plates and bring them out to the living room. They stay seated at the couch, and I leave the plate of garlic bread on the end table. I go back to the kitchen and eat my own dinner, looking out the kitchen window into the alley below.

———

After I've cleaned the kitchen and after mom is asleep on the sofa and Cal has left, I sit in my own room, on a bed that isn't mine, and I stare down at the angry, red gash on the inside of my left wrist. It makes my stomach churn, the sight of it, but that piece of glass is tucked safe under the mattress, and my fingers itch to take it out. I don't, but oh how I want to. When I wake in the morning, the gash is puckered along the edges with a sharp line of scab like a ridge.

It is raining, and I am surprised, when I step out into it to start the walk to school, to see Dylan sitting in his truck at the curb. I tap on the passenger door, and he reaches across to open it. I slide in and shake out my umbrella.

"What are you doing here?"

He looks at me for a long second before saying, "I just thought I'd see if you needed a ride. Wanted," he corrects.

"Thank you." I hop in.

We drive to school, and he doesn't say much else along the way, but when we park, he asks, "You good?"

"Yeah. I'm good." I look at him and give him a smile. "Thanks for the ride." His pale eyes search my face, but I flip the door handle and step out into the rain, jogging for the door. I stop at the guidance counselors' office before even going to my locker. I figure I should probably put in a humble appearance after all my unexcused absences these past few weeks and after leaving yesterday. The guidance office is staffed by two counselors and one receptionist. Dina, the receptionist, points me to a table where I can wait for whoever comes in first. The table is scattered with puzzle pieces and a puzzle that is over halfway complete. I pick up pieces and put them down, trying to calm my jangled nerves. I wish I had eaten something before leaving, because now it feels like my stomach is gnawing on my backbone.

Mrs. Shaw wins me in the first-to-enter drawing. She comes in, peeling off her raincoat and hanging it on the coat tree. She is tall and thick with short, black hair, pixie cut, stuck to her head. "Miss Hayes." She nods a greeting. "Come on back." She leads me into her office, a small room with no windows but filled with shelves of whimsical movement and color. Pillows that students have made for her in sewing and home ec, art with student signatures gracing the corners. It is so full of knickknacks and color that for a moment I am unable to move; it is so overwhelming. She busies herself putting away her lunch, settling the papers she has brought back from her home. She is very precise. I notice that she leaves nothing visible on her desk, except my own file, which she has now taken out of her cabinet. I expect her to sit behind the desk, but she does not. She comes over to where I am sitting and joins me on the small couch. She is not too close. She is not threatening. She is just near.

"What brings you in, Alison?"

I have tried to think all morning how this conversation might go and know that I just need to lay it out and ask for help. I let out a deep breath.

"It's been a really bad couple of weeks," I start, knowing that she knows this already. "I need to know how to get a GED. I don't think I can finish this way."

"How is your mom?" she asks, completely skirting my GED statement.

"She's okay. I think." I look down at my fingernails, looking for something to chew, but they are gnawed to the quick times ten.

"Where are you living? Did you find a place after the fire?"

I tell her we are staying in an apartment off 5th Street, and she nods. "Is there anything you need? Clothes, furniture."

"The apartment is furnished." We could definitely use clothes, but there is no way I am admitting that. The jeans and shirts that I stuffed in my backpack the day of the fire are pretty much it for me, except for the sweatshirt that I'm wearing, which I found in the lost-and-found at the laundromat.

"Can you tell me about the accident in the parking lot last week?"

"I don't know. I don't really remember it. Derrick said I swerved into his truck. I wasn't paying attention, I guess." But I remember his words yesterday in the hall, the guilt in his eyes.

"Wow." She looks me squarely in the eye for the first time. "What a month you've had." I push my hands through my hair, pulling it off my face. I let it fall again when the cuff of my sweatshirt rubs against the ridge on my wrist, and I drop my hands down into my lap again.

"Yes. What a month."

She reaches across the desk and takes my file off the desk. "You are missing quite a bit of work, but I think, with the extenuating circumstance of the past month, there can be leniency on getting that work completed. The days absent aren't going to cause you problems, so long as you can return to your normal routine. You've always been a good student and never had any attendance issues in the past. I see no reason you can't put his small blip behind you and maintain your graduation goals."

"Great. That's good to hear." I don't want her to be disappointed. She is so encouraging that I don't want to admit I've just given up on everything and don't want to have to face anybody anymore. I am so tired of hearing half-whispered comments when I pass certain people in the hall. I am so tired of the sort of pity I see in the teachers' faces. I am Moses parting the Red Sea. I am the plague ship.

CHAPTER 44

I am lost in my own thoughts when I come in to work on Thursday. I'm doing my best to suck it up at school and just stay below the radar. I hate to let Mrs. Shaw down. My mother went to her third AA meeting at the United Methodist Church last night. Faye came and took her. Rob told me while I was at work today that Faye has really high hopes for her. She told him she's requested a sponsor, and one of the women stepped forward to offer herself. I wonder why she didn't mention it to me. I made her breakfast this morning before I left for school, and we talked for a few minutes while she ate and watched the news. She did look good, though, like she had slept well, and I even told her I loved her as I walked out the door.

I have four weeks of school left, and I've talked to all of my teachers about making up the work I've missed or not completed, and for once I am happy to accept the charity of their leniency. This last week I've really done a lot to catch up, and only one report in English is still to be done, a book report on The Grapes of Wrath by John Steinbeck, which I am about a quarter of the way through. I have a hard time concentrating when I read.

I am coming back in from the sheds where I went to find Rob to give him paperwork for the lumber delivery he is taking out in the morning. I'm almost feeling normal. My body is back to normal, and even the deep bruising from the accident has faded to a faint yellow. Spring always makes me happier, and today has been a good day. It's my birthday, and even though nobody knows, it makes me feel good. One year and I will be eighteen and can do whatever I want. Twelve months. I am contemplating this prospect when a familiar face catches me up. Warren, whom I haven't seen since the Friday night when he took me to see his band play. I thought I would hear from him earlier, but when a week closed out with no sign of him, I figured he just wasn't as interested in me as I thought. I thought we had a good time, and when he kissed me in his car, all of the sparks and electricity that I remembered from Christmas were clearly still there. But he didn't come by; he was nowhere. I think I overestimated his interest.

Seeing him so suddenly this evening leaves me weak-kneed, and I try to decide if I can go back out to the shed until he is gone. Then he sees me, right before I decide to bolt, and his face lights up with that smile. I smile back and give him a little wave as I head his way. I meet him before he makes it to the door. I resolve not to ask him where he has been and to play it cool, as if I hadn't noticed that he just disappeared, but my betraying mouth says, "Where have you been?"

He laughs and holds the door open for me. "You know, just around." He smiles, but there is something in his eyes that I am not sure about.

"Uh-huh," I say, but laugh as well. He leans into me, and I feel a little ridiculous.

He closes one eye and looks at me with the other, trying to decide something, then he takes me back outside. His voice is low. "I would have come by earlier, really, but I had some stuff to take care of."

"I get it. You're a player. I get it." I say it as a joke, a big teasing joke.

"No. I'm not." He sounds a little offended, and I wish I had just kept my mouth shut. "You really think that?"

"Sort of." But I shrug, dismissing the subject. "It's okay. Seriously."

"I'm not a player, Alison."

Great. Everything is so much clearer now.

"Okay. So, what are you looking for today?" It's not like I care that he took almost two weeks to think of me again.

"You, actually."

I blow out a breath in a huff. "Whatever." I want to add "player" to the end of the sentence, but I bite my tongue.

"No, really, I was." He laughs.

"Here I am." In one of the three places I can generally be found.

He smiles but I realize there is something hiding in his stormy eyes, something uncomfortable. "Seen Cal lately?" he asks. This is not quite what I was expecting. We have not spoken of Cal except the day he told me he was his brother.

"I saw him one night last week." The night I made spaghetti for them.

"Well, he's gone," he says in a low whisper.

"What do you mean, gone?"

"Can't be found. Found his car on 57, parked with the trunk open. Three days ago. No sign of him. He's gone."

How did I not know this? I know I have been preoccupied for the most part, but, surely, Mom would have said something about him going. I close my mouth from where it has fallen open. I realize suddenly that Warren is still here, standing in front of me and that he has said something that I have missed while I was busy recalibrating my mind to see my mother for the first time. "What?" I say, shaking my head to clear it.

"You okay?"

"Yeah. I just got distracted. What do you mean he's gone?" Could I possibly be so lucky?

"I mean he's gone. Took nothing, just gone."

"No ideas?" This just gets better and better.

"Nobody knows."

"Wow." I can't help the excited tone in my voice. I am the ambulance chaser, the accident gaper that bottlenecks traffic. He's been gone for three days. That does not really even qualify as a missing person, does it? He just went somewhere, broke down, had somebody someplace else pick him up. I say as much to Warren, and he shrugs, clearly thinking this is something bigger.

I open the door to the apartment and call out. The TV is dark; the kitchen is dark. There is no light coming from under her bedroom door. There is no light coming from anywhere, and I flip switches as I move through the apartment. I open her door, and the rectangle of light from her bedroom window shows the lump of her in her bed. She is there. I start to close the door, but then I recognize the scent in the air, that vodka smell that had been gone for days, maybe a week. The light bounces on the curve of the bottle, and I find myself walking across the room, lifting the bottle, watching the slow pool of oily liquid in the bottle. So, not sober. Not sober. I had been so hopeful when Rob told me about Faye's enthusiasm. I was just excited that she actually went to a meeting or three. I set the bottle back down on the table and begin to turn. Only then do I look at her limp face, her mouth open like a cavern, her hair strewn across her face, and I reach out to move it back from her forehead and feel like I have touched a table, or a cool counter. She is cold. She is so cold.

I pull back the blanket, thinking to wake her up, but she is not waking up, and in the dim, faltering light of the window, I finally see the syringe, looking big and ominous next to her skinny arm. But not really a syringe. The plunger is missing and in its place is a tube, duct taped to the syringe, lying along her stomach ending in a bladder, a hot water bottle. I am confused by what I am seeing. Nothing about any of that makes sense. Hot water bottle, tube, syringe. "Has your mother ever suffered suicidal tendencies?" I hear this question in my mind, the one Officer Daniels had asked me. I step away, back away from her, staring down. The sight before me is very much the one that used to haunt me when I was younger, when I had the fear of finding her dead. When did I stop fearing that? Was it the day I tried to kill her or before that? I don't know. I sit on the floor for a very long time, looking at her. Not crying, not even really thinking, just etching her into my memory as she was in her last minute on Earth. I cannot reconcile the hot water bottle. That doesn't even make sense.

I pull her covers back over her, and I push her mouth closed so she doesn't look so cavernous, so wasted, so dead. I leave our apartment with the door open and knock on the door down the hall. A girl answers the door, a college-age girl, and I ask her if I can use her phone.

"Sure," she says, opening the door wide to me. "You live down the hall, right?" I nod, and she steers me toward the phone.

I dial 9-1-1. Isn't that what you are supposed to do? They'll have to figure it out. I turn my back to the girl and pitch my voice, low, embarrassed, ashamed. I'm always so fucking humiliated by my life. "This is the 9-1-1 operator, what is your emergency?" Her voice is tinny over the line, unenthused.

"I need an ambulance."

"What is your emergency?"

"I think she is dead." I repeat that I need an ambulance, ramble our address.

"Would you like me to stay on the line with you until the ambulance arrives?"

"No, I'll wait outside." I hang up the phone and turn toward the door to see the girl standing with her mouth in an "O," her hand halfway to it, tears pooling in her eyes. I nod and mumble a thank you as I go back out into the hall, past the open door to our apartment, down the stairs, and out into the night, where the air smells clean.

My mind races with images of her, my mother, going in reverse, from this desiccated shell to her crying on the floor and sleeping in my arms after Mitch left, to the day at the Goodwill when she tried to be as good as Mrs. Bancroft, to all the stories about the house we would build, to walking me home from kindergarten, buying me Milk Duds, to just her face above me, in the glow of the street lights, her voice low and singing. Beautiful in the glow, her eyes clear, her face so full of love and goodness. I feel the scream ripping through my vocal cords, and I settle on the curb, folding into my knees. "What happened to you?" I ask. I should cry, but I can't; there are no tears inside of me. I am barren and wasted, dried out.

I hear feet behind me, and the girl from upstairs has come to sit beside me, her arm around my shoulder, drawing me to her. She doesn't speak, and I don't pull away from her. She smells like lavender and vanilla. The kindest people in my life have always been strangers. The vanilla and lavender begins to fill the empty space inside of me, washing away the dirty, angry emptiness, and I realize suddenly that I am free. She is free, too, my mother, from whatever broke her life. I have to do better than she did of not breaking. I owe her that.

We wait for the call of the sirens as we sit pooled in the glow of the street lamp.

Enjoy this Sneak Peek of the
next book in Alison's Journey

THE ALISON HAYES JOURNEY

BOOK TWO

PURGUS

❀ ❀ ❦ ❀ ❀

ANGIE GALLION

PART ONE: SPRING

CHAPTER 1

The light outside the window is haloed around the street lamp, and I am sitting in the police station, on one of the metal folding chairs that line the front window. A fan whirs in the corner, moving the sultry air from one side of the room to the other. I am so alone—not so much different from every other day, really. Except it is. Today is different, and nothing will ever be like it was again.

"You can come home with me," says Leslie McGill, laying her large, square hand on my arm.

I am here because this is where they brought me after they put up the yellow CAUTION tape and began to process the scene. The crime scene. The scene where my mother had ended her life, or somebody had ended it for her. Suicide is murder—ending a life. No difference. I remember being asked months ago if she had suicidal tendencies, and at the time, all I could think was: don't we all? Back when I had sliced my own little lines of self-destruction into my skin, writing the words that defined my life on the arches of my feet, into the hollows below my ankles, and finally, just angry, wordless lines in the soft flesh of my arms.

I do not look up at her, this large, soft woman, but stare at the dark skin of her square hand, her clean, trimmed fingernails showing pink. She is fabulously big and round, in a tunic that may have been originally designed as a tent. It is every color imaginable all at once. Her black tights stretch taut over the thick muscles of her calves. I think I have seen her somewhere before, but don't have the mental capacity to figure out where. "I don't want to go home with you. I have a home," I say, looking away from her hand and back through the window, out into the night. The glow of headlights pool in the street as a car passes.

"Yes. I know you have a home, but it looks like your home is going to be tied up for a little while." She pauses, lifting her hand off my arm, folding it over the small manila envelope that sits across her lap. My name is written in the top left corner. Alison Hayes. Written in black pen, with such force that I can see where the paper has dented with the passage of the pen. "You'll just be with me until we find your family."

"I don't have any family," I say. I've been through this already, with the policeman who brought me here. "I don't have any family. I don't know my father. I don't know who my grandparents are or if my mother had siblings." It rolls off my tongue, foreign, their word, not mine.

"Yes. That's what they told me. I am sorry," she says in a quiet voice, resonant with sympathy, and I glance up at her for maybe the first time. She has blue eyes, large and slightly protruding, circled in dark by the skin around them. The dark color fades to a ruddy mocha down her cheeks, and her full lips are compressed to a tight line. "I am very sorry."

I believe her. Her eyes are pooled with liquid, and for a second, I think the liquid will spill over and run down her cheeks. But she blinks several times, looking away from me and out the window, watching as a car moves slowly past, then back. When her eyes latch to mine again, they are dry. "Won't you come with me? I have a cozy room with a nice little bed in a room you'll have to yourself."

"When will I be able to go back home?"

"I don't know, honey. It depends on what the police decide."

My mother flashes through my mind, as she was when I went into her room, her mouth open, her skin gone to gray. I close my eyes against the vision and feel my brows rising into my forehead. When I have forced the vision out, I open my eyes again and stand up. "Then let's go." I stride to the door and turn back to her as she pushes herself up from the seat, holding one leg out straight, like the knee is stiff and sore. "Can we go by and get some clothes on the way?" I ask. It isn't really clothes I want; it is my backpack that has all my money stashed inside.

"No. They won't let us in until they are done."

I nod, not surprised, and push the door open and step out into the night. She leads me to her van, a burgundy Town and Country, and I go around to the passenger side and let myself in. When she settles her bulk into the driver's seat, the van squats with a groan. She inserts a key attached to a collection of dangling fobs that jingle and clink together. She squares her bottom more comfortably in the seat, and the engine roars, taking off and down the street for the whole two minutes it takes to arrive at her house on Polk Street. I almost laugh when she pulls into the drive and turns off the car. I had thought I was going somewhere else, somewhere in another town, Mattoon, Arcola, Tuscola or Arthur, anywhere else. I didn't think I would end up just three or four blocks south of where we started. I could have walked here in as much time as it took her to get settled into her seat and out again.

The McGill house looks like a little cracker box ranch, stretching out the length of the yard. The living room, which we now step into, is long, connected and open to the dining room. A hall heads off in the other direction toward the two bedrooms at the end of the house. I take my shoes off and follow her as she walks down the hall, flipping on lights as she goes. "Mr. McGill," she says, "is a fireman. He won't be home until day after tomorrow." She motions for me to follow her, and I do, my socks sinking into the soft, blue carpet. "You know my son?" she asks, and I shake my head. "Tommy. He's maybe a year younger than you. You sixteen?" I nod, but really I'm seventeen today. Today is my birthday. "You a sophomore?" I nod. "He's a freshman. You can meet him tomorrow."

"Tommy McGill?" I ask, because there is something in the name that seems familiar. "Does he play soccer?" I am rewarded with a radiant smile that lights up the hallway.

"That's my Tommy." The pride oozes from every pore of her body, and I wonder what it would have been like to grow up with this woman as Mother. "He's pretty good with that soccer ball."

"Seems to be." I only vaguely recollect the things I have heard over the last year, about how the soccer team was excelling and how it was due to this scrawny little freshman named Tommy McGill. I feel my mouth spreading in a smile, unable to contain it in the glow of this woman's pride.

"You hungry?" she asks. We have reached the end of the hall, and she opens a door to the left and illuminates a room, dressed in pink roses from ceiling to bedspread. The blue carpet stops at the door and is transformed into a mauve-pink version, still just as soft.

I shake my head, taking in the roses peeking from the skirt of a dressing table and from the bowl of the lamp. "I guess you like roses," I say, laughing just a little.

"Charlotte likes roses."

"Who is Charlotte?"

"She was a girl who stayed with us for a time." She smiles. "She has moved on now. Got a family of her own." She pauses, a small smile on her face, "I've just never had the heart to change it."

"Where did she go?"

"Oh, she's just over in Mattoon. You'll probably get to meet her."
She says "probably" like "prolly" and I decide right then and there
that I am going to like this woman. I am going to like her and I am
going to let her be kind to me, because apparently that is the thing she
does best. Suddenly, I am weary on my feet; I'm so tired. She makes
her way through the room, showing me that there are several options
for clothing in the drawers and hanging in the closet. She tells me that
she'll be up for a while more, in the living room, if I need anything. I
almost want to give her a hug, which may be the strangest sensation
I've ever had, but I contain myself.

"Thank you for coming to get me."

"Oh, darling," she says, "we all need somebody to come and get us
from time to time."

She leaves me alone in the rose encased room and I open drawers,
looking at the pajamas and sweatpants that fill them. The scent of
lavender rises from the drawers and when I finally choose something
to put on, I sit for a very long time just holding it up to my face,
breathing in the clean of somebody else's life.

ABOUT THE AUTHOR

Angie Gallion grew up in East Central Illinois and now resides with her husband and their children outside of Atlanta, Georgia. Angie's writings often deal with personal growth through tragedy or trauma. She enjoys exploring complex relationships, often set against the backdrop of addiction or mental illness. Her debut novel, Intoxic, received the Bronze Medal from Readers' Favorite in the General Fiction category. Intoxic was well received by audiences, and reader response inspired Gallion to continue the Alison Hayes Journey, a coming-of-age series, which now include three novels: Intoxic, Purgus, and Icara.

Angie expects to release Off the Dark Ledge, her first psychologic thriller, in spring 2018, and a fourth installment in the Alison Hayes Journey in late 2018. Follow Angie at www.angiegallion.com, where she not only promotes her own novels but others' as well through her book review blogs.

BOOKS BY ANGIE GALLION

Intoxic: The Alison Hayes Journey, Book 1
Purgus: The Alison Hayes Journey, Book 2
Icara: The Alison Hayes Journey, Book 3
Off the Dark Ledge, a Psychological Thriller